PRAISE FO

'Well-drawn characters and painterly depictions of place'
THE TIMES

'A gripping, tense and highly original thriller'
SCOTS MAGAZINE

'Chilling, dark and twisty'
B P WALTER

'An emotional gut-puncher'
JONATHAN WHITELAW

'Powerful and moving'
PHILIPPA EAST

'Emma Christie is the queen of misdirection'
TREVOR WOOD

'A novel that delivers in mystery, heart, and tension'
L.V. MATTHEWS

'An absolute gem of a book'
MARION TODD

'A beautifully written story of love, loss,
guilt and redemption'
CATHERINE COOPER

WATCH YOUR BACK

Also by Emma Christie

The Silent Daughter
Find Her First
In Her Shadow

WATCH YOUR BACK

EMMA CHRISTIE

MLP

First published in 2025 by Mountain Leopard Press
An imprint of Headline Publishing Group Limited

1

Cataloguing in Publication Data is available from the British Library

Paperback ISBN 978 1 8027 9467 0

Typeset in 12/16.5 pt Sabon LT Pro by Six Red Marbles UK, Thetford, Norfolk

Printed and bound in Great Britain by Clays Ltd, Elcograf S.p.A.

FSC
www.fsc.org

MIX
Paper | Supporting
responsible forestry
FSC® C104740

Headline's policy is to use papers that are natural, renewable and recyclable
products and made from wood grown in well-managed forests and other
controlled sources. The logging and manufacturing processes are expected
to conform to the environmental regulations of the country of origin.

Headline Publishing Group Limited
An Hachette UK Company
Carmelite House
50 Victoria Embankment
London EC4Y 0DZ

The authorised representative in the EEA is Hachette Ireland,
8 Castlecourt Centre, Dublin 15, D15 XTP3, Ireland (email: info@hbgi.ie)

www.headline.co.uk
www.hachette.co.uk

For Juan. You're missed.

PROLOGUE

I'm standing by the table and she's dying on the floor.

I picture prison. If they jail me for fifteen years that's one hundred and eighty months, almost five and a half thousand days.

I've done the sums. It doesn't help.

I'll be locked up, not for good, but for all those years where choices are made about jobs, marriage, kids, houses, pets, pals, love. I'll wreck all of my expected futures.

And hers, obviously.

She's on her back, burst head inches from a spilled ashtray, and her last cigarette. I kneel down, trying to avoid the blood of her but it creeps across the tiles, seeps into my trousers. They'll wash. My hands are on her now; feeling for a pulse. Then stopping it.

I bet she never believed that smoking would kill her; was right after all.

CHAPTER 1

When the whole world goes to shit, Tink's standing in line for a school dinner, gripping a meal ticket instead of proper money. She's trying to guess what's on offer, just by the smell of it; imagining the shine of greasy burgers and the slick of fat left on the plate that she'll wipe up with buns that taste so much sweeter than any bread they have at home. And chips. She definitely wants chips. On Monday it's boiled potatoes, Tuesday they're reheated and from Wednesday onwards they're sliced and fried. They always taste best on a Friday. *Everything* is better on a Friday.

Her tummy rumbles.

She's two from the front of the queue when someone places a hand on her shoulder. Even before she turns she can tell it's Mrs Campbell from the office because the enticing smell of hot oil is swallowed by the soft scent of soap powder, like other people's freshly washed towels.

'You okay there, sunshine?'

Tink nods, then glances towards the golden glow of the serving area. This close to the front it's all clunks and clanks as large metal spoons scoop up lumps in sauce and deposit them on to heavy white plates. Most of the women who serve look ancient but happy to be there. One of them always whistles and if you can guess the tune she gives you more food. Right now she's belting out a song by ABBA. Tink's dad loves them, sometimes invites pals round for karaoke at the weekend, fills their tiny sitting room with men and bottles and ashtrays and pop songs. This one is called 'The Winner Takes It All' and it's a sad one but Tink's happy she'll get extra chips.

Her mouth waters.

Mrs Campbell's hand is on her again so she turns back to face her. She's almost as short as Tink is but right now she looks even smaller, bowing forward so their eyes are level. It reminds Tink of the way her dad always bends down to speak with strangers' dogs. They never bark. Folk say he's got a way with animals and it makes her love him even more.

'You've to come with me, hen.'

Her voice is soft and gentle as bubble bath but she's holding her lips tightly over her teeth. If Tink was to draw her now she'd put a straight line instead of a smile or frown. It was unreadable, could flip either way. It was kind and yet stern, serious.

'What about my lunch?'

'We'll get you something, after.'

'After what?'

Mrs Campbell opens her mouth to speak then shuts it again. She looks as if she wants to cry and Tink feels bad because she's made it happen. 'I'll explain in the office,' she says, then her hand moves from one of Tink's shoulders to the other and eases her out of the queue. Her arm's like a warm scarf but Tink wants to cry and kick up a fuss and with anyone else she would have, but not with Mrs Campbell. One time when Tink had a sore ear Mrs Campbell had taken her to the back office and given her blackcurrant juice and a biscuit with chocolate on one side, and told her she could call her Mrs C if there was nobody else around. Tink had never dared but she liked knowing that she could, that they were in on a secret.

She lets herself be led.

Mrs Campbell takes her into the office then flips up part of the counter so they can pass through to the staff side. The head teacher is there with a sour face and a grey suit and when she smiles at them Tink knows something is really wrong. Folk call her Cat Bum because of her mouth. Right now she looks like someone practising a smile in the mirror. Tink glances at Mrs Campbell, catches her doing that thing that adults do when they don't want children to hear;

shaping her mouth around silent words. After that the head teacher nods and leaves, says she needs to grab some food. That's what Tink needs too. All she wants is a big plate of chips and she'll be happy.

Instead, she's offered a chair.

CHAPTER 2

Jo Hidalgo drops her damp towel on to the floor next to the mess of last night's clothes. She smiles at the sight of her jeans entwined with a black bra that is not hers; would never fit. Christ, it's been a while. But, for all the unfamiliarity, their bodies had fitted together last night, and the morning had brought with it the gentle suggestion of more. If only time allowed it. She looks at her watch, knows her priorities.

Dressed, she goes to the window and watches Edinburgh wake up fifty feet beneath her. They're in a featureless tourist hotel near North Bridge but from here she can see the two faces of Edinburgh. The Old Town dribbles down from the castle, a place of cobbles and kilt shops and dank alleys, where drunks piss and students vomit and tour guides talk of hauntings. The New Town is its opposite: all sandstone and symmetry, wide streets and gated squares and glossy shops; the kind of place lawyers like to register their business.

The two sides of the city are divided by the grassy slopes and flower beds of Princes Street Gardens. The land there used to hold a filthy loch. Drained, it holds crowds of locals and visitors who flock there for picnics on sunny days. The city has reinvented itself, is living proof that it can be done. Jo's relieved. Further out folk climb Arthur's Seat, the lumpy volcanic peak that overlooks the city. Others head down to the shore, surprised to find a long sandy beach so close to the centre of the city.

After the murder of her mum, Jo felt like all beauty had been stripped from the world. But she found it again, eventually, in the big skies that rest gently on the sea at Portobello. A job offer led her there and she'd never looked back.

Now, behind her, a toilet flushes.

Jo doesn't turn when the bathroom door opens but the woman who walks out is captured on the sheen of the hotel room window; a transparent version of herself. Ari, her name is. Even her reflection is beautiful. Jo smiles, tells Ari she can see right through her. But if Ari's thinking the same thing about her, she'd be wrong.

'Enjoying the view?' That's Ari, right behind her now. Her words tickle Jo's neck.

'Something like that.'

Ari moves to the window and for a moment the two of them stand side by side, an inch apart. Jo holds herself still and wonders how an empty space can be felt so intensely. She wants to fill it, doesn't dare.

'So you're a watcher?'

'Sometimes.'

Jo's phone alarm whines so she pulls it out of her pocket, presses snooze.

'Time for work?'

When Jo nods, Ari steps closer and the heat from her skin grows legs and arms, fills the space between them. 'Can you be an hour late?'

'Not today.' Jo steps away but they keep their eyes on each other. It's like they've got magnets sewn into their foreheads. *Pull away, Jo.* She grabs her yellow leather jacket from the floor, slips it on. Zipped up, it hugs her lean body. Some folk her call *wiry* and she hates it. She's stronger than you'd think and, if you doubt that, she'll challenge you to an arm-wrestle. Ari did, last night. They both won.

'Will I see you again?'

It's Ari who's asking and just like that, Jo feels the lightness in her darken at the edges. She's annoyed at Ari for spoiling the magic of it; at herself for not leaving earlier, long before the shoots of borrowed love had time to wilt.

'I doubt it,' says Jo and that's the truth of it. She's pleased Ari doesn't make a fuss.

Ari dresses in silence while Jo makes the bed, tugs the sheets until they look unused, unloved. Force of habit. Straightening up, she heads back to the window. There's more movement now: buses, trams, cars, bikes, folk dashing through the packed pavements, probably

9

heading for the train station. Many are on their phones, talking or texting as they walk, and Jo wonders if anyone remembers how it feels to just walk, to be out there on your own and know you can't be phoned, can't be found.

Behind her a coat zip is pulled.

'We leaving together, or . . .?' *Or.* That's Ari, eager for an ending.

Something flickers in Jo's chest at the idea of them being a *we.* But it's definitely not happening. She glances towards Ari. Her hand rests on the door handle. 'Just go.'

A nod from Ari: acceptance. No kisses or long goodbyes. A back, turned, in more ways than one. When Jo looks out of the window again the traffic lights are green, the crossing a shifting weave of strangers. She stays there even after the lights have changed, even when her phone alarm screeches at her again. She waits until she sees Ari, leaving, answering a phone call as she walks away and laughing at something Jo will never be a part of. She wonders what life lies on the other end of that call. Something better.

Someone better.

When Ari disappears from sight Jo opens the dating app, saves the messages they'd exchanged before they met in person. A smile, a sigh, then she blocks her.

It's easier to break than to be broken.

She's closing the app when a text message arrives.

It's Jean, her boss at the shop. *You're late*, she says. *Assume that means the date went well?* It was Jean who persuaded her to sign up for online dating in the first place, convinced her it's how things are done now. Gay bars, begone. Her phone beeps again and a winking yellow face appears on her screen. Emojis, they're called. Jean loves them. Seems words aren't enough these days either, if they ever were. Jo's typing out a reply when Jean sends another message.

PS A big package just arrived for you. If you're not here by ten I'm opening it. Assume it's my birthday present? Another beep, another emoji. This time it's laughing, water leaking out of slitted eyes. Jo's are wide open. Her mouth follows suit.

How can there possibly be a package for *her*?

Nobody should know where she is. Nobody apart from the police, of course. They know who she is and what was lost. Her mum's murder and the grief it caused is unchanged but the killer's sentence is now over, devastating loss neatly balanced against the length of time a cell door was kept locked. And now that it's open? Jo was warned there could be trouble. And maybe, just maybe, it's been delivered to her door.

CHAPTER 3

Twenty minutes later Jo steps off the bus and through the double doors of the charity shop. The air is thick and musty and holds the smell of clothes left too long in wardrobes and drawers. They steam-clean all the donated stock but the lives of strangers linger in armpits and crotches, in the missing buttons and crumb-filled pockets. Every single thing in the shop is imperfect in some way. But they'll be bought, washed, worn again, loved again.

Or so says Jean.

Right now Gordon's manning the till, all sausage fingers and uncombed hair, purpling face focused as though he's defusing a bomb. Jo secretly calls him Beetroot. In fact she's got nicknames for almost everyone, picked up the habit from her mum and never dropped it. People have always labelled her so she does the same in return.

She heads for the staff room up the back, preparing to smile and wish Jean a happy birthday. The hinges groan and Jean's head turns at the sound. Her blonde bob wouldn't shift, even in a gale, but she'd be lifted up and carried away if a decent wind caught inside her clothes. She's always wearing baggy outfits some women called *floaty*, worn to cover up the parts of themselves they don't want others to see. We all do it, one way or another.

'Ah! I spy with my little eye . . .' Jean's smiling, arms open to give Jo a hug she never knows how to return. 'Something beginning with L. Something you *are* . . .'

'Late?'

'Lovestruck!' Jean laughs at her own joke, nods to the kettle. 'It's just boiled. I'll make the tea and you can tell me all about your date. What was the lassie's name again?'

'Ari. But . . .' Jo takes in the messy desk, the tea-stained table, the top of the microwave. She can't see a package. 'Honestly, there's not much to tell. I won't be seeing her again.'

Jean looks as disappointed as Jo feels. But it's the only way. Lying at work is one thing. Lying in love is different. Not that *this* was love, or anything like it.

'And here was me hoping that mystery package was filled with red roses,' says Jean. She pops teabags into two mugs and fills them, hands one to Jo. A faded message on the side reads *Today Will Be A Great Day!* Jo doubts it.

'Happy birthday, Jean,' she says, and they clink mugs. 'Get anything nice?'

13

'Your company, for starters.' Jean smiles, looks like she means it. 'Your box was hand-delivered, you know.' Jean seems to think this is good news. Jo does not. She blows on her tea, wishes she was made of steam, could soundlessly curl up and twist away, disappear into thin air.

'And where is it?'

'Downstairs. Thought you might want to open it in private.' Jean winks after she says it and Jo wonders how it would feel to live so lightly, to so easily see joy.

The stairs to the basement are steep and the lino is slippery, branded *treacherous* by most volunteers. Down there Jo's sealed in, protected by the stillness and the quiet. There are no windows but Jo loves to picture the world on the other side of the ceiling: the bustling shop floor, the browsing customers, the hum of traffic, the finger-smudged glass doors that are pushed open a hundred times every day as strangers come in to buy and steal and chat and donate and heat up their hands in winter. Most volunteers hate working down there. *It's like a prison*, they say, and Jo stiffens because any mention of jail automatically drags her mind to *that* prison, *that* prisoner, *that* crime; to a puddle of blood and her mum in the middle of it. She's never mentioned it at work and plans to keep it that way. They'll have read about the murder at the time, but there's no need for anybody to know she's *that* woman's daughter.

She flicks the light switch at the bottom of the stairs. The stock room lies to her left. To her right is the wide tagging desk where they label and price stock before it's taken to the shop floor. An old CD and cassette player sits at one end, extended aerial optimistically pointing skywards.

And, right now, in the middle of the desk sits a blue IKEA bag holding a box you'd need two hands to carry. Even from here she can see her name written on the top. Joanna, instead of Jo. This is not a good sign. Her full name is reserved for serious conversations and its use often precedes punishment. Now, nobody calls her that.

She eyes the box as if it's a dog with bared teeth. Edges closer, reaches out, nudges it. Definitely not red roses. Too heavy. She pulls the box towards her then tugs the strip of flimsy brown tape that seals the edges. It peels off easily and the cardboard flaps edge upwards, begging to be pulled open. It's only then that she notices the smudged logo on the side of the box, rubber-stamped with black ink. It's impossible to mis-interpret: a fancy crown and, beneath it, those three letters. HMP.

His Majesty's Prison.

She opens the box before her brain tells her not to. Reaches in, both hands. But her eyes meet the contents a few seconds before her fingers do. White envelopes. Dozens of them. All sealed, and all with her name and previous address scrawled on the front. She remembers that messy handwriting from Before, doesn't need to open the letters to know who wrote them: *Aly Chisholm, Aly Chisholm, Aly Chisholm*. The name sits like a razor on her tongue, sharpened by the memories that cling to it.

Jo's mum, at home, dying on the kitchen floor.

And Aly Chisholm, leaning over her with blood-splattered hands.

Jo pulls out a bundle of the envelopes and spreads them out on the tagging desk. They're old and dusty and some are yellowing at the edges. They've been written by Aly and sealed by Aly and addressed by Aly but not delivered, until now. Why?

It comes to her then, a memory she'd quickly and willingly buried: the final day of the court case, and Aly's last words to Jo, just after the guilty verdict. *This. Isn't. Over.*

CHAPTER 4

Panic tightens Jo's chest. She doesn't want any trace of Aly Chisholm in the new world she's built for herself. There's no place here for prisons and prisoners, for murders and convictions; for those who were there and those who remember it. Aly had lived in the same building as Jo's family. Hartfield Court, it was called, a childhood home transformed to a place of horror. All Jo wants now is a quiet life, far from all of it.

This box contains dozens – maybe hundreds – of letters. Why were they never delivered? And why have they been brought here now? Hand-delivered, Jean said. But by who? Jo stares at the box, wondering what words the letters hold, and if they have the power to change anything. Of course not. It'll only hurt to read them.

Her gut says: dump them.

Her brain says: not yet.

She returns the letters to the box, reseals it and slides it under the tagging desk. Jo's an expert in sweeping shit under carpets. Heads for the stock room, looking for distraction. It's her favourite part of the job, searching for treasure in the mountain of green bin liners that fill the room from floor to ceiling. She clambers to the top, shoes squeaking on the plastic, then makes a seat for herself and starts ripping the bags open, little by little destroying the only thing that supports her.

Usually she's fascinated by the things people throw away but today her mind and eyes are drawn to the box of letters, over and over. She's surprised by the sheer quantity of them, wonders what motivated Aly to sit down and write to Jo so many times, over so many years. Maybe she should just read one, see what Aly has to say. But why bother? No words can change what happened. No words will bring back her mum. No words can transform the years she's spent grieving that loss. Reading those letters would be like opening a can of worms that she already knows will wriggle out and bite her.

But so often we're drawn to things that harm us.

From the outside looking in Jo has a normal day at work: sorting donations and serving customers and chatting with volunteers. She's cheerful and helpful. But it's a façade. Her mind is fixated on that box, those letters, and the person who wrote them.

Eventually, she cracks.

Just before closing time she finds herself hunched down beside the tagging desk, opening the box, pulling out one of the letters. She slips a finger under the seal. It rips easily. The paper's cheap and flimsy and old. She opens the envelope and peers in. There's a single sheet of A4, folded twice. She can see the writing through the thin paper. Blue pen, messy, blotchy. Deep breath and she tugs it out and then—

'Jo! Time for my birthday drinks!'

That's Jean, shouting to her from the staff room. Then she starts thumping down the stairs. *Shit*. Jo stuffs the letter back into the box, re-seals it with the old tape then shoves it out of sight. She springs up and grabs an armful of stock, hopes she looks busy when Jean walks in, smiling like she's out for a stroll on her holidays.

'Working hard as ever,' says Jean, no irony attached. 'Barely seen you all day.'

'I like keeping busy.'

'And you like keeping secrets too, it seems.'

Jo feels sick but smiles. 'Meaning?'

'Meaning you've still never told me what was in that box. Wasn't red roses, then?'

Jean's expecting an answer that'll make her laugh or make her envious or satisfy her curiosity, at least. Jo can only offer lies, hates herself for it. 'Afraid not. You guessed right this morning. It's your birthday present,' she says. The lie comes easily. They always do. 'But I've not wrapped it yet so you'll just have to wait until tomorrow. I've got the paper at home.'

'Seriously?' Jean claps her hands. Everything she does is a celebration. 'Then I'll ask no more questions. But you really didn't have to buy me anything. It's enough having you here, part of this big family.'

Jean's always using the word *family* when she talks about the team at the shop. Jo found it a bit embarrassing at first. But not now. She's been here for six months – four as a volunteer, two as paid staff – and finally feels she's part of something that matters. That she can do some good. It's mainly down to Jean. Lovely Jean, who's coming to her now with open arms, squeezing Jo between them as if they were born of the same flesh. 'Bless you, sweetheart,' she says, and Jo wants to tell her she already feels blessed, just by being here, living an ordinary life. Instead she lies and tells her she needs half an hour to finish up, then she'll head over to the pub.

'I'll keep you a seat beside me,' says Jean, then disappears upstairs.

In the silence, Jo turns back to the box. Her gut's still arguing with her brain: *dump them, read them, dump them, read them*. First things first, there's no way she's leaving it here. All it'd take would be for some over-enthusiastic volunteer to pull open the box and prod their nose into her past. She's expected at the pub but if she turns up with the box in her arms someone – probably Jean – will demand it's opened, especially now she's told Jean it holds her birthday present. She checks her watch, a cheap digital with a black plastic strap. If she leaves now she can take the box home and get back to the pub within half an hour, as promised. And whether she decides to read the letters or bin them she can make that decision in the privacy of her own home.

Two short bus rides later, the box is at her flat and Jo's arriving at the pub.

Jean whoops and applauds when Jo walks in and the others fall into a messy Mexican wave. Most of the volunteers are here already, draining foamy pints and tiny bottles of crap wine. Jean orders vodka on the rocks then hands Jo a glass of something fizzy, adorned with half-melted ice cubes and a twirl of lemon rind. 'Your mocktail, madam. You can tell folk it's a real one.'

Jo smiles, wishes being teetotal was her biggest secret, her greatest source of shame. They clink glasses, say cheers, then join the volunteers. There's laughter, stories, music, more drinks. Jo tries to pay attention, to join in, to care. Hours pass. But all she can think of is the box, sitting on her coffee table at home.

She'll stay for one final drink then head home. The pub's full now, mainly greying men with dark jawlines and suits too tight for their loosening bellies. Staff lower the lights and turn up the music. There are queues at the bar and uncollected glasses on the tables and the dull thud of some seventies pop song, a strong woman singing that she feels love, feels love, feels love. The chorus is reaching its crescendo when it happens; Jo *sees* the face that's filled her brain ever since she opened the box of letters. It's hidden for a moment behind a mobile phone, raised to take a picture. The camera's pointing right at Jo, but then it's lowered. Eyes meet and Jo's mind blows. Nerves, tight. Heart, pounding. Skin, creeping off her bones, urging her to leave.

But she stays, stunned, staring.

Right here, right now, Aly Chisholm is standing at the far end of the bar.

CHAPTER 5

Their eyes lock for the first time since the court case. *Guilty*, the world said, and The Accused became The Convicted. End of story. But not for Aly Chisholm. As officers opened a hatch in the courtroom floor that led to the cells Aly had shouted Jo's name then screamed the three words that Jo's been hearing again and again since she opened that box. *This. Isn't. Over.*

Jo snaps shut her eyes, desperate to escape that gaze. On the other side of her lids lights flash and she hears those words over and over, despite the thump of music and the clatter from the bar and the thud of her pulse in her ears. She only opens her eyes again when she gets an elbow in the ribs from Jean. 'We boring you or something?' Jo doesn't answer, doesn't even look at her. Lights leap from green to red to blue as Jean nudges her again, harder this time. 'Will you at least let me out for a smoke?' Jo doesn't move. Her eyes are locked on the far end of the bar, to the now empty space between two blonde girls wearing matching leopard-skin outfits. Aly Chisholm is gone.

Jean tries to squeeze past Jo to get out of the booth but she knocks over an empty glass with her elbow. It rolls, falls, smashes at Jo's feet. Startled, Jo jumps, bumps into the table, sends another glass flying. Smash. Mayhem, one of those moments where you either laugh or cry. And Jean laughs, of course. 'And all because the lady loved Marlboro Lights,' she says, shoogling her packet in the air.

Jo forces a smile then stands to let Jean out, shoes crunching on the smashed glass. Jean stops in front of her, leans in, lips almost touching Jo's ear when she speaks.

'You okay, hen? You look a bit . . . shell-shocked.'

The music's too loud for any kind of conversation, thank Christ. 'Fine!' Jo smiles again to prove it. 'Thought I saw someone I knew, that's all.' The space between the two girls has now been filled by drunk men with fat wallets, creased shirts. 'I'll just nip to the loo while you're out.'

She needs a locked door between her and the rest of the world.

The bathrooms are downstairs and along a freezing corridor with three doors at the end: men, women, private. As ever there's a queue outside the women's toilet, half a dozen folk at least. They're all drunk and pretending to be pals and Jo can't be arsed. She knocks on the door of the men's bathroom, waits, then pushes open the door. Lights out, empty – perfect. She takes the first of two cubicles; locks the door, closes the seat then sits, making sure her feet don't touch the puddles on the floor. Head in hands, heart in mouth, eyes tight as if she's sucking lemons. Did she really see Aly Chisholm here, now, in this bar? Maybe it was a trick of the light, crossed wires in her brain. She's been thinking about Aly all day so maybe it's logical she'd see *that* face flash up in a crowd. Didn't mean it was real. And no, it wouldn't be the first time she's imagined a chance encounter between them. But if it *was* Aly? Then it'll be connected to the box of letters, written but never delivered until now. Maybe it's not enough for Jo to *read* Aly's words. Maybe she needs to hear them too, direct from the horse's mouth. *This. Isn't. Over.*

Suddenly, the main door to the men's bathroom swings open. Trainers squeak on wet tiles and Jo waits anxiously for the cubicle to shake when someone enters the one next to hers. Once they close the door she'll leg it. But there's no movement, no more sound, no more steps. They must be at the urinals.

Should she leave anyway? Jean will have finished her cigarette by now, will be wondering where she is. It definitely won't be the first time a man finds a woman in here, skipping the queue at the ladies' loo.

She flushes the toilet, hopes the hissing and dripping will cover the sounds of her escape. Then she opens the cubicle door, head down as she zips towards the door.

'Thought it was you.'

Jo spins around, then stops dead. Her arms and legs are ice and aye, she'd happily melt, trickle away into cracks. But she's still here, still solid, staring into *that* face.

Aly looks like a birthday balloon lost down the back of the couch, then rediscovered days after the party. Soft and sad and wrinkled. Joyless. She can almost see Aly's teenage face in there, hidden behind the wrinkles and loosening skin that's so dry it would crumble to the touch. This close she can smell minty chewing gum and right on cue Aly picks out a sticky blob, wraps it in a scrap of toilet paper.

It reminds Jo of what kids do, preparing for a kiss.

'I got your letters.' Aly flashes a nervous smile that reveals yellowing smoker's teeth: self-destruction. 'And you got mine, right?'

Jo nods, edging away. Her back hits cold tiles. She could push her way past but she doesn't want her hands on those arms, that chest, that skin.

She's trapped. Her only escape is closing her eyes but she knows what she'll see if she does. Aly, kneeling on the bloody kitchen floor of Jo's childhood home, so many years away from here. Aly, leaning over Jo's mum, so suddenly stilled. Aly, calmly checking for breath but finding none. Aly, the first one who said *that* word out loud. *Murder.*

'Jo? You in there?'

That's not the voice she expected to hear. It's Jean, stepping into the men's bathroom, holding the door open with her foot. 'The lassies in the queue told me you'd come into the men's, ten minutes ago. Looked upset, one of them said. I wanted to check you're okay?'

'I am now!' Jo forces a smile on to her face. 'I was totally bursting,' she says. 'And the queue was halfway up the corridor. The men's was empty so . . .' She shrugs, as though it's nothing. As though *this* is nothing. 'Shall we go?'

She's looking at Jean but now Jean's looking at Aly, eyes narrowed, the same way she does when she's doing the accounts at the end of each shift. Adding things up, trying to make them balance. But that won't work with Aly and Jo. There's a debt between them that won't be repaid in this lifetime. Jean's nose is twitching like a dog on a fox hunt. If she's sensing blood she'd be right. 'Sorry, am I . . . interrupting something?'

'No,' says Jo. And, at the same time, Aly says *yes*. So Jean knows one of them is lying, and by the way she looks at Jo she thinks it's her.

'I'll let you . . . finish up. See you upstairs?'

Jo nods. 'With you in a minute.'

'Timer's on,' says Jean. She's smiling but it's obviously fake.

Jo watches the door close behind her, desperate to

follow. But then Aly steps into the gap, blocking her exit. They're so close now that their clothes are touching, kicking off static. Christ knows what will happen if Aly moves any closer.

'I need to know if you've read my letters.'

'Why?'

'The very fact you're asking that suggests you haven't.' A smile comes, but there's no sparkle to it. Aly's standing directly under a spotlight but somehow all it does is make the dark parts darker, draws sadness to the surface like mould on wallpaper. 'Am I right?'

Aly stands strong and firm but Jo knows desperation when she sees it. Aly's like those statues in posh squares that look solid and heavy but if you knock on the side you realise they're hollow, easily broken. 'Answer the question, Jo. Have you read them?'

She hasn't, of course, but at least now her mind's made up. She'll go home and read every single one of them, find out why Aly cares so much. 'No comment,' says Jo and the next thing she knows those hands are on her. Rough fingers, tugging her chin upwards.

Aly's face flips to fury. '*Tell me.*'

'Or?'

For a moment they stare at each other, all hot breaths and thundering hearts and future regrets, in the making. Then, chaos. The bathroom door slams into Aly's back, pushed open from the other side. Aly curses and stumbles forward and Jo takes her chance. She grabs the hands that hold her, struggles free from their grip.

Then, she runs.

CHAPTER 6

Tink gets sent home in a taxi instead of the bus. It's the first time she's been in one because Mum says they're a rip-off. She should be excited but she's worried instead. When she arrives home the front door to the flat is hanging open and when she puts her eye to the gap she can see the hall and part of the sitting room; see her dad's framed poster from the 1992 Olympics in Barcelona. That's where he's from. She can see his hi-fi as well, and his favourite Madonna CD sitting on top. He's wanting one of those iPod Nanos that holds all your albums inside a machine the size of a matchbox. Her mum says it's a waste of money. She doesn't really like music but Dad loves it, fills every bookcase and shelf with CDs and records and tapes. Sometimes on Sundays he records the charts off the radio, pauses it whenever the DJs speak so it sounds like a real album when they play it back. When her dad's home, the flat's filled with music.

Right now it's silent and a chubby policeman with fluffy black hair is sitting in her dad's chair, hands wrapped around a mug Tink won in a raffle. There used to be a rude joke painted on the side but it's long since faded. There's a policewoman there as well. She's standing the way superheroes stand when they've just saved the world: hands on her hips, chest out, dark eyes on something Tink can't see.

Tink pushes open the door, coughs to make sure they notice her. It works. The policewoman says something Tink can't hear but she sounds foreign. That makes Tink like her right away because her dad has a funny accent too and he's always told her that being different is a good thing, despite the fact most folk at school say the opposite.

She slides off her school bag and stands in the doorway of the sitting room, wondering what she's done wrong. Her mum never cries but she's crying now. She's wearing her dressing gown even though it's the daytime. She looks drunk but she can't be because Mum says only lazy bastards drink before five. Tink doesn't know whether she's expected to sit on the sofa with her mum or at the table with the policeman. It would be easier to run away, but the policewoman looks like she'd definitely catch her.

'Where's Dad?'

Nobody answers and Tink wonders if they've heard her, or if she even said it out loud. She steps closer to her mum. 'Is that who we're waiting for?'

It definitely feels like they're all waiting for

something. Tink wants to ask about her dad again but doesn't want to be annoying so instead she stares at her mum and hopes she can feel it. Blink, sniff, sigh. Her mum looks like she'll speak then doesn't. Tink can smell unbrushed teeth and milky tea and the vinegary reek of white wine. Her dad usually drinks something that looks like water but he mixes it with Coke and ice cubes and drinks it from a tall skinny glass that Spanish people call a tube and Mum always takes the piss when he says it, says he's the only tube in the room. Sometimes Dad laughs but it depends on whether or not his best pal from work is visiting. Craig, his name is. Sometimes he brings Tink presents, like those mint chocolate sweeties that she's only ever seen at the pictures when she's sneaked inside for a pee. Maybe her dad is with him now. She wishes *she* was.

'Take a seat, sweetheart.' That's the policeman talking. He puts down the mug and pushes it away from him even though it's still full, then points to the seat opposite him. Tink wishes people would stop telling her to sit down and just tell her why. Bad news is still bad even when you're standing.

'Where's my dad?'

Her voice wobbles on the last word, then spills over into a little squeak that she tries to swallow but can't because her throat is too tight and her tongue is too dry. Tears are coming. The policeman glances at the

woman officer. She gives a tiny nod then walks towards
Tink and hunches down.

'Your mum's going to tell you everything, sweetheart. Isn't that right, Mrs Forsyth?'

They all look at her mum. Her mum looks at the
floor. Tink's throat hurts.

'When's he coming home?'

The policewoman's eyes flit over Tink's shoulder,
towards the other officer. 'As I said, your mum will
talk you through it.'

'Is he in hospital?' She pictures her dad in a narrow
bed with white sheets pulled up to his chin. She's never
been into a real hospital. Before they go she'll make
him a card with her coloured pencils and buy him a
bottle of Coke with her pocket money. She turns to her
mum, smiling. 'Is that why you took me out of school?
So we can go and see him?'

Nobody answers and Tink's cheeks throb red and
hot, as if the words had turned into hands and given
her a proper slapping. She turns back to the
policewoman.

'Have you met him?' Tink asks.

'Who?'

'My dad. His name's Juan.'

When the policewoman shakes her head she smells
like the changing rooms at the local pool. It was Dad
who taught Tink how to swim, told her he'd take her
to Spain one day so she could do ten lengths of the sea

instead of laps in chlorine. Tink didn't fancy the idea until he told her the sea there would be warm as a bath and that he'd buy her goggles to watch the fish that came close to shore.

'You'd like him,' says Tink, but she feels sad when she says it and the policewoman looks embarrassed. She squeezes one of Tink's shoulders then straightens up.

'We should go now.'

The policeman stands up as well and the room feels full and the air heavy, but Tink doesn't want them to go. They're all looking at her mum. She's gnawing on one of her thumbnails and staring at the same spot on the floor.

The policewoman steps forward, sniffs before she speaks. 'And you're *sure* you don't need assistance?'

'I've already said *I'll* tell her.'

When they leave the flat Tink runs to the window. They're chatting as they walk and the woman glances upwards as she climbs into the patrol car. For one second, maybe two, they're looking right at each other. Tink feels like the woman is sending her a message but she can't reach it and feels like she's failed. She looks away when she hears movement in the kitchen; the rattle of glass bottles in the fridge door. Tink follows the sound, watches from the doorway as her mum flips over a tumbler that's drying on the stainless steel draining board. The dregs of last night's wine are emptied into the glass then quickly drained. Her mum burps as she turns to face Tink.

'Got some news for you, hen.'

Tink's worried her mum's going to give her a hug because she puts down the glass and steps closer. She knows her mum held her as a baby because she's seen photos. But she doesn't remember how it feels, doesn't know if she'd like it. But no touch comes. Instead her mum tells Tink a horror story about her dad, adorned with words like *selfish*, *drunk*, *angry*, *bastard*. The conclusion: 'He won't be coming home.'

Her mum's head droops like a cut rose, dying. Tears fall instead of browning petals. Tink steps forward and opens her arms like that cartoon of Jesus in the school Bible, welcoming all the little children. But her mum stands still, hands in tight fists by her side.

They cry together but five inches apart.

CHAPTER 7

Jo sprints up the stairs and straight for the pub door, leaves without saying goodbye to Jean. Outside, she pushes through a group of men with slack ties and trailing eyes then runs straight into the spectacular belly of Gordon. He yelps and his lit cigarette jabs into her arm. Curses are muttered. Jo's arm's is singed and the cigarette's bent and useless.

Gordon's acting as though she's cut his balls off. 'That was my last one!' he says, scowling. 'What's the big rush anyway?'

'Don't want to miss my bus,' she says, nodding to a stop further up the street. 'I'll buy you a whole pack next time we're out, okay?'

She tosses him a smile then takes off, is almost at the bus stop when he shouts after her. 'Take it you don't want to hear about your pal, then?'

When she turns, he sneers, then slowly slugs the remainder of his beer from a plastic glass. Jo heads back towards him, eyes flitting between his smug face and the approaching bus and the pub door, in case Aly's coming after her.

'What *pal*?'

'The delivery man.' Another slurp. Foam clings to Gordon's sweaty upper lip. He wipes it off with the back of his hand. 'Turned up just before I closed the shop, right pain in the arse. It wasn't actually the same guy who brought the box but he must work for the same company. Said he'd delivered it by accident. Asked for it back.'

All the blood in Jo drains to her toes. 'And?'

'And nothing. I told him you'd left work already. But he was a right pushy bastard, kept asking if you'd taken the package with you. I mean, how was I supposed to know? I told him I had no idea, suggested he call back tomorrow, for all the difference it makes. Right?'

'Right,' says Jo. But her insides say something else.

Something is very, very wrong.

Five minutes later she's on the bus out of Portobello, heading towards the railway bridge and the big antennae. She stares out of the window at posh flats folk call apartments. They've got glossy front doors and plant pots on the front step that nobody thinks of kicking over. The bus keeps going until it reaches her side of the tracks, a place of grey tower blocks and broken lifts. Jo thanks the baldy driver as she steps off the bus and he tells her to take care, sounds as if he means it. Outside it's raining but she keeps her hood down. Safer that way. She can hear a burglar alarm ringing, a bassline beat from a distant car. For now the only footsteps are hers.

She passes the bin sheds, bracing herself for abuse from the chavs, neds, yobs, whatever label you want to give them. Jo calls them The Smoking Girls. They're usually sprawled over the benches between the bins and the main door, spend most of their lives sitting there drinking and smoking and spitting, finding ways to be noticed and not go home. A scowl from a stranger is better than a slap from your mum.

Sure enough, here they are.

They look school age but it's hard to tell with all their make-up. Lips like pincushions, eyelashes so long you could sweep the floor with them. They laugh once Jo's passed and it's probably her they're laughing at but she knows it's not personal: they'll pick on anyone who they think won't fight back. Jo quickens her pace anyway. The main door opens as she approaches then a blond guy with a bare chest strides out, doesn't say hello. Jo catches the door before it slams then gently closes it behind her. She's in, hopes she can make it up the stairs without meeting anyone else.

Someone's placed an air freshener in the entrance hall so it smells like those tinned peaches Jo's mum used to buy for a treat. She takes the stairs, knowing most folk don't. This isn't the kind of place you pop round to say hello when you move in. You keep your eyes down and your history to yourself, thank Christ.

She climbs to the third floor, reaches for her keys. *That's* when she realises she's not wearing her yellow leather jacket – and aye, her keys are in the pocket. *Shit*. It didn't even cross her mind to grab it before she legged it from the pub. She'd kick herself if she could. She'll need to take a bus back to the pub, hope nobody's swiped her jacket in the meantime. And she should phone Jean, ask her to keep an eye on it until she gets there. She glances in the direction of her flat, wishing she knew how to pick a lock.

Then realises there's no need.

Her front door's hanging open.

Jo glances up and down the corridor, panic creeping into her chest. There's nobody else there. But is there someone *inside*? The person who stole her jacket must have got here before her. Heart thumping, Jo approaches the flat, stops when she reaches the open door. It's dark inside and one by one the motion-sensor lights in the corridor click off behind her.

She steps into the hall, patting the wall until she finds a switch. The light brightens as it warms. From here Jo can see the combined sitting room and kitchen; chipped white cupboards and an old electric stove, the folding table by the window that she flips up for meals. A pile of dirty takeaway boxes on the draining board turns her stomach. She should have dumped them right away, not let them fester. Meanwhile the fridge door's packed with magnets holding menus for other restaurants she's been planning to try. Everything's exactly as she left it. To her right, the bathroom. The light switch is on the wall outside so she flicks it then looks inside. Nothing. All that remains is the bedroom. The door's closed but its edges are outlined by strips of light from the other side.

'Someone there?'

Silence, except for her thumping heart.

'I'm coming in,' she says, trying to sound hard; as if the right tone of voice might scare off an intruder. She kicks open the door and it bangs against the wall. At least she knows there's nobody behind it. Her double bed is just as she left it, sheets tugged tight. The space beneath it is empty. She learned to declutter a long time ago. It's easy when your past isn't worth holding on to.

She approaches the wardrobe. Clothes are the only thing she's got too many of, thanks to working in a charity shop. Her wardrobe's so full she doubts a human could fit in there too. But she has to check. She pulls open both doors at once, finds jackets and jumpers and jeans. There's nobody there.

Relieved, she heads back to the sitting room and flops down on the couch; lifts her feet on to the coffee table. And that's when she realises the box of letters is missing.

CHAPTER 8

Jo's brain is a broken record, playing the same lines on repeat.

Someone has stolen her jacket and stolen her keys then come here and stolen that box. But who? From their brief conversation in the men's toilets it's clear Aly knows Jo has the letters and wanted to know if she'd read them, but didn't demand she hand them back. There was no suggestion of it.

So can she cross Aly off the list of potential suspects? Maybe. But Aly was in the pub at the same time Jo was, could easily have swiped her jacket on the way out. She hates the thought of Aly here, using her keys to slip inside the building then her flat. Aly, here, touching her things, trying to work out who she is now, what her life here is like.

But what about that man that came to the shop when Gordon was closing up? He supposedly demanded the box and got annoyed when Gordon couldn't help. He'd be a more obvious suspect. But how would he know Jo was at the pub, or that her keys were in her jacket?

She's still trying to answer that when she hears glass smashing outside in the car park, followed by a roar of laughter. It's the smoking girls, still there, still drinking. They're always at the benches but would they have noticed an intruder leave with the letters?

She'll go and ask them, make sure it doesn't sound like an accusation. Kids that age and that drunk are unpredictable. But right now they're Jo's only option.

She grabs a different jacket from her wardrobe, drops her phone in the pocket and heads for the door. She'd left it hanging open when she crept inside and it's only now, with the light on, that she sees what's really happened here. The intruder didn't use her keys after all. The door's been forced. She slumps to her knees, stunned. The wood around the metal lock is splintered. Whoever came here was prepared to break her lock – and the law – to get inside. What's in those letters that she's not supposed to see?

This is the point where *most folk* would call the police for answers.

But Jo's already spent more time with police than *most folk* do in a lifetime. Plus the neighbours wouldn't appreciate her inviting police into a building like this one. It reeks of weed and poverty, breeds suspicion. She needs to deal with this herself.

She hauls herself on to her feet and marches downstairs, lets the main door slam behind her to grab the smoking girls' attention when she strides out and heads for the bench. There are seven or eight of them. They're all shades of blonde, all use straighteners, some more successfully than others. Couple of lads have joined them now, all squeezed spots and chin fluff. They're all on their mobiles.

When Jo was that age, cordless house phones were still a novelty and if you weren't home you used red phone boxes in the street that usually stank of piss. But she rarely needed one. You saw your pals at school and if you were in trouble, tough shit, you ran home. But when you laughed with your pals you looked each other in the eyes.

As Jo approaches, a girl with a pierced lip starts playing a noisy video on her phone and all the others gather round. They all laugh when she does. Jo can tell she's in charge. She stops in front of the bench, but out of spitting distance. 'Any chance of a spare cigarette?' A few of the kids glance at Jo. Most don't seem to hear.

The ringleader glares at her then pulls a cigarette from her pack and lights it, takes a drag. She doesn't offer one to Jo. 'You'll have to ask nicer than that,' she says.

'Please may I have a cigarette?'

A few folk snigger. The girl snorts, then makes a big show of pulling out another cigarette and reluctantly handing it over, along with a plastic lighter. Jo flicks, is relieved when the flame takes. It's been so long since she smoked that one tiny drag makes her feel as if she's got bubbles in her blood.

'Ta,' she says, handing back the lighter. 'What's your name, by the way?'

'What is it to you?'

'I'm new here. Just being friendly. My name's Jo.'

The girl's suspicious, probably not used to anyone caring. 'Janine. J to my pals.'

'Nice to meet you, Janine,' says Jo. Her crew whisper, laugh, shush each other. 'You girls been here all night?'

'What if we have?'

'It's just . . .' She pauses, searching for the gentlest words. She has to tread carefully. 'A neighbour told me there was someone hanging about near my flat.'

'And?'

'I wondered if you've seen anyone you don't recognise? Maybe someone carrying a box?'

'Well, we saw *you* carrying a box, earlier on.'

'So you know the one I'm talking about,' says Jo. 'But did you see anyone later, leaving with the same box?'

'Definitely might've.'

The rest of the crew are watching Janine, holding their breath, waiting to follow her lead. If she laughs, they laugh. If she fights, they fight. Right now she's chewing gum and smoking at the same time. The filth and the fresh in one hard-set mouth.

Jo knows the type – *was* the type. 'You *might've* seen someone or you *definitely did* see them?'

'That's for me to know and you to wonder.'

For fuck's sake. Janine is clearly enjoying this. Jo is not. She glances up at her flat. Most folk are asleep already so her lit-up windows are easy to find. She scans the car park, wonders if other eyes are on her. Then back to Janine and her crew.

'If you want to know what we saw, it'll cost you.'

Why do kids always assume adults have money? Jo lives *here*, for Christ's sake. But she'll play along. She glances at the lit cigarette in her hand. 'Pack of fags do?'

'Try three. By this time tomorrow.'

Jo swallows a sigh. That's thirty quid, half a day's wages. 'Let's meet in the middle. Two.'

'Deal.' Janine smiles for a second then twists round and gives evils to her crew. A few had been chatting. Now, they shut up. Jo does the same. Hush, and the queen will speak. After a couple of dramatic cowboy-style drags on her cigarette Janine's eyes slink over Jo's shoulder towards the main door.

'We saw someone sneak in, dodgy as fuck,' she says. She takes another drag, is about to talk again when a mobile phone sounds, a cheerful ringtone that spoils her attempt to be moody. Janine is fuming. Her pals are all patting their pockets and pulling their faces into exaggerated innocent expressions. Then Jo realises they're all gawking at her, notices the vibration of her phone in her jacket.

She pulls it out. Unknown number. Jo turns her back on the girls then answers.

'Hello?' First comes a breath, then an urgent whisper.

'Call the police and you're dead,' the voice says.

Then? They hang up.

CHAPTER 9

Jo stands, stunned, still holding her phone to her ear. Was that a death threat?

Call the police and you're dead, they'd said. Not mincing their words. But was that whispered voice a man? Maybe. But she can't be sure. She wishes she'd asked a question, made them speak again so she could have tried to identify the voice.

She lowers her phone then calls the number back. There's no answer but she dials again, lets it ring while she searches for a light in the dark. She hopes to see a phone screen illuminating behind the blackened windscreen of a car, hear a ringtone that will lead her right to the caller, hiding in some corner. But there's silence, darkness.

'You wantin' to know or not?' That's Janine, behind her, clearly pissed off that Jo turned her back and had the nerve to take a call when she was telling a story. She gets her strength from attention. When it's gone, so's her superpower.

Jo drops her phone into her pocket, turns. Janine's on her feet.

'C'mon, you lot.' Janine nods to her gang and they start zipping up jackets, downing the dregs of their cans. 'We're obviously not wanted here.'

'Wait.' That's Jo, reaching for her then roughly shaken off.

'Don't you dare touch me.'

Jo holds up her hands, palms out. 'Sorry, okay? Just tell me what you saw. It's important.'

'To you, maybe.'

'Please?'

'You said you'd buy me three packs of smokes, right?'

Jo sighs.

Janine smiles. 'Thought so,' she says. 'As I was saying, we saw someone slip inside, sneaked in after some blonde woman with a double buggy. The bad news is we didn't see their face. So I've no idea if it was a man or a woman.'

'That's it?' The big reveal was a huge let-down. 'You see what they were wearing at least?'

'All black,' says Janine.

Jo flushes, pictures Ari from last night. Jo had made a joke when they first met, asked why she'd dressed for a funeral.

'What about their hair?'

Janine shrugs. 'They were wearing a cap.'

Ari hadn't been wearing a hat last night but Jo's mind leapt to her profile picture on the dating app. She was one of very few people who didn't use a photo of themselves. Instead of her face she'd posted a photo of a black baseball cap.

'Was she . . . white? The woman you saw?'

'If you're racist you can fuck right off.' Janine twists her head round to look at a good-looking boy with floppy hair and dark eyes. 'Saurav here's got an Indian dad but he's Glasgow born and bred and as Scottish as they come. So watch your mouth.'

'Will you just answer my question?'

'No idea. It's dark, in case you hadn't noticed.' Then she cuts eyes contact and Jo can sense she's losing her.

'Anything else you remember?'

One of her pals mutters and Janine turns, top lip pulled up like Elvis. She doesn't like being interrupted. 'What are *you* saying?'

The girl who spoke is wearing thick glasses and a plastic necklace that spells out her name – Cally. She's the geek, the odd one out, is blushing so hard her veins must be empty. 'It's not really a description,' she says. 'But . . . they looked hard as anything.'

'Got that right,' says Janine, turning back to Jo. 'So you're fucked if they come back.' She laughs after she says it and her pals laugh along. Except Cally. With that, they leave. Jo flops on to their bench, suddenly nervous and fidgeting, sucking her cigarette to ash.

Is she safer out here or inside an unlocked flat?

She's got no idea. And she's still not sure who she's hiding from. Until a few minutes ago the main suspects were Aly Chisholm or the man who delivered the box. But now Jo's mind is throwing out an image of Ari, dressed in black. But why would she be involved? Even if she'd somehow followed Jo home she'd have been none the wiser about which flat Jo rents. The buzzer and the pigeonholes for post still hold the name of the previous tenant. She's not on social media. In theory, nobody can track her down.

And yet *someone* has.

Someone has delivered those letters to the shop and someone has broken into her flat to steal them back and someone, somehow, has her phone number so they could call and make that death threat, warning her not to contact the police.

But if she stays quiet now, will that be the end of it?

Time will tell, and there's nothing else she can do tonight.

She heads back inside, rechecks all the rooms and all the cupboards. That's when she works out how they got her mobile number: it's stuck to the fridge door with a magnet, next to all the takeaway menus. That way she's always got it to hand when she calls in an order. And that means the box thief could easily have taken a note of it as well.

One mystery solved, but she doesn't feel any better.

There's nobody in her flat, but the front door can't be locked. She just wants to go to bed knowing that she's safe behind solid walls and metal lock. She has to seal it somehow but there's no way she's calling an out-of-hours carpenter. Can't afford it, and the neighbours wouldn't thank her for power-drilling at one in the morning. Instead she drags the sofa through to the tiny hall and rams it against the door. If someone wants to get inside, they'll need to shift that first.

She goes to bed still wearing her clothes, as if jeans make her stronger than pyjamas. She leaves the lights on too. Eyes closed, head on pillow, but her mind keeps whirring. All Jo can think is: *Ari, Ari, Ari*. Then: *can't be, can't be, can't be*.

Eventually she sits up and pulls out her phone, opens the dating app and unblocks Ari as a contact. She scrolls through their exchanges, suggestions of tenderness that now seem brittle. She knows some of them off by heart. Neither of them have sent any messages since the night at the hotel, and Jo hadn't intended to. But maybe she could write one final message to remove all doubt: tell Ari she was *sure* she'd seen her near her flat tonight. See how she responds. *If* she responds. She notices a smile creeping on to her face at the idea of it. She wants to see her again. *No, Jo*.

One question, and that's the end of it.

But her plan is scuppered before it's even started. When she presses *send*, an error message appears along the top of the screen. *This account has now been deleted*, it says. Old messages can be retained but no new ones can be sent. It could be a coincidence. Or it could be evidence that Ari's got something to hide; and that she does not want to be found.

CHAPTER 10

Tink's rarely been in a room as fancy as this one. It's a place of high ceilings and black gowns and unquestioned rules and dirty sinners and those who think they're here to save the rest of us. She's sitting with her mum on a shiny wooden bench that stretches out between the panelled walls. It's hard but doesn't have a cushion and the varnish is so thick and smooth that Tink's bum slides forward when she lifts her feet off the floor. It's wooden too, but less shiny because it's been scuffed by thousands of shoes before she got there. Tink's shoes are too small and her toes hurt but Mum said she had to wear them because they're smart, and Tink couldn't understand why that mattered on a day like today. Her dad wouldn't care about the state of her shoes, would he? When she said that to her mum she got a slap on the back of her head. She never used to hit her as often as this, but she never used to drink so much either. It hurts.

Now, she gets an elbow in her ribs. 'Stand *up*,' hisses her mum and Tink imagines a pronged tongue in her mouth, flickering. A snake, a sinner. That's what they talk about in places like this. But nobody's talking now. Tink's mum yanks the sleeve of her jacket and she slips off the bench and stands up straight. Behind her there's the rustling of jackets and a thud as someone drops something hard. Her mum's warned her to keep her head down and her mouth shut when the man at the front speaks so that's what she does. He's got a white moustache and a posh accent and when he tells everyone to sit down they all do what they're told.

Tink wonders how it'd feel to have that kind of power.

The man at the front is very serious and it takes ages before he talks about Dad and when he does he starts telling stories that can't be true. Tink looks up at her mum, wants to tell her the man he's describing doesn't sound like Dad at all. Dad's a laugh. He likes to drink his special Coke and sing with his pals and cook big pots of pasta sauce with a recipe that Granny gave him. It's made from real tomatoes (not from a tin) and peppers from a multi-pack and so much garlic that their mum says the neighbours will get them evicted. That's Dad. He always drinks coffee from a special pot he brought from Spain and he snores so badly that Mum makes him sleep on the couch and he loves his own mum much more than Tink can ever imagine loving hers.

The man at the front describes her dad as *troubled*

and talks about him in the past tense and Tink feels like big invisible hands are reaching down and squeezing her chest. When she thinks about her dad, everything hurts. She wishes she'd told him she loved him and wants to tell him *now* but they're not allowed to speak until the man at the front says they can. It's stricter than school in here.

She closes her eyes, waits for the end.

When it's over Tink's mum grabs her wrist and she's tugged towards the door at the back, between rows of people with black clothes and bowed heads and sad faces. Outside, the steps are busy with other people waiting to go in and Tink wants to tell them not to bother but her mum marches on, dragging her behind her; an afterthought. Five minutes later they're inside again but this time it's a pub and for the second time that day Tink's pushed towards a polished wooden bench, told to sit down and be quiet. She hears someone call it *the funeral tea* but her mum's drinking beer instead.

Dad's best pal Craig arrives and winks at Tink from the bar then brings her a Coke. When he sits it on her table he smiles and says *Your dad's favourite* and Tink isn't sure if he means her or him or the drink and is too shy to ask. She smiles instead. But then her mum steps up and her rage swallows the pair of them. Craig holds out a hand to be shaken but instead she steps closer and slaps him, hard, like she's trying to kill an insect on his cheek. Then she calls him *filth* and spit from her mouth lands on his face. It's *your* fault, she says, then announces to the whole pub that *he's* the one who should be in a fucking box. Tink bows her head. When she lifts it again, Craig's gone.

Somehow, she knows she'll never see him again.

Tink leaves her Coke undrunk, runs home even though she doesn't have a key. There's a wooden bench near the main entrance, nailed into the slabs and splattered with dried bird shit. Her dad always said it was good luck to be shat on by birds but he never explained why and Tink regrets never asking. She's wearing her black school skirt but wants to test his theory so she sits down right in the middle of it and waits.

After a wee while she closes her eyes in case good luck works the same as birthday wishes. All she'll ever wish for now is her dad back. She'd like to print off a photo of him for her room but Mum says she's not allowed, won't even let her talk about him.

What harm could it do?

She's searching for the answer in the darkness when shadows shift on the other side of her lids. She opens her eyes and there's an older girl standing in front of her. She's dressed like a pop star in *Smash Hits* magazine but her jacket's dirty at the cuffs and her badly bleached hair is slicked back so tightly it tugs her eyebrows skywards. She's skinny and solid like a boy. But mainly Tink's looking at her face, feels like she wants to cut it out and keep it forever, though she doesn't understand why. The girl hands Tink a warm beer and, with it, the key to a world that looks very different.

'Sorry about your dad,' the girl says, clinking cans.

Tink doesn't want to drink alcohol but takes a sip because she wants the girl to like her. And right there, in that moment, life changes direction.

CHAPTER 11

Jo arrives at the shop two hours late with a coffee in each hand and an apology on her lips.

She'd called a joiner first thing, told him it was urgent, almost fallen over when he told her the price. She should phone the council or her insurance company, he said. She's got no insurance – nothing worth insuring – so the council it was. But they put her on hold then buggered off. After forty minutes of the same song, she'd hung up and called the joiner back, bartered down the price then called the pub while she waited around for him to arrive. She told them she'd been sitting with the charity shop group last night, was sure she'd left her jacket over the back of a chair. They went, they looked, they disappointed. Nothing had been found or handed in, the barman said, but they'd ask the cleaning staff later and call her back if there was any sign of it. She called the bus company as well in case she'd left it on the bus but their lost property office had no jackets that matched that description. It was gone, and her flat keys with it.

Had Aly Chisholm taken her jacket, and all that it held? Jo felt sick at the thought. But even if that was the case, the joiner brought with him a new lock, new keys, and the offer of a cheaper price if she paid in cash. Deal. The job took longer than she'd imagined but at least she arrived at work knowing her flat was secure.

For now.

She'd sent Jean a message to say she'd slept in, got a curt *okay* in reply. That wasn't like her. But she'd be hung-over, probably. Or maybe all the volunteers had called in sick after last night's party and she was running the shop on her own. Whatever the reason, coffee always helps. Jo had popped into one of the posh cafés on Portobello High Street and bought two of those extortionate cappuccinos Jean sometimes brings to work. But the moment the charity shop door comes into view she knows something's wrong. Instead of seeing Jean standing there with open arms she's met by the metal shutter, pulled down. Why would the shop be closed at this time of day?

She sits the coffees on the pavement, tugs the shutter upwards until it shifts. For a few moments the world becomes noise, the clatter of metal on metal that sets Jo's nerves on edge, no matter how often she hears it. There's another surprise inside. The bottom panes of both glass doors are cracked, lightning bolts stretching jaggedly from a centre hole that Jo guesses was made by heavy boots and brute force. The locks still work, though. She opens up with her key, holding the broken door open with one foot while she bends down to pick up the coffees.

And she's in.

'Jean?'

Silence.

The shop's lit up and everything looks normal. Packed rails of coloured-coded clothes and metal shelves loaded with kitchenware and ornaments and books and shoes that have been smell-checked before being put on display. But the till is off, which means the shop hasn't opened at all today. Jo pulls down the metal shutter behind her and heads for the staff room.

The hinges groan and Jo almost does the same when she sees who's inside.

Police. Two uniformed officers are sitting at the Formica-topped table drinking tea from chipped mugs and nodding at every word Jean says. They all turn their eyes to Jo.

'What's going on?' She already feels judged. 'I saw the front door.'

'We had a break-in last night.'

Jo's bones turn to jelly. She leans into the doorway to stop herself keeling over. 'You're *kidding*.'

'Wish I was,' says Jean, voice wobbling. 'When they couldn't break the glass they came round the back, kicked in the fire door.'

'Did they take much?'

Jean's shaking her head. She flips her gaze from Jo to the police officers then back again. 'That's the weirdest part of it. As far as I can tell, they didn't take a thing. They've obviously broken in then decided they didn't want second-hand clothes after all. Thank Christ they didn't find the safe. I'm surprised they didn't touch the computer but the officers here say burglars don't want items as big as that. Too hard to carry and not easy to sell.' Jean sighs so hard she probably lost weight. 'In all the years I've worked here, this is the first time the shop's been targeted. We're a charity, for Christ's sake. Some folk have no shame.'

Jo thinks: *and some of us have shitloads of it*. She lets the door swing shut behind her and approaches the table, hands Jean her fancy coffee. 'Got you this, to apologise for being late.'

'That's the least of my worries,' says Jean. She peels off the plastic lid, gives Jo a tight-lipped smile when she sees the cinnamon-sprinkled foam. 'Bless you, Jo.'

Jo shrugs, embarrassed by her gratitude when she suspects all of this is her fault. She breaks eye contact to escape the kindness of Jean's gaze, turns to the police. 'Any idea who did it?'

The officer who speaks has a face like an old potato. All lumps and bumps, dry skin that would benefit from a decent peeling. 'We were just telling your boss we'll be looking at the CCTV for the area, and asking neighbours if they saw anyone lingering.'

'Are there cameras at the back?'

Jean's already shaking her head. 'And the street ones at the front are probably useless anyway, don't point directly at the door.'

'Shame.'

'Aye,' says Jean. 'But maybe we'll get lucky.'

The police officers look unconvinced. Or bored, maybe. They're packing up their notepads, finishing off their tea, standing and zipping up their coats. Then Potato pauses and turns to Jo.

'Assume you were with Jean last night as well?'

'She sneaked off from the pub early,' says Jean, answering for her. 'The only sensible one among us.'

Potato's still wanting an answer from Jo. 'That right?'

Jo nods, silently wishing them away. Don't ask for my name. Don't *know* me.

'What time you leave?'

'Close to eleven. Took the bus home.'

Potato studies Jo's face, clothes, shoes, hair, thinks he knows her type. But does he know about her mum's murder? He *must*. When your life's been touched by crime, it reeks like trampled shit on shoes.

'Where's home?'

'I don't see why that's relevant.'

An eyebrow, raised. 'You live alone?'

'Aye.' But for a moment she wishes she didn't. She pictures Ari, there, in her flat instead of that hotel room. Then the image sours and she sees Ari slipping into her building at night, forcing her lock, stealing the box of letters.

'Worked here long?'

'About six months,' says Jo. 'But I don't see why that's relevant. Shouldn't you be focusing on the break-in?'

'Thanks for the advice.' He turns to Jean. 'You mind giving us a minute? Actually, wait: we'll head outside. That way your colleague here can take a look at the damage.'

Jo follows him out. He pauses to inspect the burst lock, lingers there for longer than necessary. 'Definitely amateurs,' he says, running a finger across the splintered wood. 'Now I'll ask you the same thing I just asked your boss: have you or any other member of staff received any threats recently, direct or indirect?'

'Nope.'

'Sure?'

'Sure.' Jo's jelly bones are back. She grabs the folding plastic chairs that are tucked behind that massive plant pot Jean uses as an ashtray. 'Shall we sit?' Jo flops down first and Potato studies her for a second before he takes his seat.

'You said you live alone but are you seeing anyone? Any boyfriends with a grudge? Arguments or conflicts with colleagues?'

'Nothing.' *Shit.* Did she say that too quickly?

'Issues with neighbours?'

'They don't know me, or where I work.'

'That's not what I asked.'

'I've had no problems at all.'

'And you live in Portobello, right?'

'Not exactly. Closer to Niddrie.'

'I see.' Potato clears his throat. 'Chances are your neighbours have nothing to do with *this*. But I know that sometimes they don't take well to . . . *newcomers* there. If I were you, I'd watch your back. And don't worry – I'll be watching it as well.'

That sounds more like a threat than anything else Jo's heard today. With that, Potato folds his chair and leans it against the wall. 'One final thing,' he says, nodding to the back door. Jo's chair is positioned right in front of it. 'Never, ever block your exits.'

CHAPTER 12

Five minutes later the shop's open for business and Jo's standing in the doorway, wondering if she's being watched. She thinks of Aly Chisholm at the bar last night, staring at her; following her into the men's toilets. She's looking for that face in every crowd and through the windows of every vehicle that passes the shop. Right now Portobello High Street is rammed with traffic caught behind a broken-down bus. Its hazard lights are flashing and the driver's out on the pavement, one hand pressing his phone to his baldy head, the other gripping old ladies' elbows as he helps them on to the pavement. It's the same driver she had yesterday. Dave, his name is. He's always working this route and always looks cheerful but a fiver says he's got secrets that sadden him. We all do.

'Penny for your thoughts?'

That's Jean, passing Jo on her way out of the shop. She heads for the metal bench in the bus stop just in front, sits there to light her cigarette. A girl dressed in

65

running clothes glares at her then stands up and jogs off. Jean doesn't notice.

'You okay, Jo?'

'Fine. Just feel bad for you, waking up to this. Have a fun birthday at least?'

Jean smiles. 'I did. We missed you at the dancing, though!'

'Needed my sleep.'

'Curious thing is, you look like you've slept even less than me.' Despite the drama of the break-in there's a hint of a wink in her eyes. 'Something tells me you had a second date after all?'

Jo flushes and Jean reads that as a yes, starts whistling 'I Will Always Love You'. 'Even though you're late I'm happy for you, Jo. You deserve good things.'

One kind word and there's a lump in Jo's throat so big she's sure it can be seen. 'I should get to work,' she says, turning away, hoping Jean hadn't noticed the change in her. 'I've already missed half the morning . . .'

'Was it something I said?'

Jo shakes her head, forces a smile. 'It's nothing.'

'Nothing, my arse.' Jean nods to the bench at the bus stop. 'Get over here.'

Jo stays where she is.

'That's an order, Jo. And if you disobey I'll make you work the tills with Gordon for eternity. The choice is yours. But I promise you can trust me.'

Trust. Hard to find, easy to lose. But Jean had never wavered; had taken her on as a volunteer all those months ago – then offered her a paid position when the previous assistant quit to go travelling. Jo had told her she'd been living and working abroad for years, mainly in beach resorts. She'd offered to get references from her old bosses but Jean said she trusted her own judgement better than a stranger's view. Jo had wanted a fresh start and Jean had helped her build it. She'd omitted the biggest part of herself. She doesn't want Jean or anyone at the shop to know about her mum's murder because then it'll become the one thing they define her by. They'll have questions she doesn't want to answer, will measure her actions now against the traumas of her past. She doesn't want to be looked at with curiosity or questioned about the details of it, doesn't want folk wondering how she managed to sit so still and so quiet in court while she was forced to relive the horror of that day.

Right now Jo steps around a discarded macaroni pie squashed into the pavement, flinches when her arse hits the cold metal of the bench. 'Thought they'd have invented heated seats by now.'

Jean laughs, holds out her open cigarette packet. 'Can I tempt you?'

'You can,' says Jo; she can almost taste last night's cigarette on her tongue. 'But I'll pass.' She wants Jean to believe in her, to prove she can stick to her word when she wants to. For a few moments they sit in silence, their view of the shop interrupted by passers-by. A few pause and stare at the vandalised doors, inspecting the cracks in the glass. Behind them the broken-down bus is gone and traffic rumbles up and down the High Street. Jo wonders where they're all going, where they've been, if they know how lucky they are to have any choice in the matter.

'So if you weren't on a second date, why were you so late for work?'

'I slept in,' says Jo. 'Already told you that.'

'Doesn't mean I believe you,' she says. 'You were obviously on edge last night and it's not like you to sneak home early without saying goodbye, or turn up late at work. I know you well enough to know something's bothering you. And my gut tells me it's connected to that conversation you were having last night in the men's toilets.'

'What conversation?'

'I heard you, Jo. I stayed and listened for a minute, after I left you in there. Who was that?'

'Nobody.'

'Please don't lie.'

'I'd never—'

Jean silences her, not with a shout or a slap but by gently squeezing her arm. 'I *know* you've already been lying to me, Jo. I *know* it wasn't my birthday present in that box that arrived at the shop yesterday.

Confession: I peeked inside, before you arrived. And I saw fusty old envelopes. Lots of them. So unless you've bought me a used stationery set, you're telling porkies.'

Jean's looking at Jo and Jo wants to cry, run, be anywhere but here. She closes her eyes but the view's no better behind her lids. Aly, last night, in the pub. Aly, in the men's toilets. Aly proving that those words shouted in court are as true today as they were back then.

This. Isn't. Over.

Jo's jaw is tight as a mousetrap, snapped. She just wants to be here now, start again in a place where nobody knows anything about her or her history.

'Are you in trouble, Jo?' The question's a crowbar, trying to ease her open. But Jo shakes her head.

'You sure about that?' says Jean. 'Because guess what? I saw the stamp on the side of the box, know it came from the prison.'

Jo flushes. 'Really? I hadn't noticed.'

'Nonsense. You've been out of sorts ever since that box arrived so I know it's upset you. Whatever's in those letters, good or bad, you can share it with me. Anytime.'

'I've no idea what they say, okay?'

'What did I say about lying?'

Jean sighs and Jo feels the truth slipping up her throat like a burp she's trying to hold back but can't.

'I'm telling the truth, Jean. I don't know what the letters say because . . . someone broke into my flat last night as well. Stole the box before I had the chance to read them.'

'Please tell me you're joking.'

Jo shakes her head. 'I'm late because I was waiting for the joiner to come and fix my door.'

'Jesus Christ. I assume you told the police?'

Jo thinks of that whispered phone call and immediately wishes she'd kept her mouth shut. If she tells Jean about the death threat, she'll definitely contact the authorities – despite warnings to do the opposite. But if she doesn't tell Jean then she'll see no reason *not* to call the police. She has to convince her it's not worth it.

'There's honestly no point,' says Jo. 'It's one thing reporting a shop break-in. Something else entirely when it's a flat like mine. They never find folk for stuff like this. And I don't want police turning up at my door when I've only just moved in. The neighbours aren't exactly welcoming.'

'They'll thank you if they catch the bugger.'

Jo shrugs. 'It was probably one of them who did it.'

'You think? My gut tells me it must be the same person who broke into the shop. It's an awful coincidence otherwise. That's why I think the police *need* to know. If you don't want police at the flat I'm sure they can come and take the details here? It certainly can't do any harm, can it?'

Harm is *exactly* what it might do. Jo watches, tight-jawed, as Jean stubs out her cigarette and pulls out her phone. She's always got it on her for easy access, tucked inside a bum bag from the eighties alongside her cigarettes and lighter. But today she's carrying something else too: a business card embossed with Potato's real name and the police logo. She's starting to punch in the number when Jo lunges forward and tries to snatch the card out of her fingers. But instead her hand bats Jean's, too hard, too fast. The card falls on to the pavement. At first neither woman bends to pick it up. They're stilled, staring at each other. Jean's rubbing her hand.

'I'm sorry, I didn't mean to . . .' Tears come, blur Jo's view. 'It's just . . . I'm trying to make a good impression, at the flat. And here. If the police come folk will . . . ask questions.'

'Nonsense. Nobody cares about your life half as much as you imagine they do.' Jean leans down and picks up the card, gently, like a delicate flower plucked from a field. 'And you could just have *asked* me to hang up the phone. There was no need for . . . *force*.' Jean's not looking at Jo when she says it. She slips the card back into her bum bag then rubs her hand again. Jo can see a redness there, a reminder. 'The officers said they'll be back in touch tomorrow afternoon. I'll let you decide if *you* want to tell them about your break-in before then. And if you don't, then *I* will. And I know which looks worse.' She gets up, walks towards the shop then pauses in the damaged doorway. 'In the meantime, take the day off. Get some sleep. Do some thinking. Do the right thing. And take care of yourself. Please.'

With that she turns away, crosses the shop floor and then heads to the staff room. Jo's left with the smell of Jean's cigarette smoke and a ticking bomb. In twenty-four hours Jean will call the police to report the break-in at Jo's flat and the theft of the box: precisely what Jo was warned *not* to do. Her only solution is this: find the person who stole it and assure them she *hasn't* read the letters, even the one she'd gently ripped open.

Will they believe her? Hopefully.

And if not?

Maybe, just maybe, they'll kill to keep their secrets safe.

CHAPTER 13

So far, Jo's got three potential suspects.

Fear tells her it's Aly Chisholm who's behind all of this. But the smoking girls made her think it could be Ari. And logic tells her that the person who broke into her flat and stole the letters is the same man who turned up at the shop yesterday afternoon, wanting the box back, claiming it had been delivered by mistake. And surely it was also him who called her mobile and whispered that death threat, to be sure Jo didn't involve the police. But who is he?

Gordon saw him and spoke to him. So that's where she'll start her search.

He's dealing with a shoplifter when she goes back inside, arguing with a man in a baggy anorak who's insisting he was wearing five jumpers when he came in. They've got no cameras so there's no way to prove he wasn't. Gordon bans him then lets him go without calling the police. But he's scowling when Jo approaches him. 'Should be shot,' he says, nodding in the direction of Anorak. 'Folk like that are no good to anybody.'

'Bit harsh.'

'Not in my book,' he says. 'Anyway, I thought you were heading home early? Apparently you're not well.' He doesn't roll his eyes but might as well have done. Jo doesn't react, knows people like Gordon only feel good by making others feel bad.

'Just leaving,' she says. 'But before I go, I wanted to ask if that man came back? The one who was looking for my box last night?'

'Not so far, but we've barely been open two minutes.'

'You happen to remember what he looked like?'

Gordon screws up his face. 'He was . . . ordinary. Smaller than me. Bit scrawny. Brown hair. Needed a shave.'

'What about his clothes?'

Gordon puffs up his cheeks, lets out one of those super-sized sighs folk give when they're wanting to prove how much of an inconvenience you are. 'Black trousers. Black shirt as well, actually, under his jacket.'

All black. Just like the intruder, according to Janine. And just like Ari. Again, that suggestion of a connection. Jo wants to rule it out. 'Just regular clothes or a uniform?'

'Could have been a uniform, I suppose.'

'Like someone working in security?' *Like Ari.*

Gordon shrugs. 'It's possible. There might have been a logo, now that I think about it. But my guess is that he was an ordinary delivery guy since he was here asking for a package. It's hardly rocket science. Now, if you don't mind, *some of us* have got work to do.' With that, he stomps towards the staff room.

She calls after him. 'And it was definitely a man?'

Gordon turns, curling his lip. 'Definitely. And he said he'd come back to the shop today so you can always hang about and see him for yourself. Either that or I'll phone you when he turns up, okay?'

With that he disappears into the staff room.

Jo glances at her watch, sees a countdown clock instead. There's no way she's waiting here all day on the off-chance the man comes back to try collecting the box. But all she knows about him so far is that he was dressed in black, and turned up at the shop while Aly Chisholm was hunting down Jo in the pub across the road.

Aly wrote the letters and, based on what happened in the men's toilets last night, is desperate know if Jo has read them. So it could have been Aly who sent someone to track down the box, even if that involved breaking the law. There's clearly something in those letters that Jo's not supposed to see. When Aly asked Jo if she'd read them she should have answered instead of fleeing, and maybe she'd have avoided all of *this*.

But perhaps she can fix everything by finding Aly and answering it now.

She pulls out her phone, opens the Maps app and types in four letters and three numbers. The postcode for the one place on earth she vowed she'd never return to. Hartfield Court is the block of flats where she and her mum had lived and from where a murderer had emerged, so unexpectedly, all those years ago.

And, aye, Aly Chisholm used to live there too.

Five minutes later she's on a bus, watching the blue dot move along digital streets on her phone but all she really needs to do is look outside. She recognises the grey-harled houses and the forlorn streetlamps, dull heads slumped. She sees pubs with barred windows instead of hanging baskets, that Indian restaurant that sells kebabs and that sad church with the mossy spire. She sees that narrow stretch of dog-shat pavement that curves towards a street that's all pot holes and plastic litter. Folk here carry their shopping in a one-use bag and park their crap cars on the kerb and some fly a flag in their front garden to tell you what football team their dad taught them to support. You know never to ask.

At least, Jo does.

If you counted all her days on earth she'd have spent almost half of them right here. It's familiar, in some ways. But familiar is a word built from family, and she has none, now.

The bus slows before a speed bump and then for the first time in over fifteen years she's there, driving up the street towards *that* block of flats. She's never been back, would usually take a huge detour to avoid any bus route that passed this place, those memories.

Jo was last here on the day of the murder.

But the Jo who'd walked out of that building fifteen years ago had skin that held no wrinkles and no concept of how profoundly the grief of that day would scar her. An officer with a perm and kind eyes had placed a hand on her back when they reached the street, said her name was Effie. She'd gently led Jo away from the whir of press cameras that soiled the hush death brings. Officers in white forensic suits had entered when she'd left, and the clean-up crew would have been on standby, ready to take the very worst of the stains and make them clean again. Now it seems as though developers are trying to do the same. Most of the buildings that used to line her street have already been demolished and it looks like Hartfield Court is next in line.

Jo gets off at the next stop, stands alone on the pavement until the bus moves completely out of view. And then it's just her, here, a short walk from the place where life fell apart at the seams.

She crosses the road, approaches the flimsy metal fence that now surrounds the building. A few sections have fallen over in the wind, leaving gaps she could easily slip through. The old car park is empty now apart from weeds and litter. There are crushed beer cans and traces of a small fire just outside the entrance. A pair of black boxer shorts hangs from one branch of an unloved cherry tree.

Her eyes are drawn to a glossy poster that's been

ripped off the fence and dumped on the ground. It's advertising new homes that will be built there, shows children and dogs and plants that'll be left to grow instead of being tugged out by drunk teenagers who are then called thugs. In this world there's an age-limit to sympathy and compassion. Grow up in a place like Hartfield Court and the good people of the world will pity you and try to help when you're small and dirty and not as cute as you should be; when you've got a sticky nose and dribbles on your jumper and sweets for your lunch. But it changes when you're as tall as they are and still failing your exams; when you swap sugar highs for vodka and sit in bus stops and parks because it's safer there, because your friends are more of a family than you'll ever have at home.

Jo slips through the fence, half-hoping the main door won't open. It does. She steps inside the cheerless entrance hall, almost gags when she takes a breath. There is a rot here that can be felt. The lift doors are broken, the shaft an open mouth. The unlit stairs are clad in the same green lino they always were, climbing into gloom.

There's part of Jo that wants to climb to the third floor, walk to her old front door and see if it's open. But there will be nothing left of the flat she knew, and she's not naive enough to think that closure will come in the form of fancy new wallpaper and thick-pile carpets laid by strangers to cover the stains of a killing.

She needs to stay focused, do what she came here to do. She steps over a disintegrating mattress and walks to the door of Aly Chisholm's old flat, knocks on it. The action feels absurd in a place like this; it's obvious nobody lives here. All around her, silver capsules from vapes glint on the floor. A pigeon with a limp pecks at fatty scraps in a greasy polystyrene box beside the open fire door. It glances at her for a moment, red eyes stilled, then returns to its scavenged feast. And maybe that's how the world feels too. It moves on, doesn't give a shit that she's there; that she's broken a vow and come back to the place of the murder.

She knocks again, louder this time, then tries the door handle. It opens. That's the first surprise. The second comes when she peers inside. She'd expected a wreck, a place where vandals and decay had made ruins of a life. But the hallway is more or less how she remembers it: pale pink walls and a gold-rimmed mirror, now cracked. From the front door she can see the sitting room at the far end and light from the window illuminates a couch and a coffee table, sitting where they always were. As ever it smells of cigarettes and alcohol. She wonders if teenagers come here now with beer and fags and trembling hands that creep towards trouser buttons and bra-hooks.

'Hello?' She's hoping for no reply. 'Anyone there?'

Nothing. There's relief in the silence. But as one wish is granted another one falters. If there's nobody here, she's no further forward. She's come here hoping to find Aly Chisholm so she could answer the question she didn't answer last night at the pub. No, she hasn't read the letters. And no, she won't tell the police. And hopefully that means there's no need to harm her. But she's too late. Aly's moved out and moved on.

A quick check inside, and Jo will do the same.

Jo's got one foot in the hall when she hears it: the faintest suggestion of a breath, somewhere in the flat. She stops dead, listening; stilling her body. Then it comes. A creeping footstep. Then another. More breaths, heavier now, closer now. A creak and then she sees it, a door handle, moving downwards. There's someone here.

Jo backs into the corridor, pulling the door behind her. The main exit is only ten steps away, maybe twelve. But then the pigeon coos and she jumps out of her skin and turns to see it merrily pecking at filth. She almost laughs.

Then the door of the flat bursts open.

CHAPTER 14

Tink downs her beer even though it tastes like fizzy pee. The girl laughs when she says that, then holds out a blue plastic bag that's stretched out of shape by a few more cans. She pulls out two, hands one over. When the girl opens her can it spits out foam that she sucks off the metal top. Tink's got her finger on the ring-pull but then she hesitates.

'I can't pay you back.'

'It's a present,' the girl says, taking a slug. 'You know, because of your dad.'

'Oh.' Tink opens her can, drinks as much as she can without taking a breath. 'How did you know?'

The girl shrugs. 'Everyone's talking about it.'

'Everyone where?'

'Here, at the flats. I live with my gran. Folk call me Spider.'

Tink knows the name, and where it comes from. Folk say she's a predator; that she's had sex with half the boys at school and the other half she's battered with a bike chain that she carries in her pocket, Just In

81

Case. Spider's dad's never been mentioned but her mum's in the jail so she lives with her gran who's A Drinker. Some folk say the flat is as grimy as her clothes are, that you'll stick to the sofa if you dare sit down. Tink's not sure how much of it is true and wonders, suddenly, what they say about her. She glances at a lump in Spider's jacket pocket, takes another drink.

Spider taps her can against the one in Tink's hand, says *cheers* this time, like they're grown-ups in the pub. But it makes a dull sound instead of a clink and Tink wonders if that's a bad sign. She says it back even though cheer is the opposite of what she feels. Spider downs her can really quickly then lets out a massive burp and starts laughing so hard that Tink laughs too, for the first time since all of this happened. But then a lump appears in her throat so she takes another slug of beer to wash it away.

'Did you know my dad?'

Spider shakes her head. 'I've seen his picture, though. My gran saw the story in the paper, said your dad was one of the good ones.' Tink's cheeks burn. Her dad is no longer hers. She finishes her drink then stamps on the empty can and throws it into the bushes, hoping it makes her look like a rebel. She's chuffed when Spider copies her. Just then she hears her name, hollered, and sees her mum approaching the main door, all bones and grey skin and hopelessness, shouting and slurring and smoking at the same time.

'Omygodisthatyour*mum*?'

Spider looks horrified and Tink shrinks with the shame of it.

'I better go,' she says, slipping off the bench. Her skirt rides up and she catches her bare leg on a wooden skelf that bleeds when she tries to pick it out.

'Let me,' says Spider, and Tink's body turns to sparks when she leans in really close, uses fingernails and concentration to ease it out. It should hurt but doesn't. And when her mum starts marching towards them she should run but doesn't do that either. Spider makes her feel stronger than she is.

'Got it,' says Spider, then holds up the skelf like a trophy. 'And just so you know, my dad's in the same place as yours. Maybe we can visit together one day?'

'I don't think my mum would let me.'

'Then we won't tell her.'

We? Tink smiles like she's been given a prize. It falls when her mum reaches them, grabs her wrist. 'Where the fuck did you get to? That's some way to show your *respects*.' Her mum glares at Spider then drags Tink away. 'Why the fuck are you talking to *her*?'

'She bought me some . . . juice.'

'She's scum,' says her mum. 'Her mother's had more convictions than hot dinners. Stay away from her. Got that?'

'Aye,' says Tink, then curls in on herself like a poked woodlouse. She wants to turn and wave but doesn't dare until the very last second. It's worth it. Spider's sitting, one hand holding another can of beer, the other shoved into her jacket pocket. Tink feels scared and excited at the same time when she thinks of those soft and beautiful hands, gripping the bike chain, knowing the damage it could do.

CHAPTER 15

Screeching teenage girls shoot out of Aly's flat like greyhounds at the races. But they hit a Jo-shaped wall, knock her flying. She yelps and leaps back and they look at her with wide eyes then scream some more, like kids at the fairground. Except the horrors of this place are real. Their white trainers slip and slide on the green lino as they race for the main door, the fear in them softening into laughter by the time they're outside and squeezing through the metal fences that surround the site.

Jo watches them go, pulse on overdrive, cursing them. Once her heart slides from her mouth to her chest, she steps back inside the flat. It must be empty now but she won't leave until she's sure. She flips a light switch in the hall but nothing happens. Phone out, torch on, she starts opening doors. The bathroom sink is on the floor but somehow the tap is still drip-drip-dripping. Behind it the walls are black with mould. Next, the bedrooms. The first one is bare apart from discarded beer cans, fag ends, crisp packets. The walls are peppered with graffiti, the insults and jibes of drunk adolescents. Jo would have done the same at that age, would have loved the thrill of sneaking into an abandoned building and causing havoc. The fact that there had been a murder upstairs would make it even more appealing to teenagers made bold by booze.

And that's all it is now, this place. A drinking den. There's no way Aly Chisholm still lives here. No way anybody does. She'd been stupid to think it would be as easy as that, turning up at Aly's old address, expecting open doors and answered questions. There's no trace of Aly here, or the box of letters. Hartfield Court is a dead end and the sooner she gets out of here, the better.

Jo turns around to leave, but there's one final room to check before she goes. The door to Aly's bedroom doesn't budge when she tries the handle. It's locked. She rams it repeatedly with her shoulder and when it eventually bursts open Jo stumbles forward into a room that's even darker than the rest of the house. The box room, more like a cupboard; a cell. There's no furniture in here and no graffiti or rubbish either; no sign that the neds have sat in here getting wasted like they did in the rest of the house. It's been left alone, respected. Either that or they were scared to come in here.

Jo turns, examines the yellowing walls. The paint is dotted with dozens of bright-white rectangles the same size as a standard photograph. This room had been filled with faces. But now, spaces. Whose eyes would have stared down from these walls? And is somebody watching her now? Jo pushes away the thought, forces herself to focus. There's definitely nobody living here now.

Despite that, the wee corner shop looked open when she drove past on the bus. It's got red-brick walls and wooden boards instead of glass in the windows. But maybe she'll find answers behind them.

She hurries from the flat, heads for the shop. The teenagers who burst out of Aly Chisholm's flat are hanging about outside, all stretched Lycra and tight smiles as they hand cash to a boy twice their age. He'll be buying them booze for later, knows girls are more fun when they're wasted. There's part of Jo that wants to stop and tell them it won't make things better, and the other part of her is envious of them because they still believe it might. There's hope in there somewhere, and that's more than she's got.

They mutter when she walks between them, and as the door swings closed she hears them laugh. The man at the counter is watching something on his phone, doesn't look up. She nips into the first aisle, all crisps and biscuits, with a fridge at the far end that's loaded with lumpy meats and shiny cheese squeezed tight under cellophane wrappers. She grabs a cold drink and the least-soggy sandwich then heads to the till. 'And three packs of Marlboro Lights,' she says. That's the same cigarette brand that Janine had given to Jo last night, so no doubt that's what she'll be expecting in return as 'payment' for information about the intruder at her flat. The man holds out the card machine, screws up his face when Jo hands over a tenner. 'Old school,' he says, smiling almost nostalgic-ally at the floppy, greasy note in her hand. 'And you're stuck with old-school prices as well, pal. You'll need double that just for the fags.'

Jo makes a show of searching in her purse for more money even though she knows there's none. 'I was buying for a friend,' she says, and knows it sounds like a lie or a bad joke. The man smiles then slides the tobacco into its hiding place beneath the counter. He takes an eternity to gather her change then flicks it towards her. Jo takes her coins, and a chance. 'You must be sad to see the flats go.'

'My bank balance is,' he says. 'You buying one of the new ones?'

'No chance. Used to live at Hartfield Court,' she says, testing the water. There's no trace of recognition on his face. 'Didn't know it was getting demolished. I'd hoped I might run into some of my old neighbours. Suppose there's no chance of that now.'

'Nope. But that's progress for you,' he says, clearly thinking the opposite. 'Some folk lived here their whole life and then they're turfed out, just like that. I don't blame them for fighting it.' He nods to a handmade poster by the door. *Fight For Our Flats*, it says, and below there are details of a meeting that's already passed; obviously failed. 'But we all know how this world works, don't we? There have been protests and delays but I heard they'll send in the demolition team any day now.'

'Where are they all living now? The folk from the flats, I mean.'

'Who knows? They've been leaving in dribs and drabs and most of them buggered off without saying a word. I've gone from selling these folk their papers every day of their lives to knowing hee-haw about them.' He sighs, looks over Jo's shoulder. 'I'm just hoping the builders use the shop for their lunch other-wise it'll go tits-up before the new flats are built. I can't survive on air alone. But to be honest, I miss *this*. The company. Wee conversations to fill my day. It's dire standing here all day with only my phone for company.'

As if on cue the shop door is pushed open by some of the screeching teenagers. 'Dyke!' They shout it in unison then run off, squealing with laughter. The door bangs shut and the man reddens and closes in on him-self, looks at Jo with a suspicion that wasn't there before. Changed laws don't change people. She'll milk him for info then leave.

'Just before I go,' she says, 'you happen to remem-ber Aly Chisholm?'

The man flinches and Jo can tell right away that he

recognises the name. There's definitely not much love lost there. 'Course I do,' he says. 'You a friend?'

'Not any more.'

'Good decision. Got a PhD in shoplifting, that one. Not sad to see the back of folk like that. Their mother was the same: acting like the jail was some kind of holiday camp. Not far wrong, to be fair. You know they get their own cells now, with their own toilet and a gym and God knows what else. And three hot meals, all for free. It's like one of those all-inclusive resorts, minus the booze but they've got drugs on tap in there. It's no wonder reoffending rates are so high. Folk like that probably *want* to be back in jail. But if you ask me they're parasites, the lot of them. They should be suffering for their crimes, not being rewarded for it. And meanwhile ordinary folk like me and you are footing the bill.'

Jo wants to ask what he means by *ordinary*, resists. She's heard rants like this before and knows it could go on and on. It's easy to condemn the condemned.

'You know if Aly's out of jail at the moment?'

'Couldn't tell you.'

'Know anyone who could?'

'Why you wanting to know?'

'Just being nosy. I remember the family but lost touch years back.'

The man leans in, his face pure conspiracy. 'You're not missing much. Aly's a born criminal and the other twin is a total weirdo.'

A tarnished penny drops. Jo knew Aly had a twin brother but they'd never been properly introduced. She'd occasionally see him slinking around on his own when they were teenagers and recognised the family resemblance. But even then he kept himself to himself. He was completely forgettable, one of those folk who'd die and nobody would notice. But maybe, just maybe, he was the missing piece of the jigsaw.

'What was his name again?'

'His name's Barry but the kids round here call him Big Baz because he's smaller than most of them. Scrawny wee bastard. He used to come in here and buy litres of cider and vodka, tell me it was for him, then invite all the wee neds back to his flat for a party. Poor sod thought that was how you made pals, but they were using him, plain and simple. He always left his front door open so those feral brats could come and go as they pleased. Got my Gus involved as well,' he says, thumbing towards the open door of a store-room behind him. A boy sits on a stack of beer cans, tuning a guitar. He's got a mullet and arms like twigs, a chin that's not yet been shaved.

The shopkeeper leans in. 'My Gus ended up there a few times but I skelped his arse for it. There are rumours, you see. Folk say Big Baz fiddles with the teenagers when they're wasted. Lassies *and* lads. He's stayed out of jail, so far – but given the state of his mum and twin I wouldn't put it past him.'

'It's bullshit, dad.' That's Gus, shouting through from the storeroom. 'We just went there to drink. He never touched us. And he's not *that* weird. He's got a job and stuff.'

'You know where?' Jo throws the question in Gus's direction. He answers without looking up.

'St James's.'

'The shopping centre? Know what shop?'

'Security guard,' he says. 'He was dead chuffed about it as well.'

'What colour's his uniform?'

Gus glances up, looking confused. 'It's black. That's a weird question. Why d'you need to know *that*?' Then his eyes meet Jo's for the first time and his expression changes. He puts down the guitar and walks through to the till area. He's staring at her but stands well back, like he's scared she'll bite. Jo's never seen him before in her life.

But then, it comes.

'I know who you are,' he says.

These are the words Jo dreads more than any other. Her legs turn to rubber but she tries to hold firm, look strong. 'Go on, then. Who am I?'

'You're the lassie from that weird room.'

Not the answer Jo was expecting. She screws up her face. 'What weird room?'

'At Big Baz's flat,' he says. 'He banned us from one of the bedrooms, said it belonged to his twin, Aly, and

92

it was private. But we went in anyway and it was creepy as fuck. There was nothing there except loads of photos of some lassie, stuck on every wall. Folk always said it was some girl he'd murdered but I never believed it. Not really. Baz was harmless. But that's why I shat myself when I saw you just now.'

'I don't understand.'

Gus walks around the counter, on to the shop floor, studies Jo from head to foot. 'The photos were mostly old, but there were some new ones appeared a few months ago. Before everyone moved out. Recent photos, better quality, even though they were taken from a distance. It was the same lassie, definitely not murdered because she looks much older in the new pictures. And I'm about ninety per cent sure that it's you.'

CHAPTER 16

The main entrance to the shopping centre is a wall of glass doors that never stay shut for more than a few seconds. In front is a wide flight of steps leading down to street level. Jo keeps her distance at first, watching from across the road as strangers push their way inside, empty-handed, then reappear with so many bags they're forced to open the doors with their elbows. Jo's always hated places like this, all bright lights and floor plans designed to disorientate. She'd never come by choice, never strip her life of natural light and fresh air unless under duress, or obligation. When they were younger, folk from school would flock to shopping centres at the weekend. She'd follow them, sometimes, but spend most of her time in the food court while the other girls squealed at the shit jokes of ugly boys who trembled if they stood too close.

Jo shoves her hands into her pockets and crosses the road when the green man says she can. She stops again outside the doors, tries to peer through but sees her reflection instead. Looks away, quickly. Shoppers tut and push past her, tell her to watch where she's going. She wants to push them back and tell them she knows *exactly* where she's going and that's *exactly* why she's stopped. Sweaty hands on smudged chrome. Then she pushes and steps into pure noise. Voices, laughter, screams, arguments, beeps of phones and tills and those security barriers that wail when someone steals something that's tagged. A thousand lives pushed together, the air thick with breaths that smell of chips and cheap coffee and days-old coleslaw.

It's a million miles from where she'd choose to be. For a moment she closes her eyes, conjures up an image she often uses to soothe herself: impossibly blue skies and a turquoise sea. That's the kind of place she'd described when Jean had asked Jo where she'd been working, before she took the job in the shop. She'd told Jean stories of bustling beach resorts, of working in the laundry at an all-inclusive hotel, then learning to make a hundred loaves a day in a local bakery. A life in the sun, said Jean, and Jo had nodded, didn't mention the lingering shadows cast by her mum's murder, and by Aly Chisholm.

But here, now, she'll start the hunt for Aly's twin brother.

Every shop is doorless, the gaping entrances shooting out light so bright it would split your head. Ahead of Jo are packed escalators that carry people up in a zigzag from one floor to the next. Each level is ringed by balconies over which shoppers lean; staring, arms folded, chewing gum and straws that poke out of take-away cups. Jo's amazed there are no safety nets, nothing to catch those who might fall or jump. Those who are pushed.

'Alright, hen?'

A security guard in a baggy uniform leans into her vision. He's far too old to keep anyone or anything safe but he'd be good with lost children, probably. He smiles. 'Looking for something? Can I help?'

'Kind of,' says Jo. 'I'm looking for a security guard called Barry Chisholm?'

The old man frowns then tilts his head as if the answer will clunk into place. 'Not ringing a bell, hen. Unless . . . do you mean Baz? If so he usually spends his shift skiving near the fire exit on the third floor, just past the doughnut place. Unit number seven.' Jo could tell by his smile that he was chuffed he knew the layout off by heart, hadn't needed to check the map. 'And my favourite's the walnut and honey flavour, if you're buying.' He laughs, and she joins in as best she can with a lump in her throat like a fist.

She thanks him and heads for the escalator, slips when she steps on, then grips the moving handrail all the way to the top. Here, the air smells of sugar. Outside the doughnut shop a crowd of teenagers peer into an illuminated glass counter, trying to make good choices.

And beyond them stands Barry Chisholm.

He's clearly the runt of the twin pack; reminds Jo of a tree that never properly took root. He's all bent boughs and bare branches, the one that grew up in the shade: pale, balding, thin enough for a child to snap. If she coughed hard enough she'd blow him over. And yet, and yet, and yet. She hasn't said his name out loud for years, hasn't seen him since the final day of the court case. Then, she'd turned her back on him. Now, she approaches.

She's about to say his name when he looks up, as if he's been expecting her.

For a while they just stare at each other, soaking in how much the other has aged.

When their eyes last met they were barely adults. Life was pure potential. And now? They're both locked inside bodies that are past their prime: looser, greyer, slower, sadder. She doesn't know him well enough to know who and what he dreamed of becoming, but it wouldn't be this, surely.

And aye, she could say the same thing about herself.

'Why the fuck are you here?' That's Barry. His voice sounds like an old man's, as though he's smoked sixty fags a day since she last saw him. And he might have. His skin reminds Jo of the greying yokes of overcooked boiled eggs.

'It's Aly I'm looking for.'

'Wrong answer.' He coughs after he says it then

gobs into a crumpled paper hankie he pulls from his pocket. 'You need to stay the fuck away from us.'

'Says who?'

'Says me. And let me tell you something: I'll do anything to protect my family. *Anything.*'

'You really think it's *Aly* who needs protecting from *me*?'

'Revenge is a powerful thing.'

'Who mentioned revenge?' Jo steps closer. Barry smells of crap deodorant and tobacco and something else she can't put her finger on. Drains, maybe: or the smell at the bottom of bins. 'Is that what you're both so worried about? You think I'll want *revenge* on Aly once I've read those letters? You want to tell me what they say?'

Barry sneers at her. 'I don't know anything about any letters.'

'Bullshit. I *know* you've got them.'

'And you can prove that, can you?' He smiles, thinks he's won.

Jo would happily knock out his few remaining teeth. 'I know you stole them from my flat. And I know you broke into my work first, looking for them. My boss is going apeshit. She's going to get the police involved whether I like it or not.'

His smile wilts. 'Stop her.'

'So it *was* you.'

He steps in, too close. 'Like I already said, there *are*

no letters as far as I'm concerned. That clear? And even if there were, they can't change anything, can they? Your mum was still dead last time I checked.'

'Thanks for the reminder.'

He drops his eyes, scratches the back of his neck so hard she can hear it. Dry skin falls, becomes dust on the shoulder of his uniform. 'I'm just suggesting we all try to move on.'

'That's exactly what I was doing until all of this. Just tell me what's going on.'

'You're leaving, that's what,' he says, then unclips his walkie-talkie. It beeps as he walks away, muttering something into the mouthpiece. Jo grabs the sleeve of his uniform, tugs until he's facing her. He strains under her grip.

'Tell me what's in the letters, Barry. What's the big secret? What does Aly want?'

He ignores her question. 'Make sure your boss doesn't contact the police, okay? And stay away from Aly. You'll regret it otherwise.'

'Is that a threat?'

'Call it a prediction,' he says.

At that moment, Jo's phone starts to ring in her jeans pocket. She looks down and the momentary distraction is enough for Barry to wriggle free from her. He pushes through a group of sauntering teenage boys who snort and call him a twat before he slips through a door marked *Staff Only*. And, just like that, she's lost him.

CHAPTER 17

It's Gordon on the phone, goading her.

'Enjoying your skive?'

'Loving it,' says Jo. She can almost hear him scowl. 'Not like you to phone me.'

'Aye, well, it's not every day one of your work colleagues is linked to violent crime.'

Jo flushes. Thanks Christ Gordon can't see her. 'Meaning?'

'*Meaning*, your pal's in the *Journal*.' She can hear the sound of newspaper pages being flicked at the other end of the phone, pictures Gordon licking the fattest part of his thumb to grip the corners of the newsprint. 'The one who delivered the box. He's been proper battered. And guess what – police say they're looking for—'

Suddenly, a hand grips her shoulder. She turns, tense, expecting Barry. Instead she comes face to face with the old security guard she met downstairs. The doughnut guy. He'll be wanting to know if she found who she was looking for. She smiles and points to her phone then mouths the words *one minute*, holds up a single finger at the same time. But he's not smiling. And neither's the female security guard who's just marched up beside him.

'You've to come with me, hen. *Now*.' The charm of earlier has been scraped off, exposing the rough underneath. 'You can finish your call later.'

Jo's still got the phone to her ear and her hand on the mouthpiece. But Doughnut's making no effort to speak quietly. Gordon's been talking the whole time but now there's a pause.

'Jo? Are you even listening to me?'

She doesn't hear the rest because the security guard whips her phone out of her hands and ends the call. She swipes at him. 'You can't just—'

'I just did,' he says. 'Now follow me.'

'Why? But I haven't *done* anything. This is just Barry trying to get rid of me because—'

'Because you've been stalking him.'

'What? Are you actually off your head?'

'Watch your language, missy. There's no point in denying it or kicking up a fuss. Barry told us everything. And *that's* why you're leaving and *that's* why you're not coming back.'

Jo turns towards the *Staff Only* door. Barry's standing outside, picking at the skin around his nails, glaring at her. She struggles and tries shaking off the guard but he holds her back. From there she's escorted to the doors of the shopping centre. There's no yoke and no cuffs but there might as well be. She's a sinner on parade. Shoppers throw stares and comments instead of rotten fruit and eggs. The younger folk film it on their phones, Christ knows why. If Jean gets wind of this she'll be furious.

'You're blacklisted, understood?'

'Aye,' says Jo. Story of her bloody life. They're at the main doors now and Doughnut is holding one of them open for Jo. The other security guard stands beside him, her folded arms like thick ropes pulled into a tight knot. Jo feels their eyes on her as she walks away, downhill towards the theatres and Leith Walk and the sea that lies at the end of everything. It's raining now and all around her people submit to automatic reactions: pulling up hoods and tugging umbrellas out of backpacks and stepping into shop doorways to protect themselves. Jo drops her head back, lets the heavy grey clouds do their worst. She keeps walking, a slow-motion cog in crowds that are rushing to get somewhere. She sits on a bench and stares at a statue of a giraffe that's tall and proud and elegant and built completely from scrap metal. There's hope for her yet.

Then, she pulls out her phone and returns Gordon's call.

She's greeted with a snort. 'I don't appreciate you hanging up on me.'

'I'm sorry. It was . . . an accident. You were telling me about the newspaper?'

'You should try and get hold of one. Actually, hang on and I'll switch to video.'

She lowers her phone and sees Gordon's big face on her screen. He grins. 'Welcome to the twenty-first century,' he says, then flips the camera so it's directed at the table where he's eating his lunch. She can see a mug of milky tea and a bacon roll, half-eaten. But mainly she sees the local newspaper, open at a story about a violent attack the previous evening. The article is dominated by a photo of the victim's face. The headline is short and simple. *Police Hunt Car Park Attacker.*

Gordon flips the camera again and Jo watches him stuff bits of pig into his mouth.

'That's your man,' he says, still chewing. He pauses for a second to draw a sliver of fat out of his mouth, inspects it then flicks it away. 'The one who delivered the box.' Gordon's looking at her now, still chew-chew-chewing, then using his tongue to pick out something from between his teeth. 'You won't be able to read it on the screen but basically he's had the shit kicked out of him.' He widens his eyes but keeps them on her, tongue twitching on his lips as he tries to stop his mouth sliding into a smile.

'Can I see the paper again?'

He flips the camera once more and Jo stares at the photo in the article. It shows a sunburned man with palm trees in the background, deep blue sky above.

He's abroad, and looking at someone on the other side of the camera with something like love. She knows she recognises him but isn't sure how. 'You're sure that's the person who brought the box? The other day you said you couldn't remember what he looked like.'

'I recognised him the moment I saw the picture. Want me to read it to you?'

'Go on.'

She closes her eyes as he reads, picking out key phrases. A man in his sixties was attacked in a car park close to Victoria Quay in Leith. Suffered injuries to his head and body. Police appealing for witnesses. Keen to speak to a woman seen in the vicinity, dressed in dark clothing. Victim named as pensioner Tony Burgos.

Jo stares at the name, wishing it rang a bell. If *this* was the person who delivered Aly's letters, was it him who'd kept hold of them all these years? First question: why? Second: had he read the letters? Third: would he tell Jo what they said? And a fourth and final question: is this why he's been attacked?

'You're *totally* sure it's him, Gordon?'

'Positive. And before you ask, there's still no sign of the scrawny guy who tried to collect the box last night. I'll phone you again if he turns up, okay? And at some point you can tell me why you care so much. It's the last time I'm ever accepting a package on your behalf, that's for sure.'

Jo thanks him, and already knows 'the scrawny

guy' won't be back. It's a perfect description of Barry Chisholm and all the evidence she's gathered points to him.

The only thing still unclear is why she's not supposed to read those letters.

And the only person who might tell her why is beaten and battered in hospital.

Seconds later her phone beeps. It's Gordon, sending a photo of the article. Jo skims through until she finds what she's looking for. Tony Burgos was treated at the scene, then taken to a specialist unit at Edinburgh Royal Infirmary.

If he's still alive, he'll still be there.

And soon, Jo will be too.

CHAPTER 18

When Tink goes back to school three weeks later she gets an awkward hug from Mrs Campbell and pitied by other people's parents at the gates. A group of mums stare and start whispering when Tink walks past but she hears them anyway, using words like *shocking* and *sad* and *it just goes to show*. The whole world knows about her dad dying because his face and name were in all the papers after the accident. He even got a mention on the TV news but then her mum called it trash and changed channels.

Tink would love to be famous but not for this.

Gossips swarm Tink in the playground like bacteria. Death draws in a crowd. They all know about the accident but scavenge for more details. Usually she'd have loved the attention but right now Tink wants to think about her dad being alive rather than dead; wants to tell them about his amazing karaoke sessions so they can see he doesn't belong on the page of a newspaper, his face stilled forever in black and white ink.

Now, behind her in the corridor, boys talk of body parts. Tink wishes she could close her ears, especially when they start talking about brains and how they leak out of heads if they're given a big enough whack. She turns round and gives them the same look her mum would give her dad to make him shut the fuck up. The boys keep talking but switch to whispers just like those mums at the gate. Somehow it hurts even more when you know you weren't meant to hear.

The boys are guessing how long a human can stay alive with a broken head. Tink hopes it's not long. Please, don't be long.

One of the boys says the skull was so smashed up that you could've reached in and picked out the brain if you wanted. But who would? one says. And then his pal chips in, says if it happened to him there would be no brains to find, and they all laugh and snort; a tribe.

Then fingers poke her back. 'Tink!'

Here we go. When her mum asked why they call her Tink she said it's because she's so small and her mum said Not Small Enough.

'Tink! Turn around, will you?' That's Sooty speaking. He's the boss of the bad boys at school and they believe everything he says. One time he made up song titles and asked his pals if they'd heard them on the radio and they said yes.

Tink keeps walking. She's trying really hard to act like she can't hear them.

'Tink! What's it like being the daughter of a homo?'

Tink wants to cry but tries to act casual as the boys flow around her like she's a rock and they're water, pushing, pushing, pushing. She's surrounded. Sooty's chewing gum with his mouth open, even though it's banned. He's ugly as they come, but good at football; got a portable CD player for Christmas but some folk say his dad has sex with his sister and beats up his mum. He blows a pink bubble and when it pops Tink can smell the strawberry flavour.

When Tink makes eye contact he smiles. Missile engaged.

'Is it true, then? About your dad being a poofter?'

Tink doesn't like the p-word, mainly because it's always used as an insult but she never really understood why because Elton John has a boyfriend and people still buy his albums. But obviously her dad wasn't like Elton John because he married Mum, and they'd made her. Either way, she'd rather have had two dads than no dad.

'I'm not allowed to say,' says Tink, and she's pleased with that reply because it sounds like she's in on a secret; that she's trusted and important enough to know information that's withheld from other people.

But Sooty's not impressed. He throws the phrase back at her, copying her voice, all high-pitched and pathetic. 'Are you *allowed* to say that your mum chucked him out because of it? That's what I heard.

And no wonder, eh? I hope it's not contagious or you're fucked.'

Sooty's looking at his pals and laughing and they all laugh too and that's what he's here for. Tink wonders if the roles are reversed at home, if his bruises aren't really from football. She's getting all red and hot and trying to push her way past Sooty when one of the boys behind her squeals. A hundred heads turn at once. Voices are pumped to full volume. When Tink turns, one of Sooty's pals is on the ground at her feet, holding his balls with one hand and his face with the other. That hand's red, trying to stem the blood that squeezes out from a cheek, split by the metal edges of a bike chain that's cold and hard and held tightly, so tightly, in Spider's hand.

CHAPTER 19

Jo smiles at a nurse wearing dark blue scrubs and too much perfume, says she's here to see Tony Burgos, adds that she's his niece. The woman looks at her with something like pity then directs her to a private room just past a vending machine. He's recovering from surgery, she says.

Deep breath, and Jo pushes open the door.

His closed eyes are purple and swollen, remind her of overripe plums, ready to burst. Above them he's got camel eyelashes and the beginnings of a beard that would scratch your chin if you kissed him. He's got scabs on his lips and Jo knows she's seen him before. She can picture him chewing his own flesh with squint front teeth when he's bored or nervous. But where and when have they met? Jo's grasping at memories, and for breath. The air's different in here. Heavy. Thick. Carries the scent of cauliflower and antiseptic. You can tell the windows don't open but it doesn't matter much for the man in the bed. He's breathing on his own but he's all tubed up and attached to machines that tell her nothing except he's still alive.

She hadn't considered the fact he might be unconscious, had pictured herself striding in, demanding answers and getting them. Why did you have the box and what do the letters say and what made you deliver them now, after all these years?

She steps closer, says his name, hopes he'll blink and wake up. Nothing. The medical team has pulled his sheets up to his neck but she can see the trace of bruising there as well, creeping up from his chest like wine, spilled. But his face is the worst part. She wonders about the scars it'll leave, if he'll spend the rest of his life noticing people look at him and flinch.

Right now it's Jo who flinches. Behind her, a door opens. A young doctor walks in, wearing a big smile and a white coat over a dress the colour of kingfishers. She holds out a hand.

'I'm Dr Mari Trini,' she says, meeting Jo's eyes. 'And you are . . .?'

'His niece.' If she can avoid saying her name, she will. She breaks eye contact and looks at Tony, turns eyes and attention on him instead. 'How's he doing?'

'Bit groggy. Not surprising given all the painkillers we've given him.'

'But he'll wake up, right?'

'I'm confident he'll make a full recovery, yes. Scars

aside. Speaking of which, I need to check his dressings.' She pushes her fingers into rubber gloves, wriggling her fingers to make them fit. 'Whatever weapon was used, it was a vicious attack. Angry. His wallet and phone weren't taken so it's not a robbery. But someone some-where doesn't like him very much. And given his line of work, I imagine there'll be a lot of potential suspects. How long was it he worked at the prison?'

She's asking Jo but her brain's spinning like a Waltzer. She can barely think straight, never mind speak. Tony worked at the prison? So *that's* how he had access to the letters from Aly Chisholm. Now Jo knows how he did it. But she's still no clearer on why. Meanwhile the nurse is still looking at her, waiting for a response.

'At least fifteen years,' says Jo, because that's when the first letters were written by Aly, sent then stolen by Tony.

'Oh, it's more than that,' says the doctor. 'I think he said thirty-five years. His whole career.' She shakes her head, tuts. 'But he's not having the easiest retirement, is he? First the cancer, then this. You must be at your wits' end.'

Jo nods, pressing her lips tightly together the way folk do when they're sad and don't know what to say. Hope-fully that way the doctor won't ask her any questions. It works. Dr Trini speaks to Tony instead, explaining what she's doing, telling him he's doing well.

Jo looks away, studies the room for any traces of his normal life. The wardrobe door is half-open. A blue puffa jacket hangs from a hook and beneath it there's a black backpack with a water bottle stuck in the side netting. The zips are closed but stretched tight as if there's something big and lumpy inside it. She'll check it once the doctor leaves.

'There we go,' Dr Trini says, still talking to Tony. When Jo turns back to the bed she's pulling the sheet back up to his chin then smoothing it out until there's barely a crease. Ironic, given the state of the man it binds. 'He'll be more comfortable now. You'll be staying a while?'

Jo nods.

'If you're hungry the canteen's over in A block. Bit of a hike but the food's pretty good. Oh, and you'll probably find Tony's wife in there – your aunt? She popped out a wee while ago, said she needed a bite to eat.'

Jo manages to hold her smile until the doors swings shut behind Dr Trini. *Shit.* She waits a few seconds then gently opens the door and peeks out as subtly as she can. Thankfully there's nobody there apart from the Perfume nurse she spoke to earlier. Door shut, she opens the wardrobe, kneels down, unzips his backpack. Bag open, hands in, heart thudding. She pulls out a plastic bag, peers inside, finds a pack of oat cakes. Beneath that her fingers hit a novel. She pulls it out, almost laughs when she sees the title. *To Love a Liar*, it's called. Could be her story. There's a plastic pillbox marked with the days of the week. It's loaded up, rattles when she pulls it out. That'll be for his cancer, maybe. She wonders how much time he's got, if he'll die feeling something like peace. In the very bottom of the bag she finds a mobile phone. The screen lights up when she touches it. Tony's got a family photo as his screensaver, a picture of him with his wife and two children on holiday, somewhere hot, just like in the photo in the *Journal*. When you're Scottish you believe the sun makes everything better. Jo tries to get beyond that screen but she's blocked by security, asked for a password or face ID. She glances at Tony, has an idea. She grabs the phone then goes to his bedside, holds it above his swollen face. The phone vibrates but remains locked. She'd need to pull open his eyes for the phone to recognise him.

Plan thwarted. The phone flips back to the lock screen.

She returns to his backpack. It feels almost empty now but she pulls it out of the wardrobe and, in the harsh light of the room, opens all the compartments with searching hands. Pens, hankies, chewing gum, contact lenses, receipts. She studies a few as though she's a detective but the only thing she learns is that he likes cappuccinos, same as Jean from the shop. His wife must as well, as he's always buying two.

Behind her, in the corridor, the squeak of shoes on lino floor. She stuffs everything into the bag, not caring about order; she doesn't have time to leave things as she found them. Food, pills, novel. But it's only as she's squeezing the edges of the bag together and trying to shut the zip that she sees something slipped between the pages of the book. When she pulls it out, a white envelope falls on to the floor. She picks it up, turns it over. There's no name or address on the front and it's sealed with tape instead of glue. But could it be one of Aly's letters to Jo, swiped from her box? This one has no name and no address but there's definitely a letter inside. A big one, by the feel of it.

This could be the answer to everything.

But there's no time, now, to read a letter. She hears Dr Trini somewhere nearby, talking about wounds and dressings. She shoves the envelope into her pocket, is just standing up when Dr Trini walks past the room, talking to another nurse, heading to a different room, a different patient. But her heart flips again a few seconds later when Tony's bag starts vibrating. Someone's calling him. She pulls out his mobile and now instead of his photo on the screen there's a name and phone number scrolling underneath. *Ernie, Lesmahagow.* Jo grabs her own phone, takes a picture of the details. If she can't get Tony's number directly she'll find a way via his friends.

She takes one last look at Tony then slips out, the envelope from his backpack neatly tucked in her pocket.

CHAPTER 20

Jo keeps her head down and her pace steady as she navigates the maze of hospital corridors that lead to the main doors. She's rarely been so happy to have cold air on her face, grey clouds above her. She jumps on the first bus she sees, climbs to the top deck and grabs the front seats. They're the best seats but usually taken. A sign, maybe, that her luck is changing.

The bus pulls out of the hospital grounds and it's only then that she dares open the envelope she'd swiped from Tony's backpack. She glances over her shoulder, checking to see if any eyes are on her. As ever, nobody's looking. A few rows are taken but everyone's leaning over their mobiles, and most are locked inside headphones. Two rows back a big lady with a small dog is playing a video game with the sound turned up. They'll notice nothing, are barely present.

Envelope out, finger under the seal and she pulls it open without ripping the paper. A quick glance tells her two things. One, there's no letter inside. And two, there's money. Lots of it. Crisp fifty-pound notes. Dozens of them. She's holding a small fortune.

She quickly closes it, covers the opening with her hand as the bus slows and a few folk start making their way towards the little staircase that twists to the lower deck. She waits until the new passengers settle in their seats then peeks inside the envelope again, looking for a note or letter or receipt, something to explain why he might be carrying this quantity of money. Nothing. But then a thought comes – maybe this is what his attacker was looking for. She'll need to return it, right now. If the attacker was prepared to batter Tony for this cash then they'll do the same to her if they find out she's taken it.

And anyway, she doesn't want to steal from anyone, especially not a sick man.

She pushes the red stop button and somewhere downstairs a bell rings. She'll get off at the next stop, cross the road and head back to the hospital. And if Tony's wife is in the room she'll need to wait around until she leaves again, sneak inside and leave the envelope exactly where she found it.

She stands as the bus slows, is halfway down the stairs when her phone rings. She checks the screen. A number but no name. Her blood flips from hot to cold, remembering that whispered voice on the phone last night. *Call the police and you're dead.* Was this the same person, calling back? And if not, who else had her number? She gave it to Janine last night, in case she remembered more about the intruder. But there was nobody else she could think of. Whoever it was, she didn't want to answer it here.

She stuffs the phone in her pocket and continues down the stairs, towards a grungy student who tuts as she pushes past and out of the double doors. But her phone's stopped ringing by the time she gets outside. She's both annoyed and relieved.

She crosses the road, checks the timetable. Ten minutes until the next bus back to the hospital. She'd walk, but it's raining and she's got no umbrella, and she'll be far more conspicuous if she turns up dripping wet. She sits, waits, checks the envelope is still in her pocket. Sits some more, waits some more, checks the envelope again. She's about to check it a third time when she sees the bus approach and stands up. It's one stop away, held up at traffic lights, when her phone starts ringing. That same number, again.

Whoever it is, she'd rather speak to them out here than on board a bus. She checks there's nobody around, then takes the call.

'Hello?'

'Is this Jo, from the flats?'

'Aye. Who's this?'

'Cally.'

'Who?'

'Janine's pal. We spoke last night at the benches. I'm the one with the glasses.'

So it's the nervous one, breathing down the phone as though she's been running. Or as if she's scared. 'I thought you should know there's someone here again, hanging about outside the flats.'

The bus heading for the hospital pulls in but Jo steps back, waves it on. 'Same person as last night?'

'I don't know,' says Cally. 'But they're wearing all black. Been here for twenty minutes already, watching the main door.'

Jo's heart contracts. 'Be there as soon as I can,' she says, cursing herself for getting off that first bus. It's twenty minutes until the next one. Too long. She never takes taxis because they're too expensive but she's sure Tony wouldn't mind lending her a tenner from his stash. She calls a few taxi numbers she finds online, but they're even worse, say they've got no cars for half an hour. She *can't* wait that long. Then she remembers Jean downloading some taxi app on to her phone when she helped her set it up. Jean was amazed she'd never heard of it, called her a Luddite and Jo didn't know what she meant but laughed anyway then turned the focus away from herself. She's good at that.

Right now she needs to focus on getting back to her flat.

She registers with the app, books a car, and five minutes later she's on her way.

Colour drains from the world outside the car window as they approach the grey blocks of flats where Jo lives. She asks the driver to stop on the street instead of in the parking area so she can approach by foot. More subtle that way. She pulls up her hood then crosses the length of the car park, scanning the windscreens of stationary cars. Is someone behind one of them, watching her? She can't tell from there. The only person she sees is Cally. She's sitting alone on the bench, a poor girl's throne. She's chewing her fingernails, arse on the backrest, feet on the seat. She half-waves, half-salutes to Jo as she approaches.

'She's disappeared,' says Cally. 'I just looked away for a minute and—'

'*She?*'

'Definitely. She was hanging around the door for ages, so I snuck a wee bit closer after I phoned you, got a better look at her. Daylight helps as well.'

'What did she look like?'

Cally shrugs. 'Your age. Your height. Total dyke. But apart from that, normal.'

Whatever *normal* means. 'You think she's gone inside?'

'Must have. Or back to her car to avoid getting soaked.'

'You know which is hers?'

Cally shakes her head.

'I'll try inside first,' says Jo, moving away. Then she

pauses, turns. 'Thanks for calling me, by the way. You did the right thing.'

Cally looks embarrassed instead of chuffed. 'Just don't tell Janine, okay? And don't forget to buy her those fags. She'll go mental if you don't bring them tonight.'

'I will,' says Jo, heading for the door. But then she hesitates, wondering if she's walking into a trap. Jo knows how these gangs work. If Jo had somehow made Janine look bad she'd be desperate to reassert her authority. That would involve putting Jo in her place. With fists, probably. When we're hurt, we hurt others. The worst violence is born from the softest part of us. Jo turns back to Cally. 'This isn't some kind of set-up, is it?'

Cally looks hurt, shakes her head. She's clearly nervous but trying to hide it, and clearly under Janine's thumb but happy to be noticed at all. Just like Jo at that age. She decides to trust her.

Jo steps into the communal hallway and gently pulls shut the main entrance door behind her. Folk usually let it slam despite posters pleading for the opposite. Inside all is dark, quiet, still. The hallway has beige floors and magnolia walls and ceilings yellowed by time and sneaky cigarettes. It's like living inside a dirty tooth. The lights are triggered by movement but they switch on a few seconds too late, so you're always stepping into shadow.

The only light and noise comes from the lift at the far end of the corridor. A ping, a rumble, a clue. The woman must have called it. Jo knows it's a waste of time. It takes an age to arrive and once it's loaded with passengers it takes even longer to rise. Jo quickens her pace, takes the stairs two at a time until she reaches the second floor, hoping she gets there first. The stairwell is sealed off from the corridor by two swing doors. Each has a tall pane of reinforced glass. Jo peers through, waiting. If anyone arrives on this floor or at her flat, she'll see them from here. And, best of all, she won't be seen.

She flips her phone to camera mode as the lift doors open at the opposite end of the corridor. The woman who steps out is dressed exactly as Cally and Janine had described last night, all black clothes and a black baseball cap. Jo zooms in, starts taking photos. The woman's hair's tucked inside so Jo can't tell if it's long or short. She's talking on the phone but ends the call before she starts striding up the corridor. She walks as if she knows where she's going, as if she's been here before. As ever the automatic lights click into action a few seconds too late so her face is in darkness as she draws level with the door of Jo's flat. There, she stops; and Jo's heart with it. She knows this woman. She knows that face and those hands. And aye, those hands know her. She gasps then softly whispers her name, just as she did the other night.

'*Ari.*'

CHAPTER 21

Ari, here, now, outside her flat. How does she know where Jo lives? She shouldn't know her real name, never mind her address. That was why Jo had called herself Anna on the dating app. That was why they'd agreed to meet in a hotel.

Ari looks up and down the corridor then reaches for Jo's doorbell. Her fingers are on it when Jo's phone starts ringing. Startled, she drops it. It clatters to the beige lino floor and skids into the corner, still screaming out a cheerful ringtone set by Jean. It's Cally calling again but Jo pounces on it, jabbing at the screen to silence it, then turns back towards her flat.

Now, the corridor's empty. She eases open the door, listens for the groan of the lift. Nothing. And if Ari had wanted to take the stairs she'd have come this way. So either she's thrown herself out of the window at the far end or she's disappeared.

Or gone inside Jo's flat.

Jo steps back, flops down on the stairs.

She'd convinced herself that Barry Chisholm was

123

behind all of this. But now she thinks of Ari, cutting all contact without explanation once she'd gained Jo's trust. Ari, deleting her account on the very same day the box arrived at the shop and all of this started. Ari, who told Jo she worked in security, same as Barry Chisholm.

Were they working together?

But where did Tony Burgos come into it? She thinks of him, delivering the letters and ending up bruised and battered in that hospital bed. And she thinks of the money she'd swiped from his backpack. Had someone paid Tony to deliver the letters to Jo, against the wishes of Aly and Barry? And had they dispatched Ari to do their dirty work?

Maybe. And now Jo has the chance to snare her.

If she doesn't call the police now, when Ari's here to be captured, then Jean will phone them tomorrow anyway. It's inevitable. But if she waits for Jean to make the call Ari will be long gone, and Jo risks losing the respect and friendship of her boss. This is her chance to set things right. She needs to alert the authorities, right now.

She picks up her phone and dials.

When it starts ringing a sudden sadness comes to her; some kind of betrayal.

For all her resistance there had been a connection with Ari, or so she'd thought. It was her mind that had whispered a warning to her when Ari asked to see her again. *Push away*, it said. *Don't let her in*. Unfulfilled potential was a better friend than blatant disappointment. Meanwhile her body would have leapt at the chance, lit up at the mere suggestion of that touch. But here she is, seeing the truth of it with her own eyes. This woman, whoever she is and wherever she's come from, is not to be trusted.

But how did she find her? A thought comes, strikes Jo like a penny thrown from a high building. Her phone. She'd run out of battery at the hotel and Ari had produced a charger. But the only plug point was on Ari's side of the bed. Maybe she'd waited until Jo was asleep then opened her phone and picked through all the details of her life while Jo lay asleep beside her. A virtual pickpocket, stealing details of her name and address and where she worked. But why?

When her call is answered she glances down the corridor one last time then clatters down the stairs and leaves the building. The benches are empty now, Cally nowhere to be seen. Maybe she'd been calling Jo to say she was leaving. Whatever the reason, it was atrocious timing. Jo leaves the car park, ducks into the doorway of a closed-down pub and tells the police what she's seen. She doesn't mention the box or those letters or the threatening phone call but tells them her flat was broken into on the same night someone targeted the shop. And that someone – maybe the same culprit – is inside her flat right now.

At first she's fobbed off with talk of no available patrol cars and of crimes that hold a much higher priority than this one. Then she takes a chance and asks for the only police officer she knows by name, the one who'd been kind to her on the day of the murder. PC Effie Garcia was the one who'd led Jo away, distraught, from her home; now a murder scene. She'd left behind a trail of bloody footprints and the ruin of her family. Effie had been young and inexperienced and Jo had heard her tell a colleague it was the first time she'd seen a dead body. Jo had wanted to tell her it was her first time too. She's sure Effie will remember her, and might just help.

The operator seems less convinced. She takes Jo's number and tells her someone will call her back in due course. Meanwhile Jo keeps her eyes on the main doors, heart thudding.

It goes into overdrive when her phone rings. Then comes *that* voice, from *that* day. Jo says who she is, why she's frightened.

'I'll be right there,' says Effie, then warns Jo to stay away from her flat until they arrive.

Fifteen minutes later, a black Mercedes pulls into the car park.

Effie Garcia is leaner and greyer and sadder than Jo remembers: a flower, now pressed. She's now a DS instead of a PC. Detective Sargeant. She'll have seen her fair share of murders by now and Jo wonders if it ever gets any easier; if she sleeps. With her is Potato, the sneering officer who'd come to the shop after the break-in.

Jo lets them in the main door then waits outside as instructed. She can't stop fidgeting, wishes she'd already bought those cigarettes for Janine so she could smoke one now. Or two. Why are they taking so long?

Her mind fills up with all kind of dramas, shifting snapshots from TV shows and films. Should she go inside? She could climb the stairs and watch from the same place she'd stood before. But it would be a risk. Firstly, she was ordered to stay, and the last thing she wants to do is piss off the police. Secondly, there's a chance she'll miss them if they take the lift while she's climbing the stairs. She just needs to wait. She's good at that.

Then suddenly, someone's leaving. First comes Effie Garcia, alone. Jo waits for Potato, expects him to appear with Ari behind, in cuffs. But he strolls through a few seconds later on his own and lets the door slam behind him. So where's Ari?

Jo approaches, catches the trace of an eye-roll when Effie clocks her.

'Did you find her?'

Effie frowns at Jo. 'We found one of our colleagues stuck in a broken lift and not much else. You'll be glad to know there's no sign of any intruder. In fact a senior

127

detective got here before us, didn't see anyone either. We spoke to a few neighbours on your floor but there's been no sighting of anyone, anywhere near your flat. S*trangely*, you're the only person who's seen anything . . . *untoward*.'

The word is bland and sterile on the surface but it's an accusation, smoothed down so it can hardly be seen. But Jo can feel it. In her chest, an old rage blinks and wakes up. They don't believe her, think she's crying wolf, playing the victim.

'There *was* someone here. I *saw* her.' Jo pulls out her phone, opens the photo she took when Ari was standing outside her flat. The officers glance at the screen but stay where they are, car doors held open as a barrier. Effie Garcia's trying hard not to sigh.

'In my job we work with evidence. And the only person lingering close to your flat today is *you*. Now with all due respect . . .' Whenever Jo hears that phrase, she knows what's coming. They take one look at her background and pop her in a box marked *Trouble*. 'I think you should let us do our job, okay?' Effie nods towards the branded lanyard still slung around Jo's neck, advertising the name of the charity shop. 'And we'll leave you to yours.'

With that, she drops into the car. Potato scowls then does the same. Doors are pulled shut but then Effie opens her window and leans out. 'I know we have a . . . shared history. But please, think twice before you call me. My time is *precious*.' And that comment carries the suggestion that Jo's is not; that nothing about her could ever be described using that word.

'So what happens if I see that woman again? For all I know she's trying to kill me and you lot don't seem to give a shit.'

Effie's face drops when she says that and Jo knows she's overstepped the mark. Effie switches off the car engine, climbs out. Jo's expecting the flash of a badge, the glimpse of cuffs before she's shackled. Instead Effie looks over Jo's shoulder and nods to someone behind her, the way folk do at funerals.

'Alright, boss? I was just explaining the situation to Ms Hidalgo, telling her there's no trace of any . . . *intruder* at her property. Anything you'd like to add?'

'Perhaps.' That's *the boss* speaking.

Jo's still protesting. 'I *know* I saw someone. And your colleagues here wouldn't even look at my photo.'

She spins round, holding out her phone to Effie's boss. The picture on her screen is taken from a distance but she's cropped it now, zoomed in on the figure she'd seen outside her flat. The skinny jeans, the leather jacket, the baseball cap. There's no doubt at all that it's Ari, the woman she'd woken up with less than forty-eight hours ago.

The boss glances at the screen for a second, maybe two. Then her eyes shift and they're staring right at each other. *The boss* is dressed in skinny jeans, a leather jacket, and a baseball cap. And aye, the connection that was there yesterday morning is back, with force.

Jo's jaw drops and she steps back on to Effie Garcia's feet. 'Watch it, you!' She's pushed off, tugged round, given a look that would smash a thousand mirrors. Then Effie nods again towards her boss. 'Ma'am, this is Jo Hidalgo. Miss Hidalgo, this is Detective Inspector Farida McPherson.'

The name's a mouthful but Jo already knows that, sometimes, she goes by a different name altogether.

CHAPTER 22

Spider gets suspended for battering that boy but doesn't give a shit, says her gran won't care. Nobody will notice if she's at home or not. Tink wishes she was more like Spider. Wishes she *was* her, sometimes. Everyone's talking about it, with respect, and when she announces she's banned from school for two whole weeks folk say she's a lucky bastard. She walks out of the playground at breaktime with a swagger, asks Tink if she wants to come.

She does and she doesn't. 'My mum'll be raging if she finds out.'

'Then we'll make sure she doesn't,' says Spider. 'And anyway, your mum's got way bigger shit to worry about.'

'What d'you mean?'

Spider kicks a can that's been crushed and chucked. It rattles on the ground and if there's an answer to her question Tink doesn't hear it. She wants to ask but swallows it because Spider can't know what's wrong with her mum if even the doctor doesn't. He just gives her more pills and tells her it'll pass, but it doesn't, and now she drinks instead of works.

'She still saying she won't take you to visit your dad?'

Tink feels like her blood's got warmer. 'Says there's no point.' She says a lot of other things too but Tink doesn't want to repeat them. One night a week ago, when her mum was even drunker and even sadder than usual, she had ripped up all her photos of Dad then dumped them in the bin and scraped the leftovers of their pasta dinner on top. Once she passed out on the couch Tink had picked out some scraps of his face, cleaned them with a hankie, hid them inside an old school jotter at the back of her sock drawer. So now she's got a mosaic of her dad, just for her. She won't even tell Spider.

'But you want to see him, don't you?'

They're face to face and Spider's waiting for an answer Tink can't give because when she thinks of her dad all the sadness in her turns solid and blocks her throat. She shrugs instead and then she's ashamed of that too, because if her dad could see her he'd think she didn't care.

'I'll pay for your bus,' says Spider then turns, leaves.

Tink follows.

Ten minutes later the bus comes and the driver tuts and tells them they should be at school, then looks embarrassed when Spider tells him where they're going instead. They get the best seats – top deck, front row – and sit together even though it's a squeeze. It's raining when they get off and Tink's cold and worried about getting home late but Spider doesn't even seem to notice. She's waterproof, timeproof, bulletproof. She walks faster than Tink because she's got longer legs and more years of practice. Her wet hair goes frizzy but she's still the most beautiful thing Tink's ever seen. She looks away when Spider catches her looking.

'How old are you anyway?'

'Almost fourteen,' says Tink because it sounds better than the truth. Her thirteenth birthday was last week and her mum forgot, so she'd rather skip this year anyway. 'You?' Spider's in the year above her at school.

'Old enough,' Spider says, then pulls a pack of cigarettes out of her jacket pocket. 'Want one?'

Tink's mum says it's a disgusting habit, but that's only because her dad and his best pal Craig were always smoking and it made the sitting room smell like a pub. Her dad used to let her hold his cigarette sometimes, before he lit it, but until now she's never felt the warmth of the flickering flame on the skin of her hand and chin; never realised smoking made your blood feel like it was moving in the wrong direction. Her toes are tingling and she wants to sit down and Spider laughs and leads her to a bench that overlooks the gates that lead to *that* place.

The main gates must have been part of a mountain once; but they've been chopped and smoothed down and made useful. Tink has never been to the mountains but she's seen them in films and sometimes her dad would show her old photos of the place he grew up in Spain and it was all jagged peaks, and lakes so blue they looked like swimming pools. Dad said the water in them was so cold that you'd be dead in four minutes and even now, in spite of everything, she struggles to believe a life can be lost so quickly. But the graveyard across the road is evidence that it can. Every single person in there has seen and felt and let an ending happen.

'You ready?' That's Spider, standing now, nibbling her lips so hard the bottom one is almost bleeding. She's staring across the road, watches strangers pass through the gates with their heads down and a look on their face that matches the feeling inside Tink's chest. They walk as if they're weighed down.

'We don't have to go in, you know.' That's Spider speaking.

And that's when Tink realises she's not the only one who's nervous. She gets up and stands as close to Spider as she can, without touching. She can feel her warmth, smell the cigarettes on her breath and wonders if their mouths taste the same.

'We'll go in together,' says Tink.

CHAPTER 23

Jo's hemmed in. Behind her is Effie, nursing her trampled foot. And in front, blocking her escape route, is DI Farida McPherson. Drop a few letters and what do you get? Ari.

Detectives don't wear uniform, which explains the jeans and cap. But casual clothes can't hide what lies beneath: authority. Now, Jo can sense it, feel it, wonders how she missed it the other night. When they met at that hotel Ari had told her she worked 'in security', and, given the body on her, Jo had had no reason to doubt her. But this is *security* of a different kind altogether. She hadn't quite lied, but almost.

Ari mostly keeps her eyes on Jo but they flit over her shoulder from time to time. The intimacy they'd shared is gone. And now, they have an audience.

'As my colleague said, my name's DI McPherson,' she says, the *c* of her surname sharp as a blade. 'I'd appreciate . . . a quiet word?'

Jo's pushing her back into the car door, trying to widen the gap between them.

'Why are *you* here?'

'Responding to your call, as were my colleagues.' She nods to Effie then steps towards them, brushing Jo's arm on the way past. So many sparks fly that Jo's surprised the others can't see them. 'There's no need for further investigations so I'll take it from here if you'd like to return to the station? I'll make sure Miss Hidalgo is . . . taken care of.'

Jo almost laughs. What a fucking pantomime.

Effie pretty much bows to her boss, then drives off. Farida watches them go, waits until the car's tail-lights are well out of sight before she turns back to Jo.

'We need to talk,' she says. Her voice was made in Glasgow, each word roughly chopped. But her face? It's satin that you want to reach out and touch. Jo's insides are all butterflies and fireworks and aye, she hates herself for it.

'Start by telling me why you lied about your name, maybe?'

'You tell me, *Anna*.'

There's something like a smile, shared. But it's a glow in the ashes, burns itself out before either of them are able to save it. 'I go by Farida,' she says. 'And you're Jo?'

Jo nods.

'Nice to meet you.'

'You think?' Jo steps away from her. There's two metres and a whole world between them. 'I don't understand what you're doing here. How you know where I live.'

Farida looks over her shoulder then leans in. Too close and yet not close enough.

'The officer you met at the charity shop was sure he recognised you from . . . *before*. Pulled up your file on the system when he got back. Given your . . . *history* . . . my team was alerted since we deal with serious crimes. Your name meant nothing to me but there was a photo and . . .' She's been avoiding eye contact but looks up, now. 'Obviously I recognised your face.'

'That bastard told me our chat was off the record,' says Jo. 'Didn't even ask my name.'

'He didn't need to,' says Farida. 'Says you're the double of your mother.'

Jo tightens. 'And that gives him the right to spread it round the whole station, does it?'

'He was just doing his job.'

'And you?'

'What about me?'

'Are you *just* here for work?'

Farida shakes her head, slowly. 'Not exactly,' she says. 'It's true I heard the call come in over the police radio, reporting an intruder at this address, but . . .' She sniffs deeply, as though the truth is slipping out and she's trying to haul it back in. 'The fact is, I was already here. Looking for you. But I got no answer at the flat.

Tried to leave and got stuck in that useless lift. That's when your call came in over the radio. Thankfully my colleagues arrived and rescued me and I was able to . . . improvise. Not tell them my real reason for being here.'

'Which is?'

'To talk. In private, if possible?'

'About?' Behind them someone squeals and Jo turns to see a few of the smoking girls, back at the benches, trying to kill their boredom. Cally's not with them.

Farida glances over Jo's shoulder. 'Us.'

'Forget it ever happened, you mean?'

'I didn't say that.'

'But you know who I am now, don't you?' That's Jo, gently throwing the question into the space between them. It sits there, unanswered, untouched, a bomb that could blow them to pieces.

Farida nods, once. 'I didn't know when we . . . met . . . at the hotel. But since then colleagues have informed me about your mum's . . . case.'

'Most folk call it murder.'

Farida nods again.

'And how do you feel about mixing work and . . . pleasure?'

Farida flinches. Probably as close as she gets to showing her feelings. But enough.

'Thought as much,' says Jo. 'A woman like you can't be seen with a woman like me. Or in a place like this. Right?'

'It's complicated.'

'It really isn't. We met as Ari and Anna and whatever they shared is over. There's nothing between the real me and the real you. Jo and Farida have only just met. I won't tell anyone, so you can go home, stop worrying that one night with me might wreck your career. The real Farida McPherson is safe as ever; remains flawless.'

'What about you?'

'Go and double-check my files and you'll find my flaws in no time.'

Jo turns her back on Farida and starts walking back to the flat. Striding, so she looks more confident, so she can pretend she doesn't give a shit. She's hoping Farida calls out to her, begs her to come back. Says she's sorry. But all she hears is the smoking girls: more screams, shouts, the sound of glass bottles being tossed and smashing. She slows her pace but keeps on walking, waiting for Farida's hands to gently touch her shoulder and tug her back. It doesn't happen, and when she reaches the door she deliberately looks in the wrong pockets for her keys to give Farida more time. Still nothing. Jo clamps her jaw and kids herself she doesn't feel the sink of disappointment. If it wasn't finished before, it's definitely finished now.

Over and out, Ari.

Almost. Key out, door open, and Jo looks back, expecting to see the brake lights of Farida's car, leaving. Instead she sees Farida standing at the far end of the parking area, staring at her vehicle instead of driving it. To be fair, it's a nice one, a bright red pickup that's definitely not a pool car from the police station. For a moment Jo pictures herself sitting on the inside, dogs in the back, heading up north for a weekend of big skies and birdsong; walking hand in hand through forests that smell of damp earth, freedom. *Forget it, Jo.* Her eyes flit back to Farida when she pulls out her phone, starts taking photos of the pickup from various angles.

What is she doing?

'Ari?' No response. That must be her one-night-stand name. 'Farida?'

She looks up, catches Jo's gaze then drops it again. Keeps taking photos of the pickup. Jo stuffs her keys back into her pocket and walks towards her, slowly, annoyed that she's the one who's having to retrace her steps. It makes her look weak, desperate. Maybe she is. The smoking girls are watching and Janine shouts to her on the way past, flicking her lighter. 'Where's my fags?'

'I'll bring them later!'

'Heard that before.'

Christ, even the neds don't trust her. Nobody does. But maybe that's because she doesn't trust *them*; doesn't trust anyone enough to show them every part of herself.

Jo stops before she reaches the pickup. Farida's on the other side, big red bonnet between them. She looks up, winces when she sees Jo. Not the reaction she'd hoped for. All she wants in this life is someone who's happy to see her.

Right now Farida's face is made of stone but there's a crack that tells Jo something's wrong. 'What's with the photos?'

'Come round here and you'll see.'

Jo pauses when she reaches the front of the pickup. There must be two dozen cars parked here, a mix of rust buckets and fancy models bought with credit cards and the belief that chrome paint and fat wheels would make them happier. The windows look black in the daylight. She's scouring the spaces between them when, somewhere above her, someone shuts a window. She raises her eyes, scans all the flats in her building; up, up, up until she reaches the rectangle of grey sky between two tower blocks.

Nothing. Nobody. Just her overactive imagination.

She turns back to the pickup, keeps walking. Farida's hunched down on the ground, studying the front tyre on the passenger side. There's a gap between her belt and her leather jacket and Jo wants to kneel down beside her, rest a warm hand on the smooth skin of her exposed back. But then something else grabs her attention.

Farida's pickup is gleaming, as you'd expect. But at

some point between Farida arriving and trying to leave, someone's crept up to her vehicle and written a message on the side with a black marker pen. Three words, spread across both doors.

Watch Your Back.

CHAPTER 24

When Jo drags her eyes away from the message on the pickup Farida's looking right at her. 'Those kids you were talking to . . .' She nods over Jo's shoulder towards the benches. 'Think they did it?'

'Why would they?'

'Most of them don't need a reason.'

Jo doesn't like the way Farida says *them*, like she'd have turned out differently if she'd grown up in a place like this. 'We're all born the same,' says Jo, and Farida winces as though she's just spat on someone by accident. Which in some ways, she has.

'But if it's not them, who?' Farida turns on the spot, scouring every corner of the car park. 'If I was driving a patrol car or wearing uniform I'd understand it. Expect it, even. We're not always welcome, in this part of the city. I get that. But this is my own car. My own clothes. Nobody here can have any idea that I'm with the police.'

'They can sense it, maybe.'

'Like you did?' Her mouth twitches upwards at one

side, almost a smile. She's staring at Jo and Jo's staring back, way longer than you'd ever look at a stranger. It's one of those moments that often leads to a kiss but Jo knows there's no chance of that here, now, when the eyes of others are on them. And not with a threat scrawled across the side of Farida's pickup.

Jo backs off first. She lets her gaze slip over Farida's shoulder, back towards the building, the windows, the people behind them she can't see.

'Someone must know who you are. From court, maybe? Or a different case. Or maybe they just picked your car because it stands out like a sore thumb in this shithole. Just as well you're not here on an undercover mission.'

'Depends who you ask,' says Farida, and there's a smile that's brief but shared. Then Jo pushes the focus back to the car, the graffiti.

'You worried about it?'

Farida gives the tiniest of shrugs. 'I've survived worse.'

'That doesn't answer my question,' says Jo.

'Potentially,' she says, then stands back and takes another photo of the message. 'Now, can we get some water to wash this off?'

'I'll go and grab some.'

'I'll help.'

'You really don't need—'

'I do.'

Inside, upstairs, door unlocked and opened, Jo walks in first, immediately embarrassed by the tube lights and bare walls, the tiny couch, the dirty windows. Her childhood flat was even worse but it wasn't hers. Back then, visitors felt sorry for her, but it doesn't work like that when you're an adult. Joiner aside, this is the first time she's ever let anybody inside and she can't believe it's Farida, of all people. She's ashamed to live in a place like this but wishes she wasn't. And so shame piles on top of shame, a double whammy. We waste half our lives wondering how other people judge us and the other half judging ourselves; convinced we need to do more, have more, prove something, change something. We're rarely just here, living without any filter.

And aye, right now they're both acting.

Farida's clearly pretending she doesn't notice Jo lives in a hovel, that they come from different worlds. Jo's doing the same, spewing out a pointless commentary of her every move in the hope that she'll distract Farida from sad details of her home: the absence of photographs, the tiny folding table, her clean washing crisping on the sitting room radiator because there's no room to hang it anywhere else. She looks for a bucket and fills it with warm water, hunts for a cloth under the sink. She can sense Farida standing behind her, probably doesn't want to sit down for fear of catching something.

'Can I ask you something?'

Jo's surprised she's asking for permission. Flattered, somehow. 'Go on.'

'The *intruder* at your flat obviously turned out to be me. But when you called the police you also reported a break-in, said you thought the thief could be the same person who'd targeted your shop. Want to tell me about it?'

Jo's on her knees, head poking into the fusty cupboard under the sink. She keeps it there so Farida can't see her cheeks flush. 'Not much to tell.'

'I'd disagree. The fact there were two break-ins on the same day, both connected to you, suggests something . . . suspicious. I know they left the shop empty-handed. Did they take anything from here?'

Now, a decision: to lie or not to lie. Jo grabs a few cloths and straightens up, mistruths bubbling on her tongue. Across the room Farida's now in detective mode, examining the door, rubbing her thumb up and down the splintered frame. 'So?'

She can't tell Farida about the letters, even if she's here off the record. *Tell the police and you're dead*, the box thief said. Obviously Jo *has* called the police now, but didn't tell them about Aly's letters or the death threat. Jean will be pleased she's alerted the authorities and doesn't need to know Jo hasn't told them the full story. But Aly and the box thief need to know she hasn't read the letters and hasn't told the police about anything other than the splintered door. Otherwise they might come for her; and if they mean what they say, kill her. 'They didn't steal anything of value.' Jo can't look at Farida when she says it. 'Just a delivery that I'd left on the table.'

'That's . . . unfortunate. But perhaps you can contact the company, claim it back?'

Jo nods. Farida comes from a world of right and wrong and rules that are made to be followed; a place where filled-out forms fix problems.

In Jo's world, fists do. If she wants to protect Farida, this needs to end here.

She turns to the sink, picks up the bucket. A few soapy suds spill over the edge as she holds it towards Farida. 'All yours,' she says. 'I need to get going.'

First things first, she'll head back to the hospital with Tony's cash and if he's awake she'll try to get some answers from him. Was he paid by one person to deliver the letters to Jo, then attacked by another for carrying it through? And the key question – what do the letters say? The secrets they hold are driving all of this.

She thinks again of that whispered phone call and the graffiti on Farida's pickup. Two women, two threats, two days. But is one person behind them both?

'You look . . . worried.' That's Farida, in front of Jo now, gently taking the bucket from her hands then sitting it on the ground between them. Jo's glad of the barrier.

'I'm fine,' says Jo. 'Just getting over the shock of *you* being my intruder.'

She expects a smile. But Farida looks all moody and serious, like she's about to break bad news.

Instead, she kisses her.

CHAPTER 25

When Jo wakes, her mouth tastes of Farida McPherson. She's barely slept and now lies with her eyes closed, sucking in air that smells of someone else. Farida's seeped into sheets, the carpet, the curtains. And the fabric of *her*. Jo stretches a hand across to Farida's side of the bed, hits cold sheets. Eyes open, light on.

Farida is gone.

When she goes to the kitchen she finds a note on the table. *Work called*, it says, which spells out Farida's priorities. There was no kiss, no phone number, no suggestion they'd see each other again. She was probably horrified to wake up and find herself in the kind of place she's sent to collar criminals. The world looks at these flats and thinks it's where the bad ones roam. Maybe the world's right.

Last night in bed – *afterwards* – she and Farida had barely spoken, and, when they did, they'd ignored all elephants in the room, pretended they were all part of the same circus. When Farida fell asleep Jo had nipped out and bought cigarettes for Janine and her pals,

149

finally repaid that debt. She'd half-expected Farida to be gone by the time she got back but she was still there, had opened her eyes and held out a hand to lead Jo back into the warmth of the bed, her arms.

She'd slept soundly, there. But now the show was over.

Jo showers but still feels dirty, gets dressed but still feels exposed. There's a lump in her throat so big she's sure the bus driver notices it when she steps on board and asks for a ticket to the hospital.

She should never have let Farida stay. Especially now that she knows she *knows*.

She climbs to the top deck of the bus but this morning the front seats are taken. She takes a row up the back next to a man who's eating crisps for breakfast. She'll head to the hospital before her Sunday shift at the shop, replace that envelope of money before anybody notices it's gone.

Half an hour later she reaches the right ward, spots the perfumed nurse she saw yesterday. At least she won't need to repeat her lie. She walks towards the nurses' station, trying to look relaxed but with the air of someone who's worried about a relative. Perfume looks up, then turns back to her computer. Jo keeps walking, relieved. With any luck she won't see Dr Trini and won't need to speak to anyone at all. She'll be in and out in five minutes flat, providing Tony's wife isn't in for a visit. Fingers crossed.

She pauses outside the door and peers in through the narrow pane of glass and that's when she knows something is wrong. The bed's empty and stripped of sheets. She pushes open the door, steps inside, checks the wardrobe. All his belongings are gone. Well, apart from the envelope stuffed with two thousand pounds in cash that Jo's carrying in her backpack. She's still standing there when a waft of ripe mangoes hits her nose. She turns to find Perfume in the doorway, arms crossed. 'Thought it was you,' she says, and Jo senses an accusation in the space between the words. 'Here to see your *uncle*, are you?'

'Just popping in before work,' says Jo, then makes a show of looking at the wall clock. 'In fact I should probably get going.'

'Without asking where he is?' Perfume's bunched up her glossy lips, probably thinking it makes her look hard. She's got no idea. 'Or maybe you've asked his wife already? Funny thing is, his wife told me he doesn't have any nieces.'

Jo blushes. 'Caught me red-handed,' she says then sighs long and hard, gives herself a few extra seconds to invent a credible excuse. 'You're right. Me and Tony *aren't* uncle and niece. We're . . . together. His wife knows nothing about it.'

When you've spent so many years lying, the words come easy. Jo's quite proud of this one.

'You're his *mistress*?'

Jo nods. In any other situation she'd have laughed if someone used that word, as though they're stuck in the nineteenth century and still clinging on to the morals of Adam and Eve. Woman, sinner. Especially a woman who's thirty-odd years younger than her lover. Right now Jo plays along, keeps her eyes on the floor as if she's a good girl who's ashamed of bad actions. But she can sense Perfume's eyes on her, weighing up the risk of suggesting Jo is lying.

In the end the nurse swaps the moral code for the rule book. 'It's family only for visits,' she says. 'If his wife had turned up when you were here I'd have been in deep shit.'

So now Jo sees the real reason she cares. She's not attacking Jo after all. She's protecting herself. We're all selfish at our core.

'You won't tell her, will you?'

Perfume tuts. 'I'm not that mean. And anyway, I won't be seeing them again. Good news is, he was doing much better this morning and the doctors sent him home. So you can relax. There's no danger you'll run into him or his wife on your way out.'

Jo takes the hint and leaves. But she couldn't be further from relaxed if she tried. The envelope of cash is like a rock in her backpack and now she's got no way to get rid of it. What'll happen once Tony realises the money is missing? And what happens if one of the nurses tells him he was visited by a mystery woman while he was unconscious? If the money is the reason he was attacked, does that mean she's setting herself up for the same? The questions trail her like midges all the way to work, nipping at her no matter how hard she tries to bat them away.

When she reaches the shop she spots Jean inside, stripping the mannequin that usually stands in the window. It's the first time she's seen her since their awkward conversation at the bus stop yesterday. She hopes Jean's hand isn't bruised from where she hit her by accident, trying to grab that policeman's card. At least now she can truthfully tell Jean she's reported the break-in, even describe how police came to her flat and inspected the door. She and Jean can make up and move on and nobody needs to know she didn't report the stolen letters. She can focus on finding Aly and the box thief and not worry about the police at all.

When she steps inside, Jean glances up and smiles with tight lips.

'You did the right thing, love, contacting the authorities.' Jean turns away after she says it, busies herself with her work. She tugs a blue dress over the mannequin's head and starts smoothing it out. Jo pauses, confused. How the fuck does Jean already know?

'You mean reporting the break-in at my flat?'

Jean nods. 'It was never going to look good, me phoning the police on your behalf, but I'd have done it, you know. I don't make empty threats. Just glad I didn't have to. I know you're worried but it'll be fine, okay? They're waiting for you in the staff room.'

Jo's heart implodes, or that's what it feels like. 'Who is?'

Jean's smile slips and now it's her turn to be confused. 'The detectives.'

CHAPTER 26

Jo's halfway to the staff room when she hears *that* voice on the other side of the door. She'd have recognised it underwater. Farida, here, now. Why? A thousand answers surge into her brain but all carry the same message: you've fucked up. She should never have let Farida stay over, knowing she was a detective. But she's done nothing wrong, has she? Well, *almost* nothing. But maybe Tony's noticed the missing money and someone saw her stuffing the envelope of cash into her pocket. Or maybe she'll be charged with wasting police time for calling about an intruder they couldn't find.

Or maybe *Jean* told them about the stolen box and they want to know why she withheld that detail from them. Whatever the reason they're here, Jo's sure it won't be good news.

She stops outside the staff room door, looks for a place to hide the backpack and its stash of bank notes. There's a set of purple curtains hanging from a lower rail and an empty space behind them. Perfect. She glances around to check nobody's watching then slips the bag off her shoulder, is wedging it into the gap when the door's opened from the staff room side. Gordon saunters out, licking something greasy off his fingers. He stops, belly level with her face.

'Lost something, Jo?'

She wants to scream and tell him yes, she's lost everything. But somehow, she always finds herself with even more to lose. She straightens up, backpack still in her hands, and when her eyes flit over Gordon's shoulder they meet Farida's and her heart drops to her stomach. 'Just straightening the curtains,' she says, and that's when she notices Effie Garcia's in there as well. The doors swings shut.

She could turn and run. She could dump the bag in the street then keep on going. She could leave all of this. Jean's friendship, a good job, her place in this makeshift family of volunteers and staff. It's no place for rotten apples, spreading decay.

Behind her at the till Jean's laughing with a customer but she catches Jo's eye when she turns, winks at her. Even that gesture has love in it, but Jo knows she doesn't deserve it. Maybe it's time she surrenders to her fate.

When she pushes open the staff room door it's caught and held by hands that are softer than they look, that know how to make her feel loved. Farida nods to Jo. 'I appreciate you joining us,' she says, her tone drier than sawdust. She turns towards the table where Effie Garcia sits drinking tea. 'Take a seat,' says Farida, as though this is her place of work instead of Jo's, as though she owns every place she walks into. Then Effie takes over.

'You may remember DI McPherson from yesterday afternoon? At your flat? She was first on the scene.'

'And last to leave,' says Jo, staring at Farida. She looks away. The tension in the room is so thick you have to chew your inhales.

'We need to ask you some questions,' says Effie, pulling a flimsy plastic folder from her bag. 'Informal, for now.'

Jo gently slides the backpack under her chair with her feet. 'Is this connected to the break-ins?'

'Not exactly,' says Effie. 'There's another *incident* we'd like to ask you about.'

All the blood in Jo heats up and rushes to the surface, as if it's desperate to leave. She glances at Farida, meets her eyes again, but she might as well be looking at a photo. Not a flinch, not a hint of what happened when their gaze met last night. It's as though her eyes are on standby. Jo wonders what would happen if she leaned across the table and kissed her, if they'd flicker then fire back into life.

Effie's noisily opening her folder, pulling out a photo. She slides it across the table, keeping her eyes on Jo. 'Do you recognise this gentleman?'

A laugh slips out before she can stop it. 'Fiver says that's the first time he's ever been called a *gentleman*. And it'll be the last.'

'So that's a yes?' Farida leans forward when she asks it. She's planted her elbows on the table, sniffs as if she's hunting for truth. Or lies, maybe.

'It's Barry Chisholm,' says Jo.

'And have you seen him, since you . . . returned to Edinburgh?'

'Unfortunately I have. Saw Barry yesterday, in fact. Please don't tell me he's made an official complaint.'

Farida glances at Effie, then back to Jo. 'Complaint about . . .?'

'I went to see Barry, at the shopping centre. He works in security, got me thrown out.'

'For what reason?'

'Told his colleagues I'm a stalker and they're mad enough to believe him.' Jo shakes her head. 'Bet that doesn't match his version of events. What's he told you?'

Farida and Effie share another glance then Farida leans back and Effie shifts her chair so she's looking directly at Jo without twisting her neck. 'He's not told us anything, Jo. And he couldn't, even if he wanted to.'

Jo screws up her face. 'Meaning?'

'He's gone missing. His boss contacted us when he failed to turn up for work this morning and they couldn't get an answer at home. When we spoke to colleagues several of them mentioned an . . . altercation with an unknown woman at the shopping centre yesterday, a few hours before the last confirmed sighting. And, as you've just confirmed, that woman is you.'

'That doesn't mean—'

'If you'll let me finish?' That's Effie, irritated. Jo glances at Farida, can't read her face. 'When we visited Mr Chisholm's home we found evidence of a small fire in the bathtub and within the ashes were the scraps of numerous letters that repeatedly featured your name.'

She pauses, a deliberate act. This was an accusation dressed up as a fact. Jo concentrates on keeping her face still but behind her eyes there's a whirlwind. If the letters are there, it *must* have been Barry who sneaked into her house and stole the box. She'd told Farida about the break-in yesterday but she'd not told her about *that*. If she revealed that now, Farida would know she lied yesterday. But if she didn't say anything they could take this as evidence that there had been some kind of relationship between her and Barry; that she'd been at his home. Neither looked good.

'We need to ask where you were last night between six o'clock when Mr Chisholm finished work and nine o'clock this morning when his boss contacted us to report his absence.'

Jo's silent, stunned, her eyes bouncing between the two detectives. 'I hope you're not suggesting I've got anything to do with—'

'Just answer the question.' That's Farida, her voice a bark, an order from above. She was stupid to think they could ever be on equal footing. They're suited only when they're lying down. 'And it would be . . . *useful* to know why you were visiting Mr Chisholm at his work.'

'It wasn't actually him I wanted to find,' says Jo. 'It was someone else.'

'Name?'

'Aly Chisholm.'

Farida's eyes swell like balloons squeezed at one end. She glances at Effie and they share a twitch that means something to both of them. 'Barry's twin? Why?'

'There's something we need to . . . talk about.'

'You care to share that *something* with us?'

'Not really,' says Jo. 'I don't see how the two things are connected.'

'Nothing's a certainty at this stage,' says Effie, a welcome buffer between Jo and Farida. 'But given the chequered history of Aly Chisholm I do find it surprising that a woman in your position would seek that kind of company.'

'Last I checked, I'm a grown-up.'

'And last I checked, Aly Chisholm is *notorious*,' says Farida. 'No sign of any meaningful rehabilitation. No remorse. I can't understand why you'd—'

'Aly and I . . . knew each other, before my mum's murder.'

160

That got Farida's attention. 'Do you mean ... romantically?'

'That's one way of putting it,' says Jo, and hopes Farida's jealous.

'And can you tell us your reason for hunting down Aly Chisholm *now*, this week?'

'Only if you tell me why it's relevant.'

Effie leans in, clearing her throat. 'As I said, we're still establishing facts,' she says. 'Can we perhaps bring the focus back to your whereabouts last night?'

Farida drops her head, cuts her gaze. Effie shifts in her chair. Jo traces the outline of coffee stains on the table top. Her eyes sting but she won't let herself cry. Not here, not now, not with an audience like this one. 'I spent last night with ... a friend.' Jo keeps her head down and for the first time in years wishes she had long hair to cover the burn of blood in her cheeks.

'Will this *friend* verify that?'

Jo shrugs. 'I can certainly ask.'

'And let me ask you something else,' says Effie. 'Before yesterday at the shopping centre, where and when was the last time you saw Barry Chisholm?'

'After the murder. At the court case.'

'Did you speak then?'

'Why would I? There was nothing to say.'

'And when did you last see Aly?'

'On Friday night, at the pub across the road from the shop. Aly turned up, totally out of the blue, when

I was out for a drink with my workmates. It was the same day as the break-in. We spoke but I . . . felt uncomfortable, I suppose. Left as quickly as I could.'

'Understandable,' says Effie, then pops the photo of Barry into her folder and starts spewing out tired phrases she must have said a thousand times: talk of investigations and ongoing enquiries; of looking and finding and hunting and capture. Of justice, whatever that means.

Then suddenly they're on their feet and away, and Jo's sitting alone in the staff room with a backpack of stolen money under her chair and a veiled accusation hanging over her head.

She looks up when the door swings open again from the shop side, expecting Jean or Gordon with an armful of new donations and a mouthful of questions.

Instead it's Farida. Back here, on her own.

'Can I have a word?'

'Do I have a choice?'

'People always have choices,' says Farida. 'The question is whether we're brave enough to take them.'

'Like last night, you mean? You're probably telling yourself I seduced you or that it *just happened*. But it didn't. You *chose* to stay and I *chose* to let you. Despite the fact you're a detective and I'm . . .' Jo feels a wobble in her voice, stills it. 'I'm . . . not your type, right?'

'I'm not here to talk about *that*,' says Farida,

stepping closer, hunching down so her face is level with Jo's. Her tendons are tight, her jaw held fast. There's no trace now of that smile, that laugh, those easy kisses. 'They've got CCTV footage, Jo. Of a woman lingering close to Barry Chisholm's home.'

'I'm not the only woman in Edinburgh.'

'True. But she was wearing your leather jacket. The yellow one you wore at the hotel.'

Jo squints like she's staring at the sun. 'There's more than one yellow jacket in Edinburgh as well. And actually, mine's gone missing.'

'Really?'

'Really.'

'That's an . . . unfortunate coincidence.'

'I agree.'

Farida leans in, her whispers like rough stones rubbed to sand. 'So where did you go, Jo? When you went out last night? When you said you were going to buy cigarettes?'

'Are you seriously asking me this?'

'You don't even smoke.'

'They weren't *for* me. I *told* you that. I owed three packs to the girls who sit on the benches outside my flat, promised I'd deliver them last night. And I was only gone twenty minutes. That's not enough to . . .' She swallows hard to push the massive lump out of her throat. 'You know what? I don't need to explain myself to you. Either you trust me or you don't.'

'It's not as simple as that.' Farida pulls a business card from her inside pocket, sits it on the table in front of Jo. 'Take my number. If you think you're in danger, call me.'

Jo puffs out a laugh. 'You really think you're a superhero, don't you? Some kind of Glaswegian angel, swooping in to save the peasants. Well, bad news: you're not mine.'

'I'm offering you my *help*.'

'I don't remember asking for it,' says Jo. She spits out the words like a sulking child and that's all she is, underneath. Chest burning, anger on the rise; a flash flood that'll lift her up and carry her off if she lets it. And, worse, it'll wreck anything and everything in its path. 'I don't need saving, *Farida*. Certainly not by you.'

'I know you're upset, but—'

'You know nothing about me.'

'More than I'd like.'

Jo leans in, close. 'Fuck you.'

Behind them, the door creaks open. Effie's standing there with her hands on her hips and a question in her eyes as she takes in the scene. 'Find what you were looking for, boss?'

Farida stands, quickly, pulling a small black notebook out of her pocket. 'Got it,' she says. 'Must have slipped out when I took off my jacket.'

Jo's surprised how easily Farida lies. When the door swings shut she picks up Farida's business card from the table, rubs the soft part of her thumb against the embossed lettering. Then she closes her hand into a fist and crushes it.

CHAPTER 27

Jo slips downstairs to the basement before Jean or Gordon corner her, question her. A mountain of steam-cleaned clothes sits on the tagging desk, waiting to be priced and carried up to the shop floor for selling. She loads the tagging gun then gets to work, carefully attaching price labels to collars and cuffs. Pull that trigger and boom: old clothes are ready for a new life. She repeats the process over and over, trying to keep her mind away from Barry Chisholm's disappearance, and from the word Farida used to describe Aly: *notorious*. Jo made a vow with herself years ago that she'd never search for Aly's name on the internet or via social media. She's not read a newspaper or watched the TV news since her mum's murder and has no intention of starting now.

But since she got the box of letters she's started to wonder about Aly's life, wondering what happened once the drama of the court case was over.

Jo had cut all contact at first. Silence was easier. But she had questions for Aly and it had helped, in some ways, to express the mess of her feelings with pen and paper. For a year or so she wrote to Aly once a month. But she never got a reply and gave up hoping for one, realised she was the only one who could make herself feel any better.

She knows now that Aly had got those fifteen-year-old letters two days ago, same as Jo. All thanks to Tony Burgos stealing them, then storing them for all that time. But why deliver them now? She'll find out when she tracks him down. Speaking of which, she's got a call to make.

She heads for the stairs, is halfway up when Jean appears at the top, coffee cup in one hand, unlit cigarette in the other. 'Great minds think alike,' says Jean. 'Was just about to shout you upstairs for a break.'

Usually Jo loves those moments with Jean, the two of them putting the world to rights over steaming mugs. They laugh, every day. Proper laughs too; eyes watering, bellies hurting, seeing the bright side of things. A novelty for Jo. But today, she'll opt out.

'I'm actually not feeling so good,' she says. 'You mind if I call it a day?'

Jean's got a funny look on her face: maybe suspicion, maybe disappointment. Jo's not sure which is worse. She holds out an arm, blocking Jo's path. 'Leave if you need to,' says Jean. 'But before you go. I know I said it before, love. But I'm glad you decided to contact the police about the break-in at yours. I knew they'd come down here right away. Shows they're taking it seriously.'

Jo hasn't told Jean the real reason the police were here, and doesn't intend to. She's got nothing to do with the disappearance of Barry Chisholm, despite what the police suspect, so there's no point planting ideas in Jean's head. Or doubts.

'So, do they think it's the same person who broke in here?' Jean blows on the surface of her coffee. 'I mean, it must be. It's too much of a coincidence otherwise.' She loves asking questions then answering them herself without taking a breath. 'Two break-ins in one night, in two places connected to you. Now it's out in the open the police will have more chance of catching the scoundrels. At least, I hope so. What did they say about the missing letters?'

'Not much,' says Jo. And it's true, but only because Jo hadn't mentioned them. 'They said they'll be in touch soon.' To arrest her, probably; to drag her out of the shop and down to the station and question her about what she's done to Barry Chisholm. She's glad Jean can't read thoughts. She squeezes a goodbye into a pause between the endless questions.

Gordon's on the shop floor, hoovering up a scattering of crisps, dropped by one customer and trampled into the brown carpet tiles by another. He switches off the machine and straightens up as Jo approaches. 'You skiving off again?'

'It's called Being Unwell.'

'What were the police wanting?'

'Just following up about the break-in.'

He looks disappointed, as if he was expecting her to say something else. 'So they didn't say anything about those letters?' Then he bends down to unplug the vacuum and that's when Jo sees the bruises, all up his back. As though he's been kicked. As though he's been fighting someone.

Or as though someone's been fighting him off.

She thinks of Tony, wired up to those machines in hospital. And Gordon, stumbling across the story of the attack in the paper, then miraculously remembering Tony's face. Maybe it wasn't a coincidence. Maybe Gordon knew because *he*'s the attacker.

Until now, Jo hadn't even considered the possibility that Gordon could be involved. He was the one who'd received the box from Tony in the first place – and other volunteers would have seen that happen. But they were all at the pub when the other man *allegedly* turned up, asking for the box back. Had Gordon invented the story of the second delivery man to push attention away from himself? Was it *him* who stole the letters from her flat? He'd watched her leave with the box and could easily have followed her there, or found her address on file at work. He'd turned up late for Jean's party – so he'd definitely have had time to go to Jo's flat in the meantime.

There was logic to it, kind of. But why did Gordon care if Jo read Aly's letters? And why would he damage the shop doors when he could have used his key? That part made no sense.

'Earth to Jo! Nobody ever tell you it was rude to stare?'

Jo blinks, unblurs her eyes. Gordon's on his feet now, tucking his shirt back into his trousers, hiding those stains of bruised, purpling skin before he greets a customer. A woman's just trudged in with two battered supermarket bags stuffed full of unfolded clothes. Jo can sense unsellable donations from a mile off but Gordon receives them with surprising grace, has a peek in the bags then thanks the woman for her generosity.

When she's gone he turns to Jo. 'Straight in the bin,' he says, tossing the bags under the counter. 'Can't believe the crap some folk hand in. Lucky I'm too nice to say.'

'It's called lying,' says Jo. 'You're pretty good at it.'

'I'll take that as a compliment.'

'I wouldn't, if I were you.'

Gordon stiffens, straightens up. 'Meaning?'

'How did you know what was in my box, Gordon? A minute ago you asked me about the letters, but I never told you about them. So how did you know?'

'The box man told me.'

'Which one? The one who delivered it and you only recognised once he'd been beaten up? Or the one who supposedly came to collect it when you were here alone?'

He screws up his face. Folds become fatter. 'The

second guy, the scrawny one who came in as I was closing the shop. The one who wanted the box back.'

'Thought as much,' says Jo. The man nobody else had seen. 'And let me ask you something else. How did you get those bruises, Gordon? On your back?'

He deflates when she says that, looks like a man with a slow puncture. 'None of your business,' he says, then turns away from her as an elderly couple stroll into the shop, commenting on the weather as they flip through the discarded scraps of other people's lives. Jo stares at Gordon's back, maps the bruises under his pale blue cotton shirt, and wonders where they will lead her.

CHAPTER 28

It's Tink who leads the way, pushes open the gate and steps into the hush of the graveyard. To her right is a caretaker's hut, its little window lit up by a lamp on the other side. Ahead of her it's all green grass and grey stone, a few spots of colour here and there where people have left flowers and plant pots and soft toys, made soggy by the weather. At the far end, a man in a council-issue hi-vis jacket is weeding the rose beds, pausing from time to time to sniff the flowers still in bloom.

Tink turns to Spider. She's lighting another cigarette. 'You know where your dad is?'

Spider nods then takes a draw, lips and cheeks tightening. And release. She blows the smoke away from Tink but it drifts back, lingers between them. 'You?'

'No idea.'

'We can ask the old boy,' Spider says, pointing to where the caretaker is bending to pick up a crisp packet caught in a wreath.

Tink approaches, feeling like she shouldn't be there, that's she's doing something wrong. 'I'm . . . I'm looking for my dad,' she says, then whispers his name. It's the first time she's said it out loud since he died.

The man gives a gentle smile then gazes out over the gravestones. 'Is it recent?'

Tink nods, can't speak. When does the death of your dad stop being *recent*? This isn't one of those bad feelings that fades if you distract yourself. It's part of her now.

'Sorry to hear that, hen.' He sounds as if he means it but he must get a lot of practice at being nice. 'There's a cup of tea in my hut if you need one. And I'm Arthur, by the way.'

Tink nods again then walks away before her eyes start leaking. Spider whispers to her, calls Arthur a perv, and for a moment Tink wishes she'd come alone. She walks ahead, looking for her dad's name carved into a gravestone and still half-believing she won't find it because it's impossible to think of it: him, decomposing in a box under her feet, the grass, the soil. He was solid, strong, hers. And yet not.

Most graves have cut flowers with notes attached and she feels bad that she's come with nothing. Her dad's funeral was busy, but it's only because the accident was in the papers and her dad's face all over the news. Folk just like the drama, or that's what her mum says. They want the world to think they're part of something tragic. If her dad had died in his bed when he was old they wouldn't have given a shit.

When Tink told her mum she'd seen Dad's best pal Craig crying at the church she got a slap so hard her cheek was still red the next morning. Spider was raging, called her mum a bitch, said she'd get what was coming to her.

But right now she's quiet as anything.

Tink turns, sees Spider kneeling in front of a squat gravestone that looks smaller than the others, cheaper. Even when you're dead, folk can tell. She's sniffing like she's got a runny nose but no hankie. Tink steps closer. 'You okay?'

'Be fine in a bit.' Spider bites down on her lips and stares straight ahead and Tink wishes she knew what to say but doesn't because it's too big, what she feels. It wouldn't fit on one of those little cards that people attach to their flowers.

'You get it, don't you?' That's Spider asking.

'Aye.'

One word but it binds them. A furtive smile passes between them like drugs, quickly exchanged. Then Tink keeps on walking, keeps on hoping she won't find what she's looking for.

But then, there it is.

Her dad's grave is at the end of a row. There's a big tree there and one of the branches leans right over the spot like someone sharing an umbrella, offering shelter.

You can tell it's new. The grass is trimmed, the headstone gleaming, the bouquet at its base fresh. Really fresh. It's been three weeks since her dad's funeral and she doesn't know much about cut flowers but they don't last that long. Someone's been here.

She kneels down to search for a note and finds it underneath the bouquet, soggy and torn on the grass. On other graves she'd seen cards tucked safely inside the plastic film that protects the flowers. But whoever left this one had taped it on the outside, next to a skid-mark of glue from the ripped-off price tag. She glances over her shoulder. Arthur is bent over borders and Spider's still staring, still sniffing. Tink picks up the note, carefully, so it doesn't disintegrate in her hands. The writing is totally smudged and streaked, like the ink had tried to flee the paper. She can't make out the full message. But two words had been written in capital letters, bigger than the others. Those, she can see. But immediately wishes she hadn't. Up until this moment she'd believed what the papers said: her dad's death was a tragic accident, end of story. But this note suggests someone was to blame. *Forgive me*, it says.

CHAPTER 29

Jo escapes the shop and heads to Portobello Beach. It never disappoints, never fails her. Whatever the weather it's there, a shifting postcard of sea, sand, sky, and the bumpy outline of Fife across the water. There's always someone in swimming or rowing or a dog bounding after balls thrown by their owner, but it's never the same place twice. That's what she loves about Portobello, about Scotland. The weather changes every day and takes the landscape along with it. When she tells folk she worked abroad for years they *ooh* and *aah* and think it's better than this, somehow. But warm sun on your cheeks loses its appeal if you can't remember the rain. Mid-morning the promenade smells of sausage baps and it bustles as the world wakes up. Gloved hands clutch takeaway coffee cups and the bins are stuffed with paper bags slicked with grease from expensive croissants. Dogs sniff strangers' hands and each other's arses. Cyclists and runners splash through puddles and weave through walkers. Jo steps on to the beach. Here the sand is soft and shifting. She keeps walking, over the high-tide line that's built from slimy seaweed and empty shells.

Down at the shoreline the compacted sand is hard and shiny, wet with the tide that's just retreated. She's been in for a dip a few times since she got back, loves the way cold water shocks her mind into silence, for a while. The shallows seem to go on forever but sometimes she dares herself to walk to the part where the seabed falls away into nothing; stand on the edge then let go, let go.

But not today.

She tugs her phone out of her pocket, searches the news for word of Barry Chisholm. Nothing so far. Then she deletes the first name and types *Aly* instead. This is what she vowed she'd never do. She knew it wouldn't help; wouldn't change or fix anything at all. Nothing anybody did could undo the murder. If Aly was doing well, would Jo feel pleased or bitter? And if Aly was a fuck-up, as Farida and Effie had suggested, would that make Jo feel any better or any worse about her own life? It was easier not knowing, not asking, not looking. Until that box was delivered to the shop. Until Aly followed her into the men's bathroom at that pub. Until someone made it clear that Jo shouldn't read those letters, and was willing to break the law to make sure of it. Until someone threatened her, and Farida.

She presses the search button and in the time it takes for a wave to turn then remake itself the screen fills with newspaper articles featuring *that name*. She clicks the one at the top, a court report from the *Journal*. It's brief but captures a life. Aly Chisholm, fined for repeatedly shoplifting. Jo opens the next one. Aly Chisholm, drunk and disorderly on an ordinary Tuesday, hurling abuse at strangers who'd popped to the graveyard for their lunch. Fined, threatened with a return to prison. And so it went on.

A few of the articles have photos at the top, show Aly outside court in a crap suit bought or borrowed for the occasion. But when you carry shame with you it shines through, regardless of what you're wearing. And aye, that's what Jo sees in Aly.

She shuts down the search engine but the damage is done. It only takes a second to read bad news but the impact of it has no time limit. She now knows what's become of Aly and can see nothing's really changed from Before. Crime starts with frightening folk for a laugh, for the momentary thrill of it. But Jo knows how quickly and easily these things can get out of hand. Most murders are born from ten seconds of madness, not a lifetime of badness. That's why Jo needs to find Aly, stop this before it goes any further.

But how? And, more to the point, where?

The flat at Hartfield Court has clearly been abandoned for a while but suddenly Jo knows exactly where she can find Aly's current address. She wakes up her phone and repeats the search for Aly's name; opens the most recent newspaper article.

Usually court stories feature the street name of the accused to make sure there's no confusion with other people – innocent people – who share the same name.

Jo skim-reads the page, frowns when she finds an address for Aly. It still says Hartfield Court. She checks the date, sighs. It was written two months ago so maybe the flats would still have been occupied then.

What now? She checks a few other articles but the answer is the same, over and over. There's something else that's always the same – the name of the journalist who wrote the articles.

Someone called Sandy Hamilton.

Worth a shot. Jo searches for the newspaper office's phone number, calls it. The woman who answers sounds hung-over, grunts when Jo asks for Sandy by name.

'Who should I say is calling?'

Jo hesitates. 'Jean Carmichael,' she says, just in case. She glances over her shoulder after she says it, half-expecting Jean to be standing behind her with her arms crossed and her brow creased, an expression on her face that says Jo's let her down. But there's nobody there. Just sand and, behind it, the city.

'Sandy Hamilton speaking.' The voice on the line is more cheerful than she expected for a man who clearly spends half his life in court, listening to stories about humans messing up lives. 'And you're . . . Jean?'

'Aye.' Jo squirms. She hates lying, but wonders if he'd ever sat in the same courtroom as her, if he'd recognise her full name, know her sad history. 'I'm calling because I'm trying to track someone down,' she says. 'And I'm hoping you can help.'

'Not really my line of business,' he says. 'What's the name of your missing person?'

'Aly Chisholm.'

'Ah, then that's easy. If you sit in a courtroom for more than five minutes there's a good chance you'll find Aly there, accompanied by two glamorous assistants. By which I mean prison officers.'

'I was hoping for something more specific. Your recent court reports list the address as Hartfield Court but I've been there this week and there's nobody living there. So I need an up-to-date address, today if possible.'

'Demanding, aren't you? Unfortunately for you I'm not really in the business of handing over addresses either.'

'It's important.'

'So's data protection.'

Jo sighs. Time to place her ace card. 'Look, my name's not Jean. It's Jo. My mum was Becky Forsyth, from Hartfield Court.'

He doesn't have an answer for that. Not right away,

anyway. Maybe he doesn't know who she is, doesn't remember the murder. And why would he? If he's in court every day he'll see them over and over, the quiet tragedies that unfold in ordinary homes, lives. And most of them never make it into the papers.

Silence, still. 'You still there?'

'Still here,' says Sandy. 'And I was *there* too. I covered the court case.'

And just like that Jo's back there in court, remembering the commotion every morning at the packed press bench, the sound of flipping pages as they turned witness statements into outlandish stories that would make them look clever, make readers cling to the ones they love for fear of losing them. Sometimes she'd tried to catch the eye of the journalists but they always looked away. They were there for the story and the glory it brought them at work, not the people behind it. Why would Sandy be any different?

'So you know me,' she says. Not a question.

'Aye. But forgive me if I'm just a little . . . confused. I haven't heard your name in years and suddenly today it's come up twice. Like buses, I suppose.'

He laughs. Jo doesn't. 'What do you mean, it's *come up twice*?'

He clears his throat. 'Och, I shouldn't have said anything. But your name's been mentioned as part of an . . . ongoing story. Rather fortuitous that you called, in fact.'

Jo flushes. She's waiting for him to repeat the same nonsense story Effie and Farida told her. Barry Chisholm's gone missing, hours after Jo *harassed* him at his work. And a woman's been seen, hanging about near Barry Chisholm's home – a woman wearing Jo's yellow leather jacket. She stops him before he can start. 'It's bullshit.'

'I've not told you what it is yet.'

'You don't need to. I've already had the police at the shop this morning, accusing me of all sorts. I don't need to hear it again.'

'The *police* have already talked to you about it? Who, specifically?'

'Two detectives. Effie Garcia and . . . Farida McPherson.'

Another pause. 'That makes no sense,' says Sandy. 'Listen, can we meet? Talk over a coffee or something?'

'Only if you help me find Aly Chisholm. You help me, I help you.'

'That's not how it works in journalism.'

'Be the exception,' says Jo.

'You sound like a life coach.'

'And you sound like you'd like to know more about Barry's disappearance. I'll happily tell you my side of the story, but—'

'Barry who?'

Now it's Jo who pauses. 'That's not your *ongoing story*?'

'I've heard nothing about anyone called Barry.'

'So what's the ongoing story concerned with?'

Another pause. He's a man who thinks before he speaks. And then it comes, a neatly dropped bomb. 'Your relationship with Farida McPherson,' he says.

CHAPTER 30

Jo locates the Kiwi Café from miles off thanks to the queue that trails out of the door and stretches along Portobello Promenade. It doesn't take reservations but eager brunchers swarm in from across the city and happily queue up outside. Sandy said he'd head down right away, text her once he got a table. She squeezes past the folk waiting in line, is followed in the door by tuts and mutters. A waitress approaches, smile fixed, but her eyes say what her mouth cannot. A woman like Jo was made for greasy spoons, baked beans instead of avocados.

'My friend's already here,' says Jo, searching the room, trying to match Sandy's voice to a face. She should have asked Sandy what he looked like. But *he* knows *her*. Then she spots a man on his feet in the back right-hand corner. White hair, tweed jacket, skin so pale it'd make milk look dirty. So he spends his life indoors, at work or in the pub. She guesses work.

He waves her over, then pulls out her chair as if this

is a posh hotel, as if she's someone he wants to impress. 'Wasn't sure I'd recognise you,' he says.

'It's been a while.'

'True, but . . .' Sandy's still on his feet, looking down on her now. She's used to it. 'You're the spitting image of your mum.'

Jo flushes and curses the blood in her. She pictures her mum as she was on the day of the murder; imagines herself with the same face. There must be differences, surely, but she wouldn't know. For fifteen years she's avoided mirrors; won't start looking now.

Sandy sits, is about to speak when a waiter brings a giant coffee and a slice of carrot cake that's big enough to feed a small country for a week. 'You want something?' He slides a handwritten menu across the table. 'My shout.'

Jo shakes her head. She doesn't want to owe this man any favours. He's slurping his coffee, sawing at his cake with a fork, looks like he's here for the fun of it. But it's a story he's after. 'So tell me about you and the delectable Farida McPherson.'

Jo shrugs, does her best to look nonchalant. 'There's nothing to tell.'

'Your cheeks are telling me a different story.'

'I doubt the courts would accept my cheeks as a reliable witness.'

'You should know.'

'Fuck you.'

Sandy raises an eyebrow and a woman at the next table tuts loud enough to be heard. Sandy leans in, lowering his voice. 'I'm here to help you, remember?'

'You're here to get a story.'

'I've already got it, Jo. But it'll be better for you and . . . *everyone* involved if I get your version of events instead of basing my story on rumour.'

'You wouldn't dare.'

'It's my job to dare,' he says. 'And anyway, there are photos of you two together, outside your flat, yesterday afternoon. Ring any bells?'

He smiles after he says it. Jo stares over his shoulder, wondering who saw them and how they knew it would make a cracking news story. The only other person near the flat yesterday afternoon was Cally, the nervous lassie with the glasses. But she'd been *nice* to Jo for absolutely no reason; phoned her when she saw someone hanging about outside the flats. She'd even texted later to ask what had happened with the intruder – and to apologise for leaving while Jo was inside. She'd had to go and collect her wee brother. That was why Cally had called her phone at that critical moment when 'Ari' appeared in the corridor.

It seemed unlikely she'd be so considerate to Jo then call the papers and screw her over. Unless that was her intention all along? Lure Jo to the flat so she could get a photo of her with Farida, then alert the press. But there were numerous issues with that theory. First of all, how would she know Farida was a detective? Secondly, did teenagers today even think about newspapers? Even if Cally had bought or read a newspaper, it seems unlikely she'd call an old hack like Sandy. Thirdly, why? That was easy. Either she hated Farida or she hated Jo. Both were possible, but her gut tells her Cally's *not the type*, whatever that means.

She thinks of all those parked cars and rows of windows facing out from the building; the watchers hidden behind them. But who? If the police are to be believed, Barry hasn't been seen since he left work, so that rules him out. Tony's just out of hospital but probably in no fit state for a stakeout at Jo's flat. Jean knows about Farida but knows her only as Ari, and she'd have no reason to phone the papers about it; quite the opposite. The only other person in her life who's actively hostile is Gordon. She thinks again of his bruises, her suspicions. He received the box and somehow knows it's full of letters. He spoke to the man who dropped it off and the one who wanted it back. He found the story of Tony's attack one day and arrived to work with bruises the next. But Gordon would have been working at the shop when she and Farida were outside her flat yesterday afternoon. Does that rule him out?

And what about Aly Chisholm? That's the most obvious explanation. Aly, watching, waiting, fury rising as Jo chatted with a police detective, of all people. The words of the death threat creep into Jo's mind. *Tell the police and you're dead.*

Then there's the warning on Farida's pickup. Maybe the person who left the graffiti isn't the same person who tipped off the papers – and maybe the culprit isn't linked to Jo's life at all. Farida's dedicated her career to chasing criminals, so plenty of people must hold a grudge against her.

'This tip-off,' she says. 'I assume it comes from a reliable source?'

'It was anonymous.'

'It's just . . . I doubt you'd risk messing up the career of a senior detective unless the story was rock solid.'

'Of course.'

'So how about we do a deal? You find me the current address for Aly Chisholm, and I'll speak to you about Farida McPherson.'

He looks at her, chewing on his thin lips now instead of his cake. 'Fair enough,' he says, sighing. 'But I can't guarantee that all journalists and all newspapers will share my . . . moral integrity. There's a good chance the person who tipped me off will have contacted other papers at the same time. So be prepared. You'll be hounded if word gets out.'

Jo pictures a fox, caught in the clamped jaws of a hunting dog; shaken until its neck breaks.

'Best get to work, then.' Sandy stands and shakes her hand, then gives her a business card. 'And if you think of anything else just give me a call. Any time. I'm always working.'

'News never stops, right?'

'Exactly,' he says, and then he's up and away.

Jo sits there until the waiter comes to clear Sandy's plates; gently suggests she buggers off so folk from the queue can take the table. She leaves the café, heads across Portobello Promenade and back to the beach. Maybe some fresh air will help her think straight. The sea is miles out now but a few dogs and their owners walk near the edge, leaving deep footprints that'll fill in with water when the tides turns.

She drops down on to the sand and pulls her backpack on to her knee. If Sandy does what she asks of him, then she'll soon have Aly Chisholm's new address. She can go there, assure Aly she hasn't read the letters and won't tell the police about any of it. Will that be enough to keep her safe? She thinks of Tony's battered body and Barry's disappearance. So far she's only had threats, suggestions of violence instead of the real thing. She'll do her best to keep it that way. But what if Sandy takes too long or backs out of the deal? She can't rely on one single person. Thankfully, she's got a back-up plan.

She pushes her hand into her backpack, the place a laptop should be. The envelope's still there, weighing her down, thousands of pounds in cash just waiting to be returned to its original owner. She switches her phone from internet to photos and scrolls to the photo she took of Tony's screen when he received that call from *Ernie, Lesmahagow*. She types the number into her phone and presses the call button before thoughts and fears convince her otherwise. When it rings, adrenaline surges, peaks when a man picks up. Step one, complete.

'Hi, there. Ernie? I hope you don't mind me calling but you're a friend of Tony Burgos, right?'

'Used to work with him. Who's this?'

'I'm a friend of his wife's. She's asked me to speak with all the well-wishers who've phoned his mobile. She's . . . too upset to do it herself. Tony's finding it hard to use his mobile with his . . . injuries. So his wife says it'll be better if you call the landline from now on, while he's recovering at home. Just wanted to make sure you've got the right number? They've changed it recently.'

'Really? Okay. Let me check.'

Jo holds her breath, waits, prays to whoever might be listening. The man's clicking his tongue as he searches. 'Here we go,' he says. 'I've got . . .' He recites a series of numbers. 'That right?'

Jo writes it down and reads it back. 'Perfect,' she says. 'I'm sure he'll be happy to hear from you. He's doing much better already.' And now, Jo is as well.

She ends the call, takes a deep breath then dials Tony's landline number.

It's time to make another deal.

CHAPTER 31

The graveyard visits become a weekly habit. Every time they go Tink finds an identical bunch of fresh flowers bought from a garage and wrapped too tightly in plastic. She always looks for another note, but never finds one.

Tink's convinced the source of it all is her dad's best friend Craig, though she can't understand why he blames himself for the accident. Saying that, her mum seems to. She calls Craig *That Poofter From Work* and says that if her dad had never fallen in love with him then he'd never have wanted to move out, so he wouldn't have been in his car that morning and wouldn't have smashed into that wall and wouldn't be dead. But you'll never find the one original cause for anything, not really. Life is a chain of tiny decisions, endlessly and inevitably linked to those on either side.

The accident happened near the flats.

Her dad had rammed his car into a wall and burst his head wide open. Police then found alcohol in his blood and a holdall on the back seat with all of his clothes. When Tink went into her parents' room later her dad's side of the wardrobe was empty, and when she'd asked her mum where he'd been going, she'd said: *to hell.*

They'd argued the night before he died – and it had been no ordinary fight. Her dad had kept saying he was sorry and her mum kept saying she'd never forgive him and neither the fuck would Tink. That was probably why he hadn't come in to say goodnight. She'd fallen asleep when the fighting stopped and woken up to find her dad snoring on the couch in his clothes with an undrunk glass of his special Coke on the table. He always mixed Coke with vodka, said it made him *happy, faster.* Tink had taken a sip but left most of it for her dad. She hoped he'd drink the rest when he woke up, maybe save some for her mum as well so they'd all live happily ever after.

Then she'd crept out and left for school as normal.

A few hours later her dad had left them after all, and died trying. Most people still judge him for it. Including her mum. *We don't talk about Dad*, she says. So they don't. A habit becomes a rule that's never questioned. Her mum's other catchphrase is this: *stay away from Spider.*

That one, Tink ignores.

She likes to count the days they've known each other. The bigger the number, the more solid it feels. Weeks turn to months and then years and by then

Tink can't really remember what life was like without Spider in it. Sometimes when they go to the wee shop the man who runs it says they're joined at the hip and Tink feels like she's glowing.

When Spider turns sixteen she leaves school and her gran buys her a mobile phone, so she can *keep an eye* on her. But when she calls Spider lets it ring out and says her gran's a control freak. Tink laughs even though it leaves a residue, makes her feel bad. Spider's gran must have spent a fortune on the phone because it's one of those fancy ones with a built-in camera. That's all it's good for, really, because nobody else they know owns a mobile. It's so silly, the thought that you'd always need a phone on you; that you'd ever need to urgently send someone a picture. Saying that, their summer is built of selfies, dozens of them every day. At night they sit on the benches and scroll through all the photos and Tink loves that part the most because it's proof she's part of something.

She doesn't want the holidays to end because when she goes back to school Spider won't be there and everyone else will have a tan and shell bracelets and stories from Abroad and new pencil cases. But if she doesn't turn up for classes she'll be given punishment instead of pity because her dad's face isn't in the papers any more and most people have forgotten what happened to her family. They probably think grief is a like a cut that scabs over then falls off to reveal unblemished skin.

Only Spider understands.

On the first day back at school Tink drags herself out of bed and out the door and she's trudging across the car park when Spider runs up behind her, hands her a box. 'Got you something for school,' she says, and Tink wants to cry when she opens it because there's a mobile phone inside. It's red and she loves it. 'It's got a tenner credit,' says Spider. 'And I've saved my number in your contacts. Call me at lunch, okay?'

'Promise.'

So this is how it feels to be missed. Spider walks her to the school gates and Tink hopes people notice she's not alone. When the bell rings she slips the mobile phone into her inside pocket and her heart feels fuller, warmer. A smile comes and brings with it a feeling she thought she'd lost when her dad died. But right here, right now, there's love.

CHAPTER 32

One uncomfortable phone call later, Jo's on a bus that takes her away from the soft curve of sand in Portobello and towards the home of Tony Burgos. They pass glass-fronted car showrooms and windowless carpet warehouses and once they cross the Water of Leith she sees the government offices at Victoria Quay, close to where Tony was attacked. Then comes the part of Leith that's all heavy metal and hard edges: shopping centres, factories and the industrial port. When the cityscape softens again Jo rings the bell and the bus pulls in opposite a picturesque harbour. Hand-painted fishing boats bob in the water, overlooked by a whitewashed lighthouse and the old fishing village of Newhaven. But from that historic core the neighbourhood has expanded, exploded, reinvented itself. The fish market now houses restaurants. And beyond it there are towering luxury flats, balconies laden with exotic plants and Buddha statues. A posh gym and budget hotel sit on a coastal path that's always busy with joggers and parents pushing prams, city on one side and the sea on the other. A few folk stand there with their hands on their hips, eyes on the big sea and the even bigger sky. Jo wonders if they're trying to find a sense of freedom. But it takes more than a few deep breaths, more than a place. It's your brain that traps you, not where you are, not what you do. You can wake up in paradise and still feel like shit if you've not looked inside yourself for the answers.

Right now she's hoping Tony Burgos can offer her a few more. He'd been asleep when she first called but she'd persisted until he answered, all croaky-voiced and drugged up and pissed off until she said she was calling about the money in his backpack. Then, Jo was sure she heard him whimper. He'd been released from hospital and was now recovering at home. Thankfully for Jo his wife had gone back to work; half-days, he said, until he was fully back on his feet.

Buzzer pressed, door opened, stairs climbed. When she reaches the fifth floor he's already got the door open, quickly ushers her inside as if he doesn't want his neighbours to see. He's wearing a threadbare dressing gown and his greying hair's sticking up at the back where it's been pressed into his pillow. The swelling around his eyes has loosened into puffy bruises. Jo observes his neck, the cuts that have become scabs. Life, hardening.

She refuses an offer of tea as he leads her to a sitting room stuffed with unvarnished pine furniture and jute rugs, as if he's tried to build a Mediterranean chill-out bar five floors up from the bitter Scottish sea. A bay window overlooks the harbour. 'I've got an ... *appointment* at three,' he says, taking an elderly whippet by the collar and shutting it in a bedroom.

'This shouldn't take long.'

He stays by the open door with his back to the wall. Learned behaviour. Probably thinks that'll keep him safe. 'So you've got the money?'

Jo nods. 'We'll get to that.'

He tightens, tries to press himself into the wallpaper. 'Go on, then. Spit it out. What are you wanting?'

He's talking to her as if she's a child, expects her to obey his orders. 'Respect, for starters.'

'Has to be earned.'

'I'm here, am I not? If anyone else had stumbled across your stash I doubt you'd see it again. And that's still a possibility, if you don't play along.'

'I need that money, hen.'

'You think I don't?'

'I'm begging you.'

'That's a first,' says Jo. 'I know you worked at the prison, Tony. Just retired, right?'

Tony doesn't answer, just holds his jaw tight like a hard man. Thing is, he's wearing flip-flops, and his big hairy toes curl in on themselves when he realises Jo knows who he is.

'No point in denying it. One of the doctors told me,'

she says. '*And* I know why you got yourself beaten up. It was you who delivered that box of letters to my work, wasn't it? The ones from Aly Chisholm. I couldn't understand it at first, why Aly would have held on to those letters for so long then delivered them all at once. But it was *you*, wasn't it? You've been stealing prison letters for years, keeping them as some kind of prize. Am I right?'

He closes his eyes, swallows hard. 'I never meant to cause any harm.'

'Really? And you didn't think it might *harm* me to receive that box of letters fifteen years after they were written?'

'I didn't have any choice.'

'We always have choices,' says Jo, and Farida zooms into her brain. She said the same thing to her this morning. 'It just depends if you're brave enough to make good ones.'

'Then I'm a coward,' he says, holding up his hands.

'At least you can admit it. Now tell me about the money.' She pats her backpack for effect, reminds him that it's right there, his with one pull of the zip. 'Did someone pay you to deliver those letters to me?'

He's shaking his head before she's finished speaking. 'The opposite. I was paid to keep the letters away from you.'

'I don't understand.'

'For fifteen years I confiscated any letter with your

name on it. Hundreds of them. Got a monthly payment for my efforts.'

'From?'

He sighs. 'It's all down to a guy called Barry
Chisholm. Aly's twin. I assume you know him, or
know of him. He asked me to keep an eye on all incom-
ing and outgoing mail at the prison, swipe any letters
to Aly, from you. And vice versa.'

'But why did he care?'

He shrugs. 'You'll need to ask Barry.'

'But what's your connection to him? How did Barry
find you?'

'How do you think? Through his mum.'

Jo tilts her head to one side and something slips into
place. 'From her time in prison?'

He nods. 'She was rarely out of the place. I came
across her when I was starting out as a prison officer,
met the twins – Barry and Aly – when they came in for
visits. Their mum was . . . difficult. And hard as fuck.
Wanted special treatment and more often than not she
got it. It was easier to give in to her demands than put up
with her tantrums. But I felt bad for the twins, always
tried to be nice to them when their gran brought them in
for a visit. She was more drunk than sober herself, and
the poor bastards didn't have a dad either. Broke my
heart to see them dragged in and out of that place when
they should have been outside playing with their pals.'

Jo winces, thinking of her own childhood. Those

who grow up with love and clean clothes think it's standard, something that happens automatically. It doesn't.

'So you knew both of them?'

Tony goes to shake his head then flinches with the pain of it. 'Not really. Aly always seemed a bit . . . angry. So I kept my distance. Barry was different. The quiet one. He usually came in wearing his Hearts football top and I'm a Hibs fan so I'd tease him about that, try to make him laugh. That's how we became pals, kind of. I was nice to him, and he clearly wasn't used to it. But as he got older he became more like his mum. Being *nice* wasn't enough any more. He started demanding favours and getting furious if I refused. Just wee things at first, like getting his mum extra blankets or sneaking her some tobacco. Barry made me feel like I was letting him down when I said no, painted himself as a poor wee abandoned soul that nobody wanted. And the thing is, it was true. I felt bad for him.' He shakes his head slowly. 'Then the twins' mum died. Took some dodgy drugs she'd bought in prison and never woke up. I didn't see the kids for a few years after that but I was happy when Barry got in touch again, said he'd just turned eighteen, wanted to buy me a drink to say thanks for looking after his mum so well. I was flattered, I suppose, and agreed to meet.

'The first thing Barry asked me was whether I was still working at the prison. He acted surprised when I told him, but it was just after your mum's murder so . . . he must have known. I quickly realised that was the only reason he got back in touch: he wanted to control the communication between you and his *beloved* twin. Said he'd pay me for it.' Tony winces and Jo hopes it's his conscience that's hurting. 'I didn't want to get involved but I was scared to say no. That probably sounds pathetic but the twins' mum was connected to some right bad bastards and I didn't want to end up dead. Or like *this*.' Tony points to his wounds, his bandages, his swollen eyes. 'So I did what Barry said, for years. He paid me a monthly fee and I personally ensured no letters passed between you and Aly. What Barry asked, I did. End of story.'

'Until this week,' says Jo. 'Because obviously you broke the deal when you brought me Aly's letters. What changed your mind?'

'Desperation.' His voice wobbles. 'I promised Barry I wouldn't retire until the prison sentence was over and I stuck to my word. When it ended Barry stopped paying, obviously, and I was relieved to leave all of that nonsense behind me. Then I got a cancer diagnosis. Stage four. I'm devastated but trying to beat it, want to go for private treatment. But it's expensive. I remortgaged the flat but it's still not enough.'

His gaze shifts to the windows behind Jo, the big sky, the endlessness of the sea. And still we humans are arrogant enough to think we're greater than any of it.

'I contacted Barry, told him I'd kept the letters all

that time as . . . security. Told him I'd deliver them to you if he didn't pay the amount I needed for treatment. I asked for ten grand. I was sure he'd play along: he'd paid a fortune already by then, so I knew how determined he was to ensure there was no contact between you and Aly.

'We met at the usual place and he gave me that envelope . . .' Tony nods towards Jo and her bag, the envelope zipped inside it. 'He'd never screwed me over before but I was an idiot to trust him. When I got home I realised he'd only paid a fifth of what I'd asked for. I called him, told him I was literally going to die if I didn't get that money. And you know what he said? *Good riddance.*

'I was furious, after all the help I'd given him. I'd risked my career for him. My reputation. But I let my anger get the better of me. I should have spoken to him again, tried to force his hand. Instead I went for revenge. He'd screwed me over so I decided to do the same to him by delivering the letters. I couldn't find a home address for you but I asked around, found out where you worked. And you know how that story ends.'

'Aye, but *you* don't.'

'What do you mean?'

'My letters were stolen again the same day.'

Tony's jaw drops. 'From the shop?'

Jo shakes her head. 'I took them home, but someone broke into my flat and stole them when I was out. From what you say it *must* be Barry that's behind it – or someone who works with him – but how did he find out so quickly that you'd brought me the letters?'

'Aly must have told him. After I took that box to your shop I tracked down Aly, delivered all the letters you'd written.'

'And fucked up two lives in one day.'

'It was Barry I was trying to hurt.' Tony bows his head; a sinner in line to be pardoned. He'll be waiting a while. 'If it's any consolation, I shot myself in the foot because now I don't have the money and without the letters I don't have any bargaining chips either.'

'My heart bleeds,' says Jo. 'So where did you find Aly?'

'At work. Some key-cutting place down in Leith. One look at the hand-writing and Aly knew the letters were from you; chased after me, demanding to know why I had them and what had happened to the letters meant for you.' Tony gently touches his swollen eyes, the scabs on his neck, flinches with the pain. 'I told Aly what I'm telling you now, about Barry and his bribes. Aly was furious, as you can imagine, threatened to kill me and Barry for interfering. Gave it a decent shot as well.'

'Hang on – *Aly* did this to you?'

Tony nods. 'I didn't want to involve the police but my wife insisted. I told them a stranger attacked me from behind and lied about where it happened so there was less chance they'd link it to Aly.'

203

'Why would you protect someone who wants you dead?'

'To protect myself. If I fuck over one of the twins I'm sure the other will come for me,' he says. 'And they'll be furious if they find out you've been here.'

'They won't,' says Jo. 'But only if you tell me where they live.'

'I've no idea.'

'Bullshit. You want your money or not?'

'Please, hen. I've got enough on my conscience as it is. Even if I had an address I wouldn't give it to you. Can you imagine what Barry would do to me if he found out?'

'I'm not going to hurt anyone, if that's what you're worried about.'

'That's what they all say.'

Jo could punch him for that comment but she doesn't, and aye, she appreciates the irony. 'What about Aly's work address, then? The key-cutting place where you dropped off the letters. You've got to give me *something*.'

'I can't.'

Frustration tugs at her nerves. 'Okay, last chance. Did you read the letters – the ones to me, I mean? Because I need to know what they say, Tony. I know they were written by Aly but I need to know why I wasn't supposed to read them.'

But Tony's already shaking his head. 'Barry made

me promise never to read them and I kept my word. Said they were dynamite. So if you want to know why he cared so much, you'll need to ask him.'

'Impossible.'

'Why?'

'He's missing.'

Tony turns grey. 'Missing how?'

'The police are looking for him.'

'Since when?'

'Not been seen since yesterday after work.'

Tony screws up his swollen face. 'But he texted this morning, demanding I come and see him. I told the wife I've got an appointment at the hospital.'

'What time are you meeting him?'

'At three.' Tony glances at his watch. 'He said I couldn't be late.'

'Don't worry. We won't be,' says Jo, smiling. When Tony starts to protest she pats her backpack. The money is her ace of spades. It took a while but she's got him cornered.

'I'll just get my car keys,' he says.

CHAPTER 33

Tony hasn't said a word since they left his flat. His car's neat and tidy in the front but the back is loaded with the debris children leave: sports equipment, crisp bags, crumbs from snacks. Jo can smell something like festering fruit, buried underneath the chaos.

She stares out of the window as they drive along the coast from Newhaven Harbour. Edinburgh unfolds to their left, all of it. The cliffs and the castle and the tenements resting on the haunted vaults of the underground city that few dare to enter; the factories converted into hipster homes, churches transformed into climbing centres. People complain about change then get over it. Life keeps moving, always.

On Jo's right, the sea stretches out further and deeper than the eye can conceive. Here, there's not much beach to speak of, just earth dropping underwater. And there, in the distance, something else. A squat island, jutting out in the water. Both sides are carpeted in browning grass but a huddle of trees and bushes run down the middle, from the highest point to the shore. Small beaches dot its shoreline. Jo knows this place, has been before; knows where it led her. The hairs on the back of her neck stand on end.

'Where are we heading?'

'Cramond Island,' says Tony, indicating then turning into a car park that would be packed in the summer but not on a day like today. Thick clouds shroud everything in sight. Rain threatens. It's the middle of the day but still dull, cold, grey. 'Barry and I always did our deals at a café near the prison, so Christ knows why he wants to meet here today.'

They get out and walk towards the shore. On one side of the island lies Cramond beach; a vast expanse of puddle-pocked sand bordered by a causeway that stretches for a mile between the mainland and the island. It's exposed only at low tide and one side is walled in by concrete barriers designed to keep out enemy ships during the war. Build a wall, keep them out. As if that ever solved anything.

The water here's called the Firth of Forth, a name that always tied the tongue of Jo's dad, despite the fact they lived on the edge of it. He'd explain to her, often, that this is the place where rivers meet then spill into the sea and become one. It stretches as far as you can see – the banks overlooked by towns and villages, by warehouses and shipyards. In the distance, three bridges cross from one shore to the other, vast arcs built with metal and hope and the sweat of many humans.

Tony pauses at the entrance to the causeway, looks at Jo. 'Barry said to come alone.'

'He's in for a nice surprise, then,' says Jo, stepping from dry land on to something that's a mixture of the two. Sometimes solid, sometimes water. She walks ahead of Tony, picking her way around puddles. Twice a day the causeway is exposed and twice a day it's covered again, controlled by moons, seasons, things we'll never fully understand.

She's halfway across when she sees it: the silhouette of someone on the highest point. Is it Barry? She can't tell, but quickens her pace as best she can on the sea-splashed path. Tony trails behind, slowed by his injuries.

And fear, maybe.

Jo marches onwards, reaches the island just as the figure disappears into the dark space between trees. She shouts for Tony to hurry up then climbs up towards the woodland. Paths lead off in various directions. Jo chooses one that drops downwards towards a hollow. She pushes past branches then reluctantly steps inside the crumbling walls of an old building. Whatever it was, it'd be easy for someone to hide here.

Jo stops, listens. Her body's on high alert: ears pricked, eyes aware of everything that moves. The walls are low but it's what lies behind them that worries her. She moves through the wreck of that place, slowly, cursing every twig and dry leaf that crunches under her feet.

But there's nobody. It's getting colder but she's sweating with the stress of it, the awful expectation that she's about to see a face emerge from the woodland, coming at her.

She descends again, down towards the light, sand, sea – and curves back on to the beach at the same time Tony reaches the end of the causeway, puffing as though he's climbed eight flights of stairs. He's checking his phone but looks up when she reaches him. 'Any sign of him?'

'Nothing. I thought I saw someone when we were crossing but I've lost them.'

'There can't be that many places to hide on an island this size.'

'And why would he hide anyway?'

'That's obvious, isn't it? He told me to come alone and I turn up with *you*, of all people.'

'Then we'll wait.'

Tony tuts. Then they sit, metres apart, watched over by noisy seagulls who shift with the breeze and cormorants that stand on rocks with their black wings stretched wide; letting life happen. Three o'clock comes and goes and still nobody appears.

'I'll text him.' Tony sends a message then calls Barry's mobile but the result is the same. No answer, no reply. They take another walk around the island but find nobody. 'This isn't like him.' That's Tony, getting redder in the face with every passing minute. 'We've met dozens of times for the money exchange and he's always on time.'

'I told you the police say he's missing. Obviously you didn't believe me.'

'Then why did he text me and arrange to meet?'

'Wish I knew.'

Tony slumps down on a rock, looking in the direction of Newhaven. 'I can't stay here all day. Told my wife I'd be back by five and if I'm not home she'll maybe call the hospital, find out I wasn't there at all. Traffic will be a nightmare at this time of night.'

'Then go.'

'And you?'

'I'll wait. See if he shows up when there's only one of us.'

'I really don't think that's a good idea,' says Tony. Then he steps closer, lowers his voice. 'It might not be safe.'

'I can take care of myself.'

'That's exactly what I'm worried about.'

He turns to leave but she reaches out, touches his arm. 'You forgot something.' She holds out the envelope and for a moment he just looks at it, with suspicion; as if he thinks it's a trick. Then he looks at Jo and his eyes are glossy as marbles. His hard man act is gone. And even if he'd kept it up she'd have seen through it. She's been in his home, has seen walls adorned with framed family photos, taken through the ages. Tony with joy in his eyes and babies in his arms. Tony, laughing as he looks up to teenagers even taller than he is. Tony with his wife on their wedding day, looking at each other with love. *That's* who he is underneath his uniform, for those who bother looking.

'You've done what you can,' she says, noticing now his greying skin, the scabs around his lips that point to the sickness growing in him. 'I really hope it helps.'

He sniffs, swallows hard; is not a man who likes to cry in public. 'Thank you, Jo.'

And then he's gone.

Jo watches Tony until he reaches the other side of the causeway and heads for his car. The tide is higher now than it was but she's still got a few hours left before the island will be cut off for six hours. She'll search every inch before she leaves.

Someone is here. And before she leaves, she'll find them.

CHAPTER 34

Spider builds them a new routine. She walks Tink to school and texts her at break-time and at lunch Tink goes to meet her down the street. They sit together, sharing chips and slurping cans of fizzy juice. Sometimes Spider swipes money from her gran's purse and they buy chocolate as well but usually they spend any extra on beers and cigarettes and quarter bottles of vodka that fit perfectly into the big pockets of Spider's coat. She still carries the bike chain in the other one, always.

After school they meet up the park or down the beach to get wasted because that's just what people do. It's all they've ever seen, all they've ever known, and it's good fun. When they're drunk they make silly plans about what they'll do when Tink turns sixteen and can finally leave school. They want money but not jobs, often talk about taking a trip to that beach in Spain that Tink's dad always wanted to show her. Sometimes she regrets mentioning it, thinks maybe she'd like to go there alone. She could learn Spanish and work in a bar and wake up under blue skies every day.

She feels guilty even thinking it.

And anyway, Spider says they'll go together, tells Tink her dad would be chuffed for them. She likes the idea that he's up there somewhere, looking down. That's why she drinks vodka and Coke and sometimes at the cemetery she pours some on to his grave.

They still visit their dead dads every week. Spider waits for Tink outside the school gates on Friday afternoons and they head to the graveyard by bus. The driver likes them. In the three years they've been going there he's never changed the ticket price, say they're still kids to him. Spider tuts when he says that but Tink's skint and grateful, hopes that won't change when she leaves school.

On her very last day Tink texts Spider at breaktime, says she's bored and leaving early. There's nothing to keep her there now. They meet at the school gates and head towards the graveyard even though Spider says that's a shit way to celebrate.

Tink doesn't feel as free as she thought she would.

It's raining when the bus pulls into their usual stop so they tug up their hoods and head down the stairs. But Tink's halfway down when she sees an ugly red coat she recognises. The bus door's blocked by a crumpled woman holding crap flowers bought in a garage. Wrapped in plastic. Tink stops dead and Spider pushes her from behind but her feet are rooted to the narrow metal stairway.

She turns, whispers, 'It's my *mum*.'

Then her mum shouts *thanks* to the driver in the cheery voice she reserves for other people. She lights up a cigarette the moment her feet hit the pavement, sucks in tobacco like it's saving her life. Tink holds herself so still it hurts, wills the driver to close the doors and drive away. But he knows their faces and their routine.

'You lassies not getting off?' That's the driver, twisting round, shouting to them. Her mum turns too, maybe thinking he's talking to her. That's when she sees Tink.

Then sees Spider behind her.

There's a moment of stillness, when life pauses, could go either way. But then Tink's mum tosses the lit cigarette on to the ground and hauls herself back on to the bus. Even from a distance, her fury can be felt. She's still gripping those cut flowers that look exactly like the bunches Tink finds every single week at her dad's grave.

'It's *you* who's been leaving them?' Tink stares, stunned.

Her mum glances at the flowers. They're already wilting, choked by the plastic that's wrapped too tightly around delicate stalks. 'It's a free country last time I checked.'

'You said Dad wasn't worth visiting. You banned me from coming.'

'Aye, and a fat lot of good that did.' Tink's mum grabs her arm and drags her down the stairs, pushes her into a window seat. 'Sit down and shut up. We'll talk about this at home.'

Tink is sixteen now but does as she's told. Her mum sits down beside her, wedging her in. She clamps the flowers to her lap and a bashed rose sheds its yellow petals. Her mum doesn't notice because she's watching Spider saunter off the bus, casual as anything, hands stuffed into her pockets. Then she flips her gaze to Tink.

'I warned you not to see that fucking girl, ever. Is *that* who you're hanging about with when you disappear every night? If so, it ends here. You see her again and you're sleeping on the streets. Is that clear?'

Tink doesn't answer.

'I said, is that clear?'

The question is hanging in the air, feels like something solid between them. Tink holds her breath and drops her head and keeps perfectly quiet, perfectly still. Maybe if she stays like this for long enough her mum will forget she's there.

'Don't you dare ignore me.' Tink's mum grabs her wrists and twists so hard the skin burns.

Until now she's managed to keep her voice to a whisper but even without looking up Tink can tell a few folk have heard and turned their heads. She can sense the movement, hear the rustle of waterproof jackets as passengers twist round in their seats to see what all the fuss is about. Then come mutters, words that will be casting judgement on them both.

Tink lets her eyes flit momentarily to the driver and the open doors. Spider's out on the pavement now; waiting, staring at her mum.

'Nobody ever tell you it's rude to stare at strangers?'

Her mum hisses it at first then stands up and says it again, loud as anything. She's looking at Spider but she's saying it to everyone on the whole bus, challenging them. Everyone looks away, except Spider. She's holding beers in one hand and the other's in her pocket.

'Don't forget I know what you did.'

That's her mum speaking, looking at Spider. Tink's confused because those two have never properly met, shouldn't have secrets that she doesn't know about.

'And I won't tell you again: stay the fuck away from my daughter. Understand?'

Her mum's rigid and silent beside her, waiting for an answer that doesn't come. Tink tries not to move, wishes this moment away. She wants to be halfway through next week, next year. Not here, caught between the two of them: a woman she's supposed to love but cannot, and a girl she's not supposed to love but somehow does.

'You coming, Tink?'

Spider says it cheerfully, as if it isn't really a question at all. There's no way Tink can get out past her mum and anyway she wouldn't dare ... until Spider pulls her hand out of her pocket, holds it towards Tink.

'Don't even *think* about it,' her mum says.

And Tink doesn't think about it at all. Instead she just stands up on the seat, climbs over to the row in front and leaps off the bus. Her mum erupts. Tink takes Spider's hand.

And then, they run.

CHAPTER 35

Jo starts her hunt by climbing to the highest point of the island, searches the bushes and beaches and trees for signs of movement. She keeps one eye on the causeway in case the person she's certain she saw tries to leave – and to make sure she gets off the island before the water rises. Then she ducks back into the trees, walking slowly over dry leaves. Trunks creak, branches rub, twigs snap, leaves rustle. A woodland is never silent, never still. A few more buildings crumble between the trees, walls dragged down by time or plants or vandals. She pauses a few times and listens for breathing or feet snapping the undergrowth. Nothing. It's just her and the island. She heads for the furthest beach, down on to the sand that's slowly disappearing under gentle waves. There's nothing, nobody.

But the silence doesn't last.

She's searching the next beach when she hears the thud-thud-thud of an approaching helicopter. Seabirds screech and rise, alarmed. Jo holds her breath and searches the sky, spots red on the grey. It's a search and rescue helicopter, flying towards the island, low enough that she can see the open door and the figure it frames; jumpsuit, helmet, boots.

Are they looking for Barry Chisholm?

She steps back into the trees and watches it pass overhead and keep going, still watching, searching, but not here. Relief feels like a hot bath. She steps back on to the beach and heads for the causeway. The tide's rising. Dusk, falling. She needs to leave, accept the fact that all she's found here is another dead end.

Why had Barry arranged to meet Tony here at three o'clock if he had no intention of coming? It's possible Tony had lied about their meet-up plan – but why would he? As far as Jo can see, he'd gain nothing from it. So the facts were this: Tony received a text from Barry's phone, arranging to meet. But was it definitely Barry who typed the message and made the plan? The police say he's gone missing, so maybe his phone's in someone else's hands. Or maybe he *did* send the message but hid from Tony when he saw Jo had come too. She's *sure* she saw someone.

So far she'd searched in silence but maybe that wasn't the right approach. She's got nothing to lose. She cups her hands round her mouth, takes a deep breath and shouts his name.

'Barry! Barry!' She turns on the spot, throws her voice to every corner of the island. It's her last hope but the wind is doing its best to sabotage her plan. Throat sore, hands cold, she turns back to the causeway. The path's wet and will soon be submerged. Her time is running out. She needs to hurry.

She's halfway back to shore when she pauses, takes one final look at the island behind her. From this perspective she can see something she didn't see before.

A dark shape, in the water.

It's close to one of the beaches, rising and falling with the movement of the waves. Jo narrows her eyes, tries to make out the details. It could be a log or a seal or a bank of seaweed. Or it could be a man.

She retraces her steps, quickly as she can, shoes splashing in growing puddles that punctuate the causeway path. When she reaches the island again she speeds up, races over spiky grass and over the rocks then down to the far beach. The man's five or six metres from shore, on his back, eyes open and pointing at the sky. She keeps going, forcing herself through the freezing water. Cold hits her skin like a thousand blades. She gasps but keeps going, grabbing for his outstretched arm just as a wave carries him inches further from shore. A few more steps and she'll have him. The water's shallow here so if she can bear the cold she can make it. A wave throws water on to her face, feels like a slap. She edges closer, grasping with frigid hands until she grips his feet and drags his heavy body towards the shore.

Barry looks dead and feels dead but she pulls him out of the water and as far up the beach as she can; then drops to her knees and frantically searches for signs of life.

Overhead, seagulls squawk and circle, hunting small fish that have been chased to the surface by those that are bigger. Stalks of stiff seagrass whisper as the wind rubs them together. And all around this tiny island the sea rises and falls, rises and falls, rises and falls: the breath of the earth, the beginning and the ending of everything.

Jo's done all the courses, practised the ABC of how to save a life on dummies with plastic mouths. But here, now, there's no instructor, no pals to remind her where to push and how, and when to give up. There's no breath, and when she offers Barry her own lips his are cold against hers. She starts chest compressions, waiting, waiting, waiting for a groan or a blink, some kind of twitch that'll show she's done a good job; saved a life.

Then, a voice comes instead.

CHAPTER 36

For a moment it feels as if somebody's pressed the pause button on Jo's brain, body, life; or maybe they've pressed rewind. She's silent, soaking up the scene in front of her.

Her and Aly and a body between them. Again.

'You're too late,' says Aly.

The words are pushed out through nibbled lips. Jo knows that look, that voice, the impending panic Aly tries to fight off by chewing down on the softest parts of herself. Later she'll fill herself with beer and vodka so the parts that hurt start to blur. Some people never change.

Jo's still kneeling on the ground. She restarts the CPR, still convincing herself there's hope Barry will survive this. Whatever *this* is, she's sure Aly's behind it.

'What have you done, Aly?'

'Nothing you wouldn't do.'

Jo hates Aly in that moment. The air between them is so thick and heavy it might have been made from bricks, hurriedly laid in rows and fixed with oozing cement.

'But he's your *brother*, Aly. Your *twin*. Why would—'

222

'He's the reason we're not together, Jo. He deliberately drove us apart. He came between us.'

'So did a prison wall.'

Aly had looked so calm in court, even when the murder was described in vivid detail, from the first awful blow to the final breath. They'd both known what would happen next. The jail sentence that was handed down had gobbled up the joyful milestones of a normal life: gone was the possibility of celebrating your eighteenth and twenty-first and thirtieth birthdays. Gone was the notion that adulthood meant freedom. Gone was the two of them, together, a first love that had dazzled them both, then shot out sparks that blazed so wildly it destroyed everything and anything in its path. First, Jo's mum. Now, Aly's brother. Jo's still got her hands on Barry's chest but there's no heartbeat now; no chance. She straightens up as Aly drops on to the sand and hugs her knees.

'Letters would have kept us together even if walls kept us apart,' she says. Jo wonders if she'd read that line somewhere and rehearsed it. But surely, *surely*, she couldn't believe it. 'We're not together thanks to *him*.' Aly pushes one foot forward, nudges her brother's stilled cheek. His mouth falls open. No words fall out. 'I wrote to you every day, Jo. For years.' She's staring at the ground. 'Can you imagine? *Me* of all people, sitting down with a pen and paper, thinking I was some kind of poet or something. When I didn't hear back I thought maybe I'd read everything wrong, imagined the bond between us. But that kiss—'

'Was fifteen years ago.'

'*Exactly*, Jo. That's the whole point. It was fifteen years ago and I can *still* feel it.' She looks up at Jo, desperately.

Jo looks away, embarrassed. But the truth of it was this: in spite of everything, she remembered it too. That kiss – all those years ago – had been like a sunrise after endless months of impending dawn that both of them had pretended they couldn't see.

But then darkness had fallen, fast.

Jo closes her eyes even though she knows what she'll see. Mum, blood, Aly, police.

'That's why I kept writing, Jo. Maybe not every day but every week, then every month. I was convinced that eventually you'd write to me and say you felt the same.' There's a hint of a smile on Aly's face, a flicked lighter that doesn't quite take hold. 'And now I know you *did* write. Eighteen times, to be precise. So now I *know* you care. Now I *know* you love me. But all that time you thought you weren't loved back.' Aly's jaw tightens, clamping fury. 'And then in your very last letter you tell me you won't write again because, thanks to Barry, you'd never heard from me. You felt totally abandoned, and I did too. But that all changed when I got your letters on Friday, hand-delivered fifteen years late by that spineless fuckwit.'

'You mean Tony?'

'Of course I do. He dropped the letters at my work then tried to leg it. But when I saw your handwriting I chased him, caught up with him before he reached his car, forced him to explain.'

'With your fists?'

Aly shrugs, as if violence is the only obvious response. 'I needed to know if he'd given you the letters I wrote. He told me he'd dropped off the box at your work before you arrived for your shift and I made him tell me the address. Then I called Barry.' She laughs, to herself. Jo's not sure what's funny. 'I told him I knew what he'd been up to all these years, bribing Tony to hide the letters so you'd think I didn't care, and vice versa. Then I told him his big plan had backfired because now I had your letters I *knew* the truth of it: you feel the same way I do. I told him I was going to find you, that we'd get back together anyway. Barry laughed when I said that, said I was fucked because if you read my letters now you'd run a mile. And he was right, wasn't he? Because that's exactly what you did when I came to find you in the pub.'

'I haven't read them, Aly.'

'*What?*'

Jo shakes her head. 'They were stolen from my flat before I could read a single word. I'd assumed that was down to you, or Barry.'

'It *was*,' says Aly. 'Barry got your address off some

225

dodgy contact of his. He stole the box but said the seal was broken, and at least one of the letters had been torn open.'

'True,' says Jo. 'But not read.'

'Seriously? So why did you run away from me?' Aly swallows hard after she asks that and when she speaks again her voice is softer, sadder. 'I've read *your* letters, over and over. And I've spent most of the weekend parked outside your flat, waiting for the right moment to knock your door and ask if you still meant what you said when you wrote them. You said I'd saved you, that you'd never laughed as much with anyone. Me and you forever, you said. But then I saw you, with *her*.'

Jo doesn't need to ask who. So it was Aly who'd seen her with Farida. And most likely Aly who'd called the press and left the graffiti on her pickup. *Watch Your Back*.

'I called Barry, told him he'd been right all along, that it was finally over between us. The smug fuck sounded quite pleased, said it was for the best. He didn't realise then that I blamed him for it. *Hated* him for it. I suggested we burn the letters and dump the ashes at sea. Make sure there was no chance that anyone else could ever read them. We did the burning at his flat then came here. He was thick enough to think that would be the end of it. Then he realised I wanted to dump *him* at sea as well.'

Again, she nudges her brother with her shoe. This

time his head falls to one side and now his dead eyes are looking at Jo.

'When I went to dump his mobile I found dozens of messages from Tony, begging for more money. He's so pathetic. But I realised I could kill two birds with one stone. Blame Tony for killing Barry. He's been bribed by Barry for years so the motive was already there. An ex-screw like him would have a terrible time in jail and it would serve him right for keeping me and you apart. But he *really* fucked up my plan bringing you with him. I needed him to be seen *alone* on the causeway. Then I'd claim Barry invited Tony here to talk, but got killed instead. Witnessed by me. I'd have made sure Tony got done for the murder. God knows who they'll blame now.'

'Me, probably.'

'I won't let that happen.'

'So you'll confess?'

Aly smiles but it's a sad one. 'You'd like that, wouldn't you? Then you'd get rid of me once and for all.'

'I don't want to get rid of anyone,' says Jo. 'I just want to understand what's really behind all of this. It must have cost Barry a fortune to pay off Tony for all those years, and all because he didn't want me to read what you'd written? They're just teenage love letters, right? It's not as if there are any secrets between us.'

Jo expects a nod of agreement. But that's when Aly flinches.

CHAPTER 37

It was a tiny twitch, a cloud passing momentarily over Aly's face. In any other moment, Jo might not have noticed. But here, now, it means something.

'What's the secret, Aly?'

But she's not listening. Aly's eyes dart from Jo to Barry, then towards the causeway. She leaps up; steps over Barry as if he's a shit she doesn't want to stand on. 'We need to get off the island, *right now*. Before the tide gets any higher.'

'What about Barry?'

'What about him?' Aly's already walking away and it's only then that Jo notices Aly holding a yellow leather jacket in her hand. 'Come on, Jo!'

'Where did you get that jacket, Aly?'

'Why does it matter?'

'Tell me where you got it.'

'Some charity shop,' she says. Face straight, she tugs it on. Jo spots a fresh stain on the sleeve and pictures Aly hunched over her brother, pressing the jacket over his face until there was no air left, the way you'd do with armbands before you packed them away. So it was Aly who stole her jacket from the pub, as a souvenir, maybe. Or to disguise herself as Jo. Pass the blame. And if Farida was to be believed, this was the same yellow jacket caught on cameras near Barry's home just before he was declared missing. Aly in Jo's clothing. Mystery solved. But the bad news? That same jacket might now have been used as a murder weapon. The worse news: Jo's got plenty of reasons to want Barry dead.

She turns back to him, desperately checking again for signs of a pulse, a breath. 'We *have* to call an ambulance, Aly. And the police.'

'Have you seen the tide? Come on!'

Jo knows – remembers – how Aly always expected Jo to obey her, to follow. Instead, she pulls out her phone. She's only pressed the first of three nines when Aly whips the phone out of her hand. She wraps her fingers around Jo's, too tightly. Her hands are shaking. 'It'll be better for us both if you don't call the authorities. You of all people should know what'll happen.'

When Jo tugs her hand away Aly lunges for her, grabs her wrist so tightly that the skin stings. Little balls of saliva are gathering at the corners of her mouth. 'Come with me, Jo. We've both been waiting for this, haven't we? We can leave Edinburgh, go somewhere else and start again. Together. It's *us*. Me and you.'

'Against the world?'

A smile flickers on to Aly's face then burns out, a match caught in a gale. 'Why not?'

'Why not *with* the world?'

'Because it fucks you over, that's why.' She glances at the causeway. 'Come *on*.'

'We can't just—'

'We *can*. You think there are rules but it's you who's making them. Just *undo* them.'

Aly hauls Jo up then runs, dragging her behind her. The ground is dotted with puddles that most folk would step around. They go right through them. Jo's a dog, pulled; a child strapped into one of those harnesses. She used to like it when Aly did this. When they were teenagers they'd go drinking up the park then wreak havoc. Break stuff, steal stuff, kick the shit out of folk who had more stuff or better stuff than they did. Aly always had plastic bags loaded with drink and a brain packed with mischief and the nerve to turn thoughts to actions. It was a thrill for Jo to be chosen, to be pulled into the mess of it with her. But now being chosen is the last thing she wants. She can see so clearly now what she couldn't see then: Aly won't stop until she gets what she wants.

Back then, she'd run with Aly until her lungs burst. Now she wants to run *from* her. Barry's dead and Aly's the killer, doesn't even appear to be sorry. But how can someone you love commit the most hateful of all acts? Easy. You think it's hard until it happens.

And it happens every day. All killers were once loved. And aye, Jo wishes it was as easy to hate Aly now as it had been to love her back then. But she sees the pain that lies behind all of this. Killings are born from suffering, plain and simple. She'd never justify anyone taking a life. But most murderers are convinced their crime will make them feel better, happier, a little more whole. And it'll work, maybe, for a few fiery seconds. Killing is the ultimate power rush, controlling who lives and who dies. It's not just playing God, it's *being* God. If you believe the papers you probably think killers are different beasts, humans who are wired wrong. But if Jo's learned anything it's this: in most cases they're *exactly* like us, and that's the scariest part. They're just like you. They're someone's parent or child or sibling or friend. They're the person you once so deeply adored.

Aly slows on the downward slope towards the causeway and Jo reaches out, grabs a tree branch. They slide to a stop, out of breath. Aly's red in the face with the effort of it.

Jo tugs her hand free. 'I *said* I won't just leave him here.'

'So you're a *martyr* now, is that it? Here's the reality, Jo. If you stay here and call the police, you're fucked, because you'll be the only person on an inaccessible island with the body of a man you hate. If you stay here and *don't* call the police, you're fucked, because sooner or later some cheerful dog-walker will find you both and call them anyway. The only sensible option is to get the fuck off this island before the tide comes in. We leave Barry here and once we're back on dry land we can talk. Okay?'

Aly zips up that yellow leather jacket, all the way to the top. Once her lips are chewed to hell she'll start on the zip, gnaw cold, hard metal until she tastes blood in her mouth. She's always liked it, finds it a comfort to know she bleeds like everyone else. She steps forward now and pulls Jo close enough to kiss her. Jo doesn't struggle or resist, lets their breaths mingle for a moment. She can still remember that first moment they stood this close; her helplessness in the face of a power like that one. Love, or something like it. They resisted, for a while; but in the end it just made the surrender even sweeter. It would be so easy now to lean in, let such a simple thing as touch be the guide of her. Difference is, she knows now where it will lead.

'I'm staying,' says Aly.

The silence that follows is broken only by their breaths and breaking waves. Then Jo's mobile starts ringing in Aly's hand. She glares at it then tosses it on to the ground, unanswered. 'No need for mobiles where we're going,' says Aly, and the only phone-free place Jo can think of is heaven. Or prison. Two ends of the spectrum, for most. Aly's tugging her towards the causeway and Jo's still hanging on to that tree branch but it's bending and ready to break. Then her phone starts ringing, again, the screen lighting up the sand around it.

'You're popular today.' Aly releases Jo, then reaches down and picks up the phone. 'It's your voicemail,' she says, then answers and presses the hands-free button so both of them can hear.

And suddenly *that* voice floats out of the handset and into the air between them.

'Jo? It's . . . Farida. *Please* pick up. Or call me back. I'm not sure what's going on with you but . . . I promise it'll be better for everyone if you get in touch. I want to . . . help, okay?'

'How sweet,' says Aly, then pulls out her own phone and takes a photo of Farida's number on the screen. 'Never know when you might need a detective,' she says, winking at Jo as if this is all a game, a joke, something they'll laugh about later down the pub.

'Wait,' says Jo. 'You *know* Farida?'

'We've had a few . . . encounters.'

Jo flushes, thinking of those hands on Aly instead of her. *Surely* not. 'You mean—?'

'We fucked? No. I'll leave that to you. But she fucked me over, good and proper. Almost got sent back to prison thanks to that bitch. Makes me sick to think of you and her . . . *together.*' That last word is squeezed out through tightly clamped teeth. 'It broke my heart, Jo, when I saw you talking to *her.* Standing so close. *Too* close. Even a blind man could tell something had happened between you two.'

'It's nothing.'

Aly laughs. 'Really? So why did she stay so long? I waited outside for hours before I gave up and went home. I was desperate for her to leave, but she didn't. In my books that's not *nothing*.' Aly's all tensed shoulders and clamped jaw and whitening fists but just for a moment she loosens, like an elastic band stretched so far it snaps. Jo wonders if she's used up all the fight in her, if she'll wilt and flop on to the beach. 'When I got your letters I felt hope, Jo, for the first time in years. Hope that we weren't finished. That we'd get back together. But when I saw you there with Farida – *of all people* – I knew then that I'd lost you, for good this time. And it was all Barry's fault for keeping us apart and Tony's fault for helping him and Farida's fault for stealing you on the very same day I was coming to get you.'

'So it was you who wrote that warning on her car?'

'Aye. And I meant it,' she says, then lobs Jo's phone towards the water and starts running towards the causeway, feet splashing on the path as she tries to beat the rising tide.

Jo watches until the darkening sky swallows Aly's outline then hurries back to the beach and triple-checks Barry's body for signs of life. Nothing. After that she scours the darkening beach for her phone, eventually finds it nestled in a bed of puffy seaweed that would have cushioned its fall. She calls the police; it's the only thing she can do now. They'll come, quick as they can; bring help, boats, questions.

She hangs up and waits. The rising tide covers the causeway, cutting her off from the mainland. Aly's gone. Barry's dead. For now it's just Jo and the body and a shifting sea that seems to be whispering at her, taunting her like the bad kids at school.

Maybe she should have run. Maybe she should have saved herself.

Instead, she's suspect number one.

CHAPTER 38

Once they're sure Tink's mum is off their trail they stop at a wee shop and Spider flirts with the track-suited boys outside so they'll go inside and buy them more booze. Then they get on another bus – top deck, front row, again – and stay on board for ages, rumble through streets that Tink's never seen before. They don't speak. Tink rests a warm cheek against the cold glass, tries not to think about her mum as they pass through thousands of lives without being seen. Tink doesn't know the names of these places but she can tell just by looking which ones are posh. More money means more sky and more space. In the rich parts of the city, rugby pitches are spread like plush rugs between houses with no upstairs neighbour. The roofs here don't have moss or satellite dishes and cars in driveways aren't held up by bricks. Tink's never felt so far from home.

They pass a sprawling golf course that leads them back to the sea then Spider rings the bell and motions for Tink to get off. They're at a massive beach.

Shallow stretches of seawater streak hard-packed sand that's shiny from the retreating tide.

'Where are we?'

'Not there yet,' says Spider, pointing to a concrete path drawn by the straightest ruler, leading from the beach to a tiny island. A sign at the entrance warns of tides and times and changes in the weather but Spider strides onwards, through puddles that Tink pauses to step around. The right-hand side is guarded by slanting concrete blocks twice as tall as she is and Spider says they're something to do with the military. But the other side is wide open. Waves suck both sides of the path as she walks and Tink feels a little bit like Jesus when he walked on water but decides not to mention it. It takes twenty minutes to reach the island and Tink wants to stop and cram it all in so she doesn't forget how beautiful the world can be but she can do that later, come here again. Instead she follows Spider up a hill and through a woodland and past a ruined house and on to a sandy beach on the far side that feels a thousand miles from everything. Spider flops down on the sand. Tink copies her.

'*Now* we're here.' Spider pulls out two beers that spit out warm fizz when they open them. And so they drink and they laugh and regret not buying crisps. When they're finishing the first beer and opening the second Tink remembers she's got some salt 'n' vinegar

Discos in her backpack and when she pulls them out Spider says *omygodiloveyou* and they stare at each other for ages and it should be awkward but it isn't.

They can see the city from here, the sea a darkening lake between them and the hard edges and slanting roofs of buildings. And so they sit, arses turning to ice on the sand as the endless sky darkens above them and sucks all the colour from the bricks and rocks of Edinburgh. Then the whole place is dotted with stars made of street lamps and the headlights of cars, of TVs in windows and security lights screwed to walls to make folk feel safe. Beyond the outline of the city, more nature. For the first time it seems obvious that the trees were here first.

Tink can feel the beer bubbles in her veins and some of them have floated up into her head. It helps ease the weight of her thoughts, which have been stuck on repeat since they saw her mum at the graveyard. Right from day one Tink's mum had banned her from visiting her dad's grave, hadn't even told her where it was. She'd offer Tink a pick 'n' mix of stupid reasons that were always changing, depending on the day and how much she'd drunk: he'd let them down, shamed their family, wasn't worth grieving for. She didn't want Tink wasting her time and love on a man who was better off forgotten.

But all the while *she'd* been visiting him on her own, leaving flowers and apologies for the man who died trying to leave her. But surely if anything it should be her dad apologising to her mum for leaving, not her mum apologising to her dad now he's dead? None of it makes any sense.

But most of all, it hurts.

Tink smiles when Spider opens another warm can. This time she pops a bendy straw into the opening, says you get drunk quicker that way. Tink gives it a try and feels better and that means her dad had been right all along. Drinking makes you *happy*, *faster*.

Spider downs her can in one then burps and turns to Tink. 'So, you been here before?'

Tink shakes her head. 'But I'll come back.'

'You mean *we*,' says Spider, and Tink wants to stay there forever. Spider gets out her posh camera phone and takes a photo of them, side by side, cheering as they hold their cans in the air. The photo's grainy and they both look drunk as anything but Tink likes it because you can tell they're on an island, see the sea behind them. It looks exotic. They take loads then huddle over the tiny screen, laughing at each other's expressions. The phone doesn't have a flash so the quality fades with the light and soon all you can see is eyes and teeth in the dark. Spider leaves the phone with Tink when she goes to pee. Tink's flick-flick-flicking through the photos when Spider shouts to her from the rocks at the end of the beach. 'We're in deep shit,' she says.

When Tink stands up she sees why: seawater is creeping over the edge of the causeway, cutting off their escape from the island. 'We might make it if we leave now,' says Spider, tugging up her trousers. 'Otherwise we'll be stuck here for hours and I'm guessing your mum won't be happy if you get home at two in the morning.'

'She won't be happy anyway,' says Tink, and all the bubbles in her burst. She's annoyed at Spider for mentioning her mum. 'I'm staying,' she says, then flops down on to the sand. Suddenly it feels colder, damper. She doesn't care.

'Come on, Tink. We'll freeze to death if we stay here.'

'My mum's going to kill me anyway, for storming off that bus.'

Spider runs back to where she's sitting then kneels down. Their faces are so close that Tink can feel Spider's breath on her cheeks. It's hot like a dog's but smells better.

'I'll come home with you.'

'That'll probably make things worse,' says Tink. 'Mum totally hates you.' She expects Spider to slag off her mum again but instead she looks away, stares into the dark. Tink wonders if she's thinking about what happened on the bus; what her mum meant when she shouted at Spider. *I know what you did*, she said.

But what had Spider done?

The question's been lodged in Tink's throat since

they got here and won't seem to budge, no matter how much she drinks. But now, quietly, it slips out.

Spider stands up and edges away. The dark sky sucks all the colour from her face.

'You really want to know?'

'Aye.'

'Let's get off the island first. Then I'll tell you every-thing. Deal?'

'Suppose.' It's not really a deal at all, but Tink agrees because it's the only way she'll get an answer. Spider helps her on to her feet and they sprint, hand in hand, across the sea-lapped causeway. They're both knackered when they reach the mainland and their shoes are soaked. They find a bench and hang them-selves over it, puffing and groaning. Tink gets her breath back first but when Spider starts speaking her heart starts thundering again. She feels like she's got a bouncy ball trapped in her chest.

'You've got to promise this won't change anything. With us, I mean.'

'Promise,' says Tink. *I know what you did*, her mum had said. And now, finally, Tink would know as well.

Spider clears her throat, a drum roll. 'I know why your mum's been leaving flowers at your dad's grave. I know what she feels guilty about. And I know why she hates me. She thinks I tried to fuck her over but I promise I was just trying to help.'

'Help with *what*?'

Spider's tugging ragged skin around one of her thumbs. 'Help the police. After your dad's accident,' she says and Tink's mouth goes dry, like she's licked a carpet.

'You were *there*?'

Spider nods and a cold breeze slips into the space between Tink's jacket and jogging bottoms; between the two of them.

'But why would she hate you for that?'

Spider closes her eyes, chews her lips for a few seconds before she speaks.

'Because I saw the whole thing,' says Spider. 'The police asked me what had happened and I told them. And . . . the thing is . . . your mum caused the accident that killed your dad. It's her fault he's dead.'

CHAPTER 39

Jo's phone battery dies right after she calls the police and coastguard. When they arrive about half an hour later by boat the sounds of the island are lost to diesel motors and fuzzy radios and the shouted instructions of people in uniform. Jo's greeted with warm blankets and veiled disapproval, asked where they can find the body. Then booted feet thunder over rocks and leaves and sand. She wants to stay and explain what happened but instead she's loaded on to the rescue boat. Now's not the time for words. From there they bump over the waves away from Edinburgh, towards the nearest coastguard station at South Queensferry. Jo twists round, watches police officers and paramedics cross the island then disappear from view as they dip down to the beach where she'd tried breathing life into Barry's body. The high tide was clawing at his shoes when she left him and seagulls watched from the rocks. She once saw a gull drag a chicken carcass along Portobello High Street, sickens herself now picturing a flock of them pecking at Barry, tugging at his clothes, hair, lips.

'You alright, sweetheart?' That's one of the coast-guards, inspecting her. 'You're looking a bit peaky. You should focus on the horizon.'

She does as she's told, stares straight ahead, wishes she could empty her head of all those images and tip them into the water. She's seen too much already. Why do beautiful memories fade faster than the bloody ones?

A few minutes later the boat slows and she's offered a dry hand as she climbs from the boat to the coast-guard's base. The world here is cold and damp, smells of diesel and seaweed. Two pickups with neon stripes are parked outside a building of sand-coloured bricks and a pitched roof. The coastguard flag flaps loudly above Jo's head as she's led inside and ushered to a sofa in the reception area that's too hard and too small to offer much comfort. She's given tea, blankets, dry clothes, directions to the loo and assurances that they'll be right back. Wait here, they say. Again, she obeys. Sometimes life's easier when you're told what to do and just do it. It means you don't need to think, don't need to worry about what's coming next because you're not the one deciding. She sips her tea, feels it warm her from the inside out. The coastguard team have gath-ered in a room at the end of the building. They've got a TV on, news by the sounds of it. But the volume's too low for her to hear. She wonders if Barry's disappear-ance and death have made the news yet, if Sandy and other hacks will be sent down to cover the story. She won't speak to any of them, knows how it feels when your family becomes public property to be picked over and commented on; judged and pitied on printed pages.

Jo closes her eyes, tries to process what's happened, then jumps out of her skin when someone places a hand on her arm. Eyes open and she's looking into the eyes of the coastguard who'd helped her off the boat.

'You're wanted, hen. Through here.'

Jo tugs the blanket around her shoulder and follows him to a small meeting room with a table and chairs. Two are occupied. One by a police officer she's never seen before. The other by DS Effie Garcia. 'This is becoming a habit,' says Effie, then nods to a seat in front of her. 'If you don't mind?'

Jo sits, tugs her blanket tighter, then looks Effie in the eye. 'Did you find him?'

Effie tilts her head. 'Who do you mean by *him*?'

'Barry Chisholm. Your missing man.'

'I was under the impression *you'd* found him.'

'I did. But he was already dead. I tried CPR but . . .' Jo remembers the coldness of his cheeks and lips, wishes she could brush her teeth. 'He was gone.'

'And you're sure about that?'

'Positive.'

Effie glances at the other officer, makes no attempt to stifle a sigh. 'The thing is, Jo, there's no body on that island.'

'Impossible.'

'We've had a team searching it for the past hour.'

'Then he must have been washed out to sea.'

'Convenient.'

Jo screws up her face. 'Why?'

'It allows you to continue this little game of yours; all this ridiculous attention-seeking behaviour.'

'What are you talking about?'

'One day your place of work is broken into but nothing is taken. Then you invent a story about an intruder at your flat. Next day you invent finding a body. What's next?'

'It's all true.'

'You know what else is true? Wasting police time is a criminal offence, Jo.'

'You're the ones wasting time. I *know* who's behind all of this.'

'Go on then. What's his name?'

'It's a *she*. Aly Chisholm.'

'Barry's twin sister?' Effie screws up her face. 'Nice try. But it was Aly who reported Barry missing in the first place. She collected him from work late afternoon, they went for a woodland walk then she dropped him off at their home. She's not seen him since.'

'She saw him tonight.'

'Where?'

'On the island. She was *there*. And it was her who killed him.'

'And you witnessed the murder, did you?'

'No, but—'

'So you're speculating?'

'I *spoke* to her.'

'And she confessed?'

Jo hesitates, then nods. If she protects Aly they'll just blame her instead. 'She told me she wanted to pin it on Tony Burgos, the retired screw who was beaten up. The papers said you lot want to speak with a woman seen close to the place he was attacked, right? Well, it was Aly Chisholm. And she's the woman caught on camera near Barry's flat as well.'

Effie widens her eyes and holds them still, as though she's trying really hard to stop them from rolling. 'And you have *evidence* for all of this, do you?'

'Just my word.'

'I work with facts. I talked to Aly on the telephone an hour ago and she was at home; tells me she's been there all day.'

'And you *believe* her? You said yourself she's got a terrible record.'

'I think you're forgetting how you and I first became acquainted.'

'If only.' Jo blinks and sees it again: the scene of her mum's murder. She wonders how it looked through Effie's eyes. 'So what happens now?'

'We get out of here, that's what. *Someone* has alerted the press. We'll be swarmed in no time which is why we'll move to the station to . . . continue this conversation. If you'll accompany me to the van?'

No chance. Jo's been there, done that, remembers hard benches, barred windows, and, metres away, paramedics zipping her mother into a bag. She couldn't, wouldn't.

'I'm fine here.'

Effie's eyes slip over Jo's shoulders to the room where the coastguards sit with their monitoring equipment and mugs of tea. Jo doesn't turn but feels dozens of eyes on her back as Effie calmly packs away her notepad and pen then stands and motions for Jo to do the same.

'It wasn't a question,' says Effie.

CHAPTER 40

Effie's on her feet, framed by the door; a portrait of power. She's got one eye on Jo and the other on a window that overlooks the car park at the harbour. It's dark now so Jo can't see what she sees but she can tell there's more movement than when she arrived: headlights tossing light through the window; the thump of car doors closing. Effie frowns. 'That's the press here. I'll get the van brought to the door and then we'll leave.' She presses the button on her radio, gives the same instructions to the driver. 'Be right there,' he says, voice cloaked in static.

'How long's the drive?'

'Half an hour or so, depends on the traffic.'

'It's just, I need the toilet again. Must be the nerves.'

Effie glares at her, then glances at the wall clock. 'You've got two minutes.'

Jo pushes back her chair and hurries out, does the kind of half-run people do at pedestrian crossings. The toilet's at the very back of the building, the opposite end from the door. She'd gone when she first arrived, was handed a towel to dry off and offered a pair of grey jogging pants that they kept there for people like her. Saved, but soaked. They gave her socks too but didn't have any shoes that fitted so with every step she's squelching in sea water, remembering the slap of the waves on her skin; the weight of that body once she'd dragged it to the beach.

Jo had never seen a body until her mum's murder; had certainly never touched one. She'd been shocked how quickly she turned pale and cold, how obvious it was that life was no longer locked inside of that skin. Racing blood, stopped in its tracks.

But will Jo be stopped in hers?

Her plan is simple. The toilet has one of those tiny windows above the cistern that's opened only to release bad smells. And maybe, just maybe, bad people. Light on, door locked, window open. The toilet seat clunks loudly and slides to one side when she steps on it. She stops, breath held, eyes closed, ears pricked. Would Effie have heard? She waits, heart thumping, but nobody comes. She sticks her head out of the window to see what lies on the other side. Mossy tarmac, swirling crisp bags, two seagulls with their heads tucked under their wings, sleeping. Nothing that can harm her. She tries to lift her leg to the window frame so she can climb out feet-first but the space is too small, the risk of making more noise too big. Head-first it is. If her shoulders fit through the space, that means the rest of her will as well. Good news. But there's nowhere to grip on the other side of the wall so once she lets go of the window frame she'll slip out and on to the ground, face-first.

She's half in, half out, fingers clinging to the frame, when someone knocks on the bathroom door. 'Get a move on. The van's here.' That's Effie, impatient. She'll kick down that door if she needs to. One, two, three and Jo lets go, arms and hands and fingers out-stretched, trying to break the force of the fall. It's a silent and slow-motion crash but when her soft body meets hard ground it knocks the breath right out of her. She curls up and holds still, a dog expecting a beating. But no more blows come. Her lungs refill. Her hands sting and throb but they're still moving. When she opens her eyes one of the seagulls is awake, toddles towards her then tilts its head. On the other side of the window, fists hammer a door and Jo can hear an approaching siren. She pictures traffic, splitting. The good people of the world slow and pull in to one side of the road when they hear a siren. They feel helpful, and glad it's not them. But the bad people of the world have a different response. Jo's body is warming up for a fight or a flight, her heart a revving motor. The siren's getting louder, closer. And, with it, a decision to be made. Stay or go? Go.

Then she's on her feet, running, Christ knows where to, but away from the sea and the harbour and the police and the press. She heads uphill, follows the street lights towards the cobbled high street then turns right, heading in the direction of the bridges. Up ahead a bus is pulling into a stop and she speeds up. It's heading for Edinburgh. She slows, tries to catch her breath as she joins the queue behind two Spanish tourists complaining about shit Scottish food. She's got one foot on board when she hears another siren. Hood up, head down, silent prayers muttered to whoever might be listening. We're all believers sometimes. The Spanish girls move and Jo lifts herself on board, smiles at the driver as if he's her long-lost brother.

'City centre, please.'

The driver nods, pushes buttons on his side of the protective plastic screen that separates them. Nobody's safe these days. 'Cash or card?'

Jo pats the pockets of her trousers, looking for money. Then her face falls. She's wearing those ugly jogging bottoms donated by the coastguard. Her jeans are still hanging over a radiator in reception with her wallet tucked into the back pocket.

She pulls a face, hoping for pity. 'I've not got any cash on me.'

The driver rolls his eyes like a puggy machine at the pub. 'We've got contactless,' he says, and Jo pulls out her phone but it's dead, of course. Has been for hours. She shows him the black screen. 'Not your day, is it? Sorry, pal.' Some folk were born arseholes. His eyes move over her shoulder to the next passenger and Jo retreats, back to the cobbles, and glances around for the cameras that hang over every street these days. She's got no money and no phone and no way of getting back to Edinburgh without it. And the moment Effie realises she's gone she'll have the police on her tail as well. And the press. She wonders if Sandy will have heard about Barry and put two and two together; how long it'll be before he calls her and pretends he's not just there for the story.

Where now? She starts walking away from the main street then turns uphill towards houses that used to belong to the council but have now been bought and painted, made into something folk are proud of. From there she can hear the endless whoosh of cars on the new bridge, racing over the water and on to the motorway that leads to the city. There's no way she can walk to Edinburgh from here. It'd take hours and anyway she'd probably get picked up by traffic police then dragged back to Effie.

Her only solution is charging her phone. She'll need to find a pub with plugs, and a helpful barman. Then she can pay for a bus ticket or maybe phone Tony and see if he fancies another drive. Once she gets power, she's got options.

She heads back downhill to a street that looks like a postcard, all exposed stone walls and hanging baskets. The perfection is tainted by a group of rugby lads with red faces and upturned collars, singing lurid songs they find hilarious. They'll be here to drink cocktails in the posh bars that overlook the water, get wasted while gazing at the three bridges that span it. They swagger down the street, oblivious to the fact locals are staring at them and muttering abuse. Jo's pleased they're drawing eyes away from her.

She chooses a pub where she won't stand out, one with frosted glass on the windows and tarnished brass on the door. Inside it's poorly lit and smells of decades-old tobacco. A few customers sit at tables with newspapers and others stare absently at a TV in the corner even though the sound's turned down. Jo edges into a space between two old men gripping pint glasses with dry hands, their elbows planted on the wooden bar. Behind it stands a red-faced man with a beard like a musketeer and a huge smile that exposes squint teeth.

'What can I get you, darling?'

Jo pulls out her phone. 'Any chance of a charger? I'll buy a drink as well.'

'It'll cost you extra.' He laughs after he says it. Jo manages a weak smile then hands it over. The man inspects the phone's power inlet then turns towards the till, tugs on a tangle of wires that hang from one side. 'You're in luck,' he says, plugging it in.

And outside, by the shore, the tide turns.

CHAPTER 41

Jo sips the last of her fizzy water, eyes locked on the pub's oversized wall clock. It's shifting second hand screams at her, tick-tock, tick-tock, underlining how long she's been waiting. Last time she asked the barman to check her phone he said it wasn't even at ten per cent, blamed the ancient cable. Not to mention her ancient smartphone. Jean had given it to her when she first started working at the shop, said it would do in the meantime. She barely uses it so there's never been reason to upgrade. Now she's regretting her resistance. A ten per cent charge on that phone won't even last one phone call.

She needs to wait, be patient, use the time to work out what she's going to do next.

Every time the door hinges creak she tenses but it's just the wind, or her imagination. The pub is quieter now and the only other customer is curled over a newspaper in one of the corners, underneath a framed photo of Edinburgh castle. He's holding a chewed pen and a warming pint. From time to time his phone beeps and

Jo jumps and the man tuts and the barman glances up from his own phone. He's watching short videos with the sound turned up, reminds Jo of the way her mum would endlessly flick from one channel when they got a TV with a remote control. It used to make Jo dizzy but she only mentioned it once and got a slap round the head for her troubles. Then, she said nothing. Now, she asks the barman for another drink, tries to act casual when she asks him to check her phone again.

'Almost at fifty per cent. Half full, half empty, depends on your point of view.' He laughs. 'Either way you're in for a treat. It's not stopped vibrating since it came back to life. You're obviously popular.'

'Something like that.' Jo feels sick but laughs instead and realises this is what people do, always. We never really say what we mean or feel. Instead we use words as walls we can hide behind. The barman flips the metal lid off her fizzy water and pushes it across the counter, bubbles shooting towards the neck of the bottle. 'All yours.'

'You know what? I'll take my phone now. Curious to see who's been calling.'

'Curiosity killed the cat,' he says, then winks and hands over her mobile. She pays her tab using her phone then heads back to the table. She's got dozens of notifications on her screen. Missed calls, voicemails, text messages. *All* from Jean. It still blows her mind, the power of these tiny machines. She grew up in a world of letters and envelopes and stamps; of phones nailed to walls, of coiling cables that always ended up in knots. She still remembers the day her class sent an *electronic mail* to pupils at a different primary school, the astonishment one week later when they received a reply. But they'd laughed at the idea that a trick like that would continue beyond the dull walls of their computer studies class. Letters would live on.

And aye, some do.

Aly's letters are the reason Barry's dead and the reason Tony got his head kicked in. They're the reason Jo fled from the police and the reason she must get back to Edinburgh. She needs to find Aly and force her to confess to the killing and the beating. And hopefully before she's dragged back to jail she'll tell Jo what those letters say.

She'll head for a bus as soon as she gets through all of Jean's messages. Deep breath and she clicks on the first text.

Hi, Jo. Can you call me please? Ta.

On to the next one.

Jo, the police have turned up at the shop, looking for you. Get in touch.

And the third.

Are you okay? Call me x

And a fourth.

There's now a journalist here, asking for you. Will you come?

Another.

Jo, please respond. I just saw this. We need to talk.

Under that message there's a link to the website of the local newspaper. Jo clicks it, dread flooding her chest when it opens and she sees a picture of herself on the screen, hanging head-first out of the toilet window at the coastguard centre.

Jo scans the text of the article. *Police and coastguard teams are searching the sea close to Edinburgh's Cramond Island after a member of the public alerted them to the presence of a body in the water. Police are looking for this woman to help with their enquiries.* The article is an hour old and pretty vague on details; has no names except for the one she really doesn't want to see. Leading the investigation is *formidable city cop*, the one and only Detective Inspector Farida McPherson.

Jo reads the article dozens of times, as if that might change the ending; what it means. But the reality is this: her face is on the news and Farida's on her trail.

It's only then that she notices a shift in the atmosphere, hears voices in the pub that weren't there before. She can't hear the tick-tock, tick-tock any more. Maybe that's because time has run out. The barman has flipped up part of the wooden bar and he's standing in the middle of the floor, feet planted on a sticky-looking rug as he points a remote control at a wall-mounted TV. He's turned up the volume and even before she turns to look at the screen Jo can tell it's the news and it's local and aye, it's being broadcast live from the harbour just down the road. She twists round, sees her face on the screen then feels the barman's eyes upon her. The other customer is looking up from his crossword as well and for a moment nobody says anything. The space between them is filled with words from the TV: *body*, *water*, *fled*, *hunt*. And along the bottom of the screen there's a scrolling tickertape holding the words that define her.

Convicted killer Joanna Forsyth wanted by police.

A red-faced man in a waterproof jacket steps on to the screen. He's holding a furry microphone and a serious expression as he tells viewers what and who they should be frightened of. 'Fifteen years ago, Joanna Forsyth murdered her own mother. Today she's wanted in connection with another brutal killing close to the city . . .' He keeps talking but Jo doesn't hear it. Now, there's only one word lodged in her brain and it's this: *run*.

CHAPTER 42

So Spider was a witness. She was skipping school and drinking; saw Tink's dad, leaving. Her mum, storming out after him, shouting and screaming and crying and pleading then stepping in front of the car as he sped off. She saw Tink's dad swerving to miss her mum then braking, but not fast enough, not hard enough. She saw his car slam into a wall.

She saw Tink's dad, dead.

Tink turns and runs towards the causeway. She wants to be back on the island, on her own, keep the whole sea between her and the rest of city. But she's too late. There's only water, only waves. She trudges back to the bench then flops on to the ground instead. It's hard and cold against her back but she stays there for ages, staring through tears to clouds made grey by nightfall. All she can hear is the sea, high tide rising.

Then Spider leans into her view.

'I'm sorry, Tink.' Spider lies down beside her and they lie there, side by side, in silence, eyes on the sky and fingertips almost touching but not quite, not quite.

'So my dad's accident was *my mum's* fault?'

'Aye.'

Tink's throat hurts. She feels as though she's swallowed a brick and now it's lodged in her chest, weighing it down. 'Why didn't you tell me before now?'

'Your mum . . . made it pretty clear that I shouldn't.'

'She threatened you?'

'More or less,' says Spider. 'Said that if I told you what happened she'd call social services, tell them my gran's a drunk and couldn't look after us. Said me and Barry would end up in care. I don't know why she cared so much. It was still an accident, right? The police knew what happened and didn't press charges. But your mum obviously felt guilty and didn't want you to know *she's* the reason it happened. I didn't think she'd seen me there but a few days later she grabbed me in the corridor at the flats, warned me not to say a thing to anyone. And to stay away from you.'

'But you didn't.'

'I tried,' says Spider. 'But then I saw you after your dad's funeral, crying your eyes out on that bench. I know how it feels, remember? I just wanted to make sure you were okay. And once we got talking, I . . . liked you. Still do.'

When Tink shivers Spider tells her to sit up. Then she pulls the vodka from her bag and wraps her jacket around Tink's shoulders. Bottle open, throats burning, false medicine easing the sting of open wounds.

Tink hands back the bottle then slips her cold hands into the pocket of Spider's jacket, hits hard metal. The bike chain. That's why the jacket always hangs to one side; a silent warning, to those who know. She pulls it out, surprised by the weight of it.

'Want a try?' That's Spider, and Tink's amazed because she never lets anyone touch it, never mind use it. It's her superpower; the one thing she can hide behind and still be seen.

Tink smiles, nods. 'Might help.'

They spend the next few hours whipping the heads off flowers and leaves off bushes and snapping at fat seagulls that peck the ground close to their feet, hoping for crumbs. If anyone could have seen them they'd call them vandals and ask them if their parents would be proud of them, and it's a useless question because obviously the answer is no and that's the whole point. Another favourite: *You not got a home to go to?* And that question is stupid as well because of course they do but they'd rather be out *here* than in *there* even though it means being cold and hungry and angry and sad but trying not to show not it.

Tonight of all nights, Tink doesn't want to go home.

Every time she thinks about her mum the *happy, faster* feeling disappears and she's angry instead. Like mother, like daughter. This must be what drinking does: flip your moods from one extreme to the other. She thought she'd feel better, not worse, with the vodka. And she thought she'd feel better, not worse, knowing the truth of what happened. But her mum had lied and kept on lying. At least now she understands why her mum was so desperate to keep her away from Spider. She knew that eventually she'd tell Tink the truth: it was her mum's fault that her dad ended up dead. End of story.

And end of the bottle.

Spider pours the dregs of the vodka into the last can of Coke and they take turns drinking it, don't even wipe the can between turns. But then it's gone and the only thing left to do is go home. The part that comes next is here.

'Game over,' says Tink, stumbling as she stands. She tosses their empties into the bushes even though there's probably a bin somewhere. But that isn't the point. When they chuck rubbish they're like dogs, lifting a leg wherever they please; marking their territory. It's a way to break rules, quietly, even if you're the only one who knows you did it. If nobody sees the damage you do, does it mean any less? Hurt any less?

Now, she'd ask her mum the same question.

CHAPTER 43

Jo sprints out of the pub and away from the town centre, pounding over the cobbles, shoving past tourists who've paused to take a selfie with the illuminated bridges in the background. She can't go to the road and she can't go to the shore and she can't stay in town so there's only one option left. Her legs burn as she pushes up and on to the gloomy path that leads to the middle of the three bridges, the one that looks like the Golden Gate in San Francisco. It used to be the main one for cars but these days it's only buses and taxis and pedestrians who use this one to cross from Edinburgh into Fife. Thankfully for Jo, not many do. It's one and a half miles long and forty-four metres high, can easily take half an hour to walk across. Jo knows because she came here once when she was wee and was stunned by the beauty of the world and the size of the sky, had spun round and round so she could see it all at once without blinking. When she got dizzy and stumbled close to the railing her dad had crouched down beside her, told her to *hold on, hold on, hold on*. Sometimes beautiful things are dangerous, he said.

The following year one of her teachers jumped off on purpose and they were all expected to go to the funeral even though nobody ever liked him. Jo's dad said he must not have liked himself much either. She'd not understood it at the time. She did a few years later, after her dad had died in that car accident and her family had crumbled into something unrecognisable. Her dad, dead but still hated, and mocked for being gay in a world that wasn't ready for that kind of love. Her mum, destroying herself as punishment; slowly mutating from a working mother to a woman in ruins. And Jo, an angry teenager who got drunk and took things too far.

Jo, her mother's killer.

Now, she keeps walking until she reaches the middle. On her right is the bright red railway bridge; three giant steel diamonds laid end to end, spanning the water. On her left, the newest of the three bridges; a towering white harp, played by the breeze that never stops blowing up here. All three are brightly lit, and perfectly reflected on the water beneath. She turns in the direction of Edinburgh, thinks of the city that visitors see, the polished version captured in calendars and the backdrop of selfies. But that Edinburgh was never hers, feels as foreign to her as it does to the tourists who roam there.

Beneath her, a boat passes, carrying cargo and workers paid to keep it safe.

And where is a safe place for her, now?

She pulls out her phone, refreshes the Breaking News story to see if there are any updates. Nothing. She wonders where Aly is and if she's seen it.

Jo's only hope is to track down Aly and force her to confess, *again*. And this time she'll need to either record it on her phone or make sure there's another witness. But how and where will she find her? She looks towards Edinburgh. There's no way she can walk but she can't risk public transport when her face is plastered all over the news. A taxi, maybe. But first, she'll call Tony and ask for a lift into the city centre. She plans her request as it rings, will frame it as one good deed in exchange for another. If he answers.

Now he's got his money back, he'll probably ignore her. Or, worse, stab her in the back and report her for stealing it in the first place. But she could report him for theft as well. Jo had been held in a young offenders' institution for the first few years of her life sentence. When she turned twenty-one she was moved to an adult women's jail that was part of the same massive complex. Some staff moved between the youth and adult sites which is how Tony was able to steal her mail for the duration of her sentence.

Right now, wherever he is, he's not answering his phone.

Who else can help? The only other numbers she's got are Sandy and Jean and Gordon and Farida. Sandy will want a story and he'd risk his career if he helped her out now. Gordon she doesn't trust as far as she could throw him, and that isn't far. Farida will probably trace her call and get her arrested if she phones her.

There is only Jean. Lovely Jean.

She calls Jean's mobile before her brain tells her not to. She's always got it to hand. It rings once, twice, three times. Four rings, then five. She'll wait for ten and then she'll hang up, give up, start walking. What direction, she's not sure. Maybe up the bridge, maybe down the bridge, maybe off the bridge.

'I'm here, sweetheart.' Jean's voice is like music. She's an angel with a smoker's cough. 'Did you see my texts?'

'Aye. And I just saw myself on the news.' Jo stares over the edge of the bridge, watches a gull float effortlessly beneath her, wings spread, held by air. 'I've done nothing wrong, Jean.' She's embarrassed by how childish it sounds; as if she'd broken a vase, secretly eaten the last piece of somebody else's cake. 'I know you might not believe me but—'

'I do,' says Jean. 'I trusted you right from the start.'

'Only because you didn't know who I was.'

'That's where you're wrong.' Jean's lighting a cigarette; Jo hears the flick-flick-flick of her lighter, then the long outbreath that'll shroud her in smoke that smells just like her. 'I've always known, Jo. About your mum. About the murder. About your conviction.'

'How?'

'I always do a thorough internet search on new volunteers, just in case. But there was no record of anyone called Jo Hidalgo, the name you'd put on your form. No photos, no social media accounts, nothing. That's the first time it had ever happened and it made me curious. I called the hotel you said you'd worked at, in Spain, and of course they'd never heard of you. At that point I was ready to reject your application. I don't *do* lies, as you know. That's my number one rule.'

'So what changed your mind?'

'It was more of a *who* than a *what*, and I think you'll be surprised by the answer. It was Gordon. I asked him to look you up, see if he'd have better luck. But once he saw you he didn't need the internet at all. He knows you from school, Jo. Worked in the kitchens. Says all the canteen staff loved you to bits and were stunned by . . . what happened. He says you won't remember him because he was usually behind the scenes. And he worked out why I couldn't find you online. Told me that when you were little you were always telling folk you had two surnames, one from your mum and one from your dad, just like they do in Spain. Full name, Joanna Forsyth Hidalgo. I'd been searching for your new name – Jo Hidalgo – not your old one, Joanna Forsyth. Mystery solved, and when he told me about your conviction I understood why you'd want to change it. As for the murder . . . Gordon told me you'd had a tough time growing up. Got in with a bad crowd. But he assured me you were solid, had a good heart.'

'*Gordon* said that?'

'Aye. And he was right.'

'So why is he always so rude to me?'

Jean clicks her tongue. 'Think it might be a touch of jealousy? You and I clicked right away but I never had that kind of connection with him. He has a rough time at home too. Bullied by his overbearing dad. Think his attitude is some kind of misplaced defence mechanism. Automatic, maybe, when he's spent his whole life being attacked.'

'Know the feeling.'

'Then you've got more in common with him than you think.'

Guilt pokes Jo's heart. Every time you judge yourself you're strengthening that muscle and soon enough the judgement extends to other people. She'd got him wrong.

'But if you knew about the murder . . . why didn't you say anything?'

'I was waiting for you to come clean and tell me yourself,' says Jean. 'But as the weeks went on I realised it didn't really matter either way. I liked you. And I *trusted* you. We've all got things in our past that we'd

269

rather keep to ourselves. But you can talk to me, if you want. When all of this ends.'

'*When?* I think we're definitely still on *if.*'

'Call me an optimist.'

'I'm fucked, Jean. The police are—'

'You said you've done nothing wrong. Right?'

'Right.'

'Then tell me where you are,' says Jean. 'I'm coming to get you.'

CHAPTER 44

When Jo wakes the next morning the pillow is softer than usual and smells of someone else. She keeps her eyes closed, trying to remember where she is and who she'll see beside her if she rolls over. She hopes she's in another hotel, with Farida. Then she remembers Barry in the water, the helicopter, her face on TV in that pub; and she remembers standing alone on the bridges wondering which way to walk.

After that, her mind's blank. She opens her eyes and rolls over at the same time; yelps as she rolls off the edge of the single bed and on to the carpeted floor, knocking over a mug of undrunk tea on the way. It looks like piss, smells like fermented flowers. A ticket hanging from the teabag says *camomile* and suddenly everything clicks into place. Jean's always telling folk that it helps her sleep, soothes her nerves, keeps her calm.

Jo wishes she'd drunk it.

She sits up, studies the room. Every single thing in here is teal blue, apart from the numerous sets of fairy

271

lights. A handmade sign above the bed reads *Grace*. Jo assumes it's a name and not a noun. Either way, it doesn't apply to her. Jean has never mentioned a daughter but it definitely looks like a child's room.

'Jo! I heard a thump! You okay in there?'

Little by little, the memories return. Jean had collected Jo from the car park of a hotel that overlooks the bridges, across the water from the coastguard station and the police who lingered there. They'd driven to her home in Aberdour to warm up and calm down. But Jo hadn't intended to stay for long, definitely hadn't meant to fall asleep and stay overnight. The haze of sleep hardens into something else and she hauls herself to her feet, heart zipping into overdrive.

She needs to find Aly.

'Can I come in?' Jean asks, but her head's already popping round the door, followed by a hand holding a steaming mug. 'Made coffee if you want some?'

Jean pushes open the door, hands Jo her drink and sips her own. She's wearing a pink robe and fur-lined slippers and, for once, no make-up. She looks younger, somehow, as though there's nothing she's trying to hide. 'You crashed out before your head even hit the pillow. Been sleeping for ten hours.'

'*Shit*. What time is it?'

'Don't panic. It's only nine o'clock. I'm just glad you slept okay in the fish finger.' She motions to the narrow single bed that Jo had just fallen out of. 'That's what our Grace always called it; said she'd buy herself a double bed the moment she left home.'

'And did she?'

Jean's face drops. 'Didn't get the chance. Drugs got her first. But she'll have a king-size up there, I'm sure.' She looks at the bedroom ceiling and smiles, as if she sees the gates to Heaven, hidden somewhere between the damp patches and the crumbling Artex swirls.

'I'm sorry, Jean. I didn't know.'

'Why would you? Everyone's got a hidden tragedy. And I'll tell you something: that's why I don't really believe in good and bad. *And* I believe in giving second chances. All that happens is that some folk are better than others at dealing with the shite life throws at us. I try to keep that in mind but it's not always easy. Talking of which . . .' She pulls her phone out of her pocket and turns the screen to Jo. It's open at the local newspaper website. 'I've been awake for hours, refreshing it every few minutes, waiting for breaking news. There's nothing official from the authorities yet but a few of these amateur sleuths on social media are claiming that police divers have just found Barry Chisholm's body. They're saying he was killed on Cramond Island but was then carried off by the tide. And if that's true, then—'

'It's now a murder inquiry.'

Jean nods.

'So I need to leave.' Jo looks around the room for

her clothes, finds them hanging over the radiator. Next to them, those ugly grey jogging bottoms they gave her at the coastguard base; just like the ones handed out in jail. She'd ask Jean for some trousers but they'd never fit. Prison garb it is, for now. At least she looks the part. 'I'll get dressed and go. If it's me they're looking for I can't be here, with you. And don't worry, I won't tell anyone that you helped me, Jean. I'll say—'

'You've done nothing wrong, remember?'

'Try telling that to the police.'

'That's precisely what I was going to suggest, Jo. Drink your coffee and have a shower and we'll head down the station, together. We'll explain what happened. They can't have proof of something that didn't happen. And without proof, you're a free woman.'

'True, but in the meantime they can hold me for questioning. And I *need* to find Aly.'

'But why, love? Leave that to the police.'

'There's something she's not telling me, Jean. Something about those letters. I still don't understand why Barry was so determined to ensure I didn't read them. Obviously I can't ask *him* any more. The only other person who knows what's in those letters is Aly. And if she's jailed and doesn't agree to see me, I'll never know. This is my last chance.'

'Then I'm coming with you,' says Jean. 'No arguments.'

*

Half an hour later they're back in Jean's car, clean and caffeinated. Gordon's looking after the shop, under strict orders to keep the press pack out. Answer no questions, Jean had warned. He agreed. But now she's the one who's asking.

'Where to?' Jean glances at Jo as they roar on to the motorway that leads back to Edinburgh. 'You think Aly'll be somewhere near the island?'

Jo shakes her head. 'Not any more. I'm pretty sure she'll have legged it.'

'Any other ideas?'

'Just one.'

Jo picks up her phone. Still nothing from Sandy despite the fact that he's the only journalist with the mobile phone number of the most wanted woman in Edinburgh. But if she calls him, will he turn her in or trace her call? Maybe, now, she doesn't have a choice. Barry is dead, Tony isn't answering and Farida's the one she's trying to escape from. The longer she runs, the guiltier she looks and the reality is this: she's got no alibi and no way to prove it wasn't her who killed Barry. There's video evidence and witnesses to prove she harassed him at work the previous day. Letters with her name on them were found at his flat. She can't prove Aly was on the island and can't explain why she let her leave. And to top it all off, she ran away from a detective the moment she started asking difficult questions. The only way to prove her innocence is to find Aly and hope she can persuade her to confess to the police. And, before that, tell her what was in the letters.

Sandy said he'd call her if he found Aly's address but that was before *this*, before Barry's body was found and Jo was in the frame. The police had issued a statement, appealing to the public to help hunt her down. It was formal and polite but in essence it said: *Wanted, dead or alive.* A year or two back, Jo might not have minded either way.

But here, now, she does care.

And Sandy is her last chance.

CHAPTER 45

Tink and Spider walk for a while then grab a night bus back to Edinburgh. Mostly the streets are dead but a few folk are hanging about at bus stops and in shop doorways, drinking and smoking and shouting and eating greasy kebabs. They have to walk the last part because no buses stop near the flats at this time of night. Tink feels dizzy and hot, thinks she might fall over. Somehow Spider can Just Tell. She puts an arm around Tink's shoulders, leads her to a park on the way, sits her on the only bench that's not been burned. There's movement near the swan pond. Then voices.

'Fucking lesbians!'

The call is followed by a laughter that grows and grows. Boys, in the shadows. Spider stiffens. 'Say that once more and you're getting it.'

'Lesbos! You're just too ugly to get a boyfriend!'

Spider's on her feet and in her hand, the bike chain. The boys find it hilarious, egg on the one who shouted. It's Sooty from school, the one who first called Tink's dad the p-word. *Poofter.* He saunters towards the bench. His pals follow. Spider holds her ground. They're gladiators in the arena except this stage is made of muddy grass and cracked cement and vomit puddles. Sooty laughs at them again. Tink's body is full of vodka and rage. She leaps up, stands between Spider and Sooty, then reaches for the bike chain.

'Let me,' she says.

Tink swings the chain, misses. Everyone laughs. Her rage inflates. Sooty makes a shield with his arms to protect himself from the second swing. Palms out, eyes closed, gaping mouth. She misses again and this time there's uproar, hoots and shouts and laughter and booing, and she hates herself almost as much as they do. Spider tuts and grabs the chain from her, stands firm. 'Like *this*,' she says.

It must be the speed of her swing that makes the smooth edges a blade. It slices open Sooty's cheek like a ripe peach, split.

He's bigger than her as well, could probably have decked her if he'd been able to stand up. Spider only hits him three times because it's harder to get a good aim when he's rolling about on the ground. But it's enough. She's proven herself. She pockets the chain and kicks him in the balls then grabs Tink's hand. 'Now, run,' she says, and they do; don't stop running until they reach the car park outside the flats. This is usually where they spend half an hour saying goodbye, standing in the welcome dark of the covered doorway.

But tonight the boys are chasing them and getting closer. Tink's hands are shaking but she manages to unlock the main door and they throw themselves into the communal entrance hall. The door swings shut behind them, automatically locks. Unless the boys smash the glass or ram the door they won't get in but Tink and Spider don't want to risk being seen. They leg it up the stairs to Tink's floor, stand a few doors down from her flat. The boys won't find them here. They're safe for now, but there's a tension so thick and heavy that Tink can't breathe properly. Or maybe it's the lump in her throat. Disappointment, made solid. If her mum gets her way, this will be the last time Tink and Spider see each other. And as if that's not bad enough, Spider's probably embarrassed by her for messing up that fight. Tink tried to be tough and became the opposite. Now she's wasted everything. She hangs her head and that's when she notices tiny splatters of blood on her fingers.

'Think Sooty'll be alright?'

Spider shrugs. 'Don't give a shit.'

'Me neither,' says Tink and hopes that's the right answer. She's rubbing her hands on her trousers, trying to get them clean before she goes inside. 'Anyway, I should go.'

Spider nods, doesn't look at her. 'You be okay? With your mum, I mean.'

'She'll be asleep.' Tink's hands are shaking so she

stuffs them in her pocket but then she notices Spider's are doing the same. 'You cold?'

'Nervous,' says Spider.

'Because of the boys?'

'Nope.'

'Because of my mum?'

'Nope. Because of this.'

Time stoops and Spider leans in and it's right there, in that moment, that Tink realises there are parts of her body she cannot control. And worse than that, more bewildering: she's not the girl she thought she was. Spider's beer-scented mouth, on hers. Sticky tongues, touching.

Tink's lost in the impossibility and inevitability of it. Her mind is blank and useless, no rival for the softness and the weight and the taste and the urgency. There's just the two of them and something like love. The world could end right now and Tink wouldn't even notice. There's only this. Only them.

At least, that's what she thinks.

CHAPTER 46

Sandy answers right away, like he's been waiting for her call. Even before he says hello she hears seagulls and sirens. So he's at the harbour with the rest of the press pack, hoping he's the one to catch the scent, hunt her down. Jo almost hangs up but thinks of her dad on the bridge when she was wee, telling her to *hold on, hold on, hold on.*

'Sandy? It's Jo.'

She can hear him breath but for a long time he says nothing. Then comes a sigh and footsteps as he walks to somewhere quieter. He wants her for himself. 'You're alive then?'

'And kicking.'

'So I hear.'

Beside her, Jean has lit a cigarette and the car's filling up with fumes. Jo inhales deeply. It'll help, maybe. 'Remember that woman I asked you to look for?'

'I do.'

'It was her, Sandy. She killed Barry Chisholm.'

'And you know this because?'

'I was there.'

'Can I be frank?' He doesn't wait for an answer. 'The police have spoken to me off the record and it's a closed case as far as they're concerned. You were rescued from the island and the body was found just offshore a few hours later. They're still checking CCTV but so far nobody else was seen in the vicinity. And given your history—'

'Aly must have found another way off.'

'She a good swimmer?'

'Christ knows.'

'Trouble is, Jo, the whole thing's somewhat aggravated by the fact that we've got several witnesses saying you harassed Barry Chisholm the previous day at his work, and there's CCTV recordings to back them up. Why didn't you tell me the full story when we met at that café? The police had already spoken to you about Barry's disappearance. Did you think I wouldn't find out?'

'The opposite. I *knew* you would, sooner or later, and I *knew* that would change how willing you were to make a deal with me. I wanted to make sure you got me Aly's address first.'

'That wasn't fair.'

'Is anything?'

Sandy sighs. 'For what it's worth, I tracked her down.'

'Aly? When? Where is she? And why didn't you contact me?'

'I had to be sure Aly *wanted* to see you before I handed over her address. Standard practice, no offence intended. My plan was simple: phone Aly, ask permission to share her address, then call you with the details. But the moment I introduced myself I got a mouthful of abuse. Aly accused the *Journal* of letting her down, said she'd been promised anonymity when she called in with the story. I was confused. This wasn't about a story, I said. I was calling for an old friend who wanted to see her. I hadn't even named you at that point but then she started slagging off Farida McPherson, saying she'd stolen the love of her life, that Farida was the reason you two weren't together. And it all fell into place. I realised it must have been Aly who tipped off the paper about your . . . encounter . . . with Farida. She insists she saw the two of you, together, outside your flat on Saturday evening. Claims you talked for a while then moved inside.'

'And did she also tell you she left graffiti on Farida's car?'

'No, she didn't. But thanks for confirming her claims,' says Sandy.

Jo's heart drops to her stomach. 'When will it be printed?' She could maybe warn Farida, at least. But if she called her she'd be traced and hauled to the station with a murder accusation on her back. Lose–lose.

'I've actually decided we won't publish,' says Sandy. 'After speaking to Miss Chisholm I realised she's . . . a little . . . unstable, shall we say. And I'd suggest you don't go anywhere near her.'

'I'll make that decision for myself,' says Jo. 'Give me the address. Please. I won't do anything stupid.'

'It's not *your* behaviour I'm worried about. You've literally just told me that Aly murdered her own brother and beat up that prison guard. It wouldn't be safe for you to go there, however good your intentions.'

'I can handle myself.'

'Maybe, but I refuse to put you in danger. You're not getting Aly's address.'

Jo ends the call without saying goodbye, head spinning. Jean's saying something but Jo can't hear her. Instead her brain replays the words of Aly on the island, when Jo asked why she'd killed her brother. *He came between us*, she said. *He's the reason we're not together.* And if Sandy's to be believed, Aly said the same thing about Farida yesterday afternoon. And it was Aly who'd seen them, Aly who'd phoned the papers in an attempt to expose their relationship and potentially break it up. And after Farida left Jo a voicemail on her phone, Aly had photographed her number and then fled.

Jo types her own name into Google, followed by *breaking news*. The first article she opens confirms a body has now been found that is believed to be missing Edinburgh security guard Barry Chisholm. Police would be in contact with the family to arrange formal identification. *Family* meant Aly. And if this was now a murder case, then probably a detective would be sent to see her.

And maybe, just maybe, that meant Farida.

She calls Sandy back but he doesn't pick up. Not surprising, given the fact she just hung up on him. She tries again, same result. *Come on, come on, come on.* Third time, and a fourth. He picks up on the fifth. 'Want a harassment charge added to the list?'

'I just want Aly's address.'

'And I've already said I won't give it to you. It's for your own good.'

'And what if I told you Farida's the one at risk here? They've found Barry's body and I think she's on her way to see Aly. You *need* to tell me where she lives.'

'Farida won't go there alone,' says Sandy.

'That doesn't mean Aly can't hurt her.' Jo's trying to sound calm, rational, reasonable. All the things she's not, right now. 'Aly's already killed her twin brother for keeping us apart and now she blames Farida for coming between us. But it's *me* she wants, so she won't hurt me. I'm sure of it. I just need to reach Aly before Farida does. Trust me, Sandy. That's all I'm asking. I'm trying to save a life here.'

Sandy is silent for so long Jo thinks he's hung up. 'You still there?'

'Only just,' he says. 'The big irony is, you already know the address, Jo. Aly still lives at Hartfield Court.'

'What? But I was there the other day and her old flat's empty.'

'That's because she moved into *yours*,' says Sandy. 'That's why the demolition has been held up for months. All the other neighbours left ages ago but Aly refused to go. The paper's written stories about it, but I hadn't made the connection until today.'

'Why on earth would anyone want to stay *there*? It's a wreck.'

'Simple. So you'd always know where to find her.'

'Very funny.'

'I'm being serious. That's what she told me when I called her yesterday afternoon. After the murder your flat was cleaned and made available for a new tenant. Aly told me that she'd actually contacted the council and *requested* it but since she already had a flat with her gran and brother downstairs they gave it to another family. So she stayed put and after the gran died it was just her and Barry for years, until the demolition was announced. Barry left, same as all the other residents. But Aly had a different idea. Once the family moved out of your old flat, Aly moved in. Refused to budge despite eviction orders and police pressure. She told me yesterday that she'd promised you she'd wait for you, *right there*; hoped that you'd come home from prison and see that nothing had really changed after all. It would just be you and her, together again. You'd finally get your happy ending, she said. And she sounded like she really believed it.'

Something like pity rises in Jo's chest, making her eyes sting. So there's the awful truth of it: Aly's spent her whole adult life waiting for Jo to be released from jail, but all the while she was locked in a cell of her own making. If Jo's prison was made of high walls and window bars, Aly's was made of false beliefs and the desperate need to feel as though she was part of something that mattered. *This isn't over*, she'd shouted, as Jo was led, handcuffed, from the courtroom to the cells. But *what* they were had ended there and then, because *who* they were was changed forever. Jo had become a before and an after, a child turned into a criminal. Aly had stayed the same, it seemed, or wanted to.

Jo hangs up the phone, tells Jean the address. For the first time since the murder she'll return to her childhood home, face the memories of that ruinous night with Aly.

It had started with a kiss.

And ended with a killing.

CHAPTER 47

It's Tink who hears it first, the muffled whoosh of her front door being pushed open over the badly fitted carpet in the hall. If the significance of the sound had registered in Tink's love-soaked brain then maybe, just maybe, she'd have pulled away from Spider before her mum stepped out of the flat. She had two seconds to react, maybe three. For years afterwards she'd think about those few seconds of life; how a whole world changed in less time than it took to say *hello*.

Her mum roars. If there are words wrapped inside, Tink can't make them out, but there's no need for specifics. The blame is already on her.

Spider leaps away from Tink, slips on the lino and falls. The drink won't have helped. In any other moment they'd have laughed at the sight of her, folded over like a newborn calf on the floor. When Tink's mum marches over to her, Spider holds up her arms up like a shield, same way Sooty did when she hit him. She looks like she's done that before; been there. 'You're barely worth the effort,' her mum says, then bends down and grabs Spider's feet with both hands, drags her towards the stairs. Spider's kicking and trying to wriggle free and when her mum finally drops her legs she's up and on her feet in seconds, but she's still holding her hands up; surrendering. 'I'll go, okay?' She's edging towards the stairwell. 'But you need to know this isn't Tink's fault.'

'Takes two.'

'I started it.'

'Well, I didn't see her pushing you off.' She's snorting and snarling, a human pig. 'I've not slept, been worried sick, sitting by the phone, thinking you might be adult enough to phone. More fool me. Do you want me to suffer, is that it?' She's looking at Tink now, stepping closer. Then she stands with both hands over her mouth as if she can catch the next scream on its way out. Breathing hard, pumping out breath that's bitter with wine and whatever else festers in her. 'This is finished, okay? For good. Now get inside.'

Tink bows her head, studies the blood stains on her tracksuit bottoms. They'll disappear in the wash. The shame in her will be more difficult to shift. She's desperately looking for words that might ease the tension but then those hands are on her and she's being dragged, drunk and useless, along the corridor and in the front door. Inside, her mum slaps her so hard her ears start ringing. 'Can't take a warning, can you?' she says, then slams the door. Or tries to. But it hits something and springs back. Spider's got one foot in their hall.

'If you lay another finger on Tink you'll regret it.' That's Spider, glaring at Jo's mum.

'Funny, I was about to say the same thing to you.'

'Too late.' Spider smiles at her mum but it's sharp as a nettle, made to sting. She's still at the door, but not leaving. Tink wants her to stay because she doesn't want to be alone with her mum but she also wishes she would go. Escape the attack. Save herself from the venom. Instead she pushes her way inside and kicks shut the door.

'Get out of my house.'

'Or what?'

'You *know* what.'

Spider doesn't say anything. Instead her and Tink's mum are just staring at each other, all tight jaws and ugly mouths. Then her mum spits and it lands on Spider's shirt.

'Now fuck off and leave us alone.'

Spider slips her hand inside her sleeve, wipes off the saliva. 'I *knew* we shouldn't have come here.' Then she's backing away and Tink knows she's losing her and it's all her fault. They should have stayed on the island until the morning. They should never have hit that boy. Then they'd never have come here, now, and never been caught by her mum. Everything she touches turns to shit. That's what her mum always said, and she was right. Now Spider's leaving and her mum's saying good riddance and Tink's full of love and hate at the same time. A storm, brewing.

'I know the truth, Mum. About Dad. I know the accident was *your* fault.'

'And who told you that? *Her?*' Her mum looks at Spider, and every part of her tightens like a noose. 'Is *that* what she's been telling you? Your mum's a big bad wolf and she's the hero swooping in to save you? Well, I've got news for you, hen. It's the other way round. *She's* the one who caused your dad's accident, staggering around drunk in the middle of the road. I saw it happen. He swerved to miss her and *that's* why he crashed. *That's* why he died. Life would have been better for all of us if he'd put his foot down instead of braking; flattened her. He'd still be here. And *she'd* not be missed.'

'Fuck you.' That's Spider, slurring; a girl made of rage.

Tink wishes Spider had denied what her mum said even though she knows it couldn't be true because Spider is the only good thing that's happened to her for ages and her mum is just jealous because she loves Spider more than she loves her.

She *loves* her. That's the first time she's had that thought and let it linger, grow. It makes her feel bigger than she is, stronger than she ever has. And free, kind of.

'You're lying.' That's Tink, to her mum. She's

expecting a slap in reply. Gets a sob instead. That's a first.

'I saw it happen, hen. And I saw her leg it afterwards as well. That's why I told you to stay away from her. And I've never told the police because it wouldn't change anything, would it? I actually felt a bit sorry for her, knowing how fucked-up her family is. I told myself she was just a sad wee girl who made a mistake, that I should forgive her. But turns out she's a lying wee bitch as well. And she's got you fooled good and proper.'

'It's not true, Tink.' That's Spider, stepping closer. They're not touching but Tink can feel the warmth of her body, can still taste Spider's saliva in her own mouth.

'We saw your flowers, Mum. At Dad's grave. And that note asking Dad to forgive you. So there's no point in denying it.'

'I'm not denying I feel guilty, but it's *not* for causing the accident. I feel guilty that my last conversation with your dad was a blazing row. I feel guilty for all the awful things I said to him when he told me he was leaving me for that . . . *man*. I feel guilty that I told him to fuck off and leave this house even though I knew he was drunk.' She bites down on her bottom lip to stop it trembling. 'But *she's* the one who forced him to swerve. *She's* the one who killed your dad. And I know you think you're in love with her and she's in love with you but it's not real. She's making an arse of you, same way your dad made an arse of me.'

'It *is* real,' says Tink. 'You're just jealous because you've got nobody. And it serves you right for . . . what you did. And you know what? I'm not surprised Dad didn't love you.'

Then, there's a moment of silence. Tink's mum turns to face her, slowly steps closer. When she speaks again her voice is softer, quieter; but the words sting like poison.

'He never loved you either, hen. Never even *wanted* you. Who would?'

And that's it: the last moment Tink can remember with total certainty.

The words are a trigger, pulled, and all the logic in her is lost. She becomes the fire that blazes in her. She becomes the rush and the rage and the roar of it. She becomes someone she doesn't recognise and can't control; something that cannot be stopped.

CHAPTER 48

Jean pulls in at the far end of Jo's old street but leaves the car engine running.

'I wish you'd let me come in with you.'

'You've done enough,' says Jo, opening the passenger side door. 'Aly won't want anyone else there and if it all goes to shit I don't want you involved okay? Wait at the end of the street like we agreed and I'll call you when I'm done. Promise.'

Jean looks ready to argue but instead she reaches over, squeezes Jo's arm before she climbs out. 'Whatever happens, I'm on your side,' she says. 'I hope you know that.'

Jo nods, so simple a gesture for words that meant so much.

Then she's out, on the street, running until she reaches the flimsy metal fence that surrounds Hartfield Court. Right away, Jo knows she's too late. New laminated signs now dot the perimeter, warning intruders that there's Danger of Death if they enter the site. Today is demolition day. The space between her and the front door is now earth, exposed; churned up by heavy tyres and the jaws of diggers. A few men are wandering the site, all scuffed boots and stained jeans and faded hoodies that have been washed a thousand times. On top of that they wear neon-yellow waist-coats, unfastened. On their heads, hardhats. On their chins, stubble. On their breath, a blend of cigarettes and the sausage rolls some carry as they arrive, grease staining the white paper bags from the bakery. None of them pays Jo any attention.

But there's no way they'll let her in.

Jo steps forward to look closer. A heavily tattooed man appears from a Portakabin set up in the car park. He pulls a cigarette from behind his ear and lights it inside a cupped hand before he walks the length of a huge machine that dominates the site. He inspects it carefully, occasionally leaning forward and wiping its smart yellow paintwork with his sleeve. He pauses for a moment to finish his cigarette, stubs it out on the sole of his boot then heaves himself into the little cab up top. When he turns on the ignition, birds rise up from hidden spots on the ground. Then the giant arm stretches out and the driver makes the scoop flip one way then the other, like it's warming up before a fight, testing its reflexes. It rises to the full height of the building, hangs overhead. Jo's eyes creep to the kitchen window of her childhood home, picturing every detail of the room that will soon be destroyed forever.

Then, between one breath and the next, the metal arm drops. Serrated metal teeth slice effortlessly through slate, beams, plaster, ceiling. Jo imagines filth shooting into her neighbours' flats along with light from the sun that shines bright and warm overhead. Now the driver pushes the scoop of the excavator against a side wall, taps it with one of the protruding metal teeth. If walls could fall to their knees then that's what happens to this one. It buckles then falls forward, crumbling as it topples. The only sounds that reach Jo are the harmonies of a home falling down; crunches and cracks and thuds and groans. Endings.

From time to time her eyes flit to the driver. She wonders if he thinks of the lives once lived inside of the places he pulls down, if he goes home with the imagined memories of others flickering in his mind. He'll know the story of this one if he's local, no doubt. The murder flat, destroyed. It'd make a good story. She wonders if he'll tell folk down the pub later, if he'll glance over his shoulder then lean in over his fourth pint and admit he'd felt some kind of tiny glory when he'd pulled the walls to the ground.

Good riddance, he might say; and nobody would argue.

Only Jo knew it wouldn't make any difference to anything. The impact of her mum's murder reverberated far beyond walls and windows and doors and things that could be torn up and broken down.

Crash. Bang. Wallop. Another wall demolished. Half the building is gone. A house becoming a mole-hill. The driver lowers the excavator's scoop towards the pile of rubble then poke-poke-pokes, breaking the unbroken pieces, tidying the scraps of her old home into a neat pile. The metal hand rises into the air again, preparing for another strike. But then suddenly it pauses, slackens. The driver sticks his head out of the window then kills the engine, pushes open the door and runs towards the Portakabin. He sticks his head in the door then turns and sprints towards the ruins of the building. A group of men follow, matching his pace. Then comes shouting and pointing and pacing. A few men pull phones out of their pockets, make calls. But none of them takes their eyes off the build-ing. The driver then pulls out another cigarette and lights it with shaking hands. He sucks in the filth of it then blows out smoke that floats skywards, towards the window of Jo's old kitchen. And it's right then, through the hazy smog of demolition, that Jo sees a woman's face at a window.

CHAPTER 49

It starts with a push. Tink shoves her mum and her mum does the same in return. Trouble is, Tink's way stronger than she looks. Drunker too. Trouble is, her mum falls and smacks her head on the edge of the radiator. It could have stopped there, with Tink bending down and helping her up and holding a damp cloth, tightly, against the wound all the way to hospital. It could have stopped there, with a big comedy bandage wrapped around her mum's head. It could have stopped, there.

Trouble is, it doesn't.

Tink's shocked at first by the quickness of the blood that comes. There are splatters on the radiator and the floor and on her mum's cheeks.

'You've split my head, you bastard.'

That's her mum speaking. Defiant, even when she's down. But she's still down. She's making a barrier with her arms and it's a novelty for Tink to be with her and feel like the stronger one.

Tink pokes at her with her shoe. 'Take it back. What you said about Dad. And about Spider.' She's crying now and annoyed at herself for being so pathetic. Her mum will find this hilarious: Tink trying to be hard and sobbing her heart out at the same time.

'I *know* Dad loved me.'

'Is that right? He was gutted when I got pregnant. At least now we know why, eh? There was me, thinking we were happily married. That I'd found the love of my life. But all the while he was shagging those . . . *boys* . . . behind my back. And now *you're* turning out as bad as *him*. I was the only one who loved you, hen, but you know what? You don't deserve it. Not now. You *disgust* me, the pair of you.'

That's when Tink's hand slips into the pocket of Spider's jacket and her fingers touch sticky metal: the bike chain. Tink thinks of the boy Spider had attacked in the corridor at school just after they met, and of Sooty screaming his head off tonight. He was probably still bleeding. Time and again Spider had protected Tink, and not only that, she'd proved she wouldn't take any shit from anyone. A quick flick of the wrist and she'd taught them a lesson, shown them she was worth more than they thought. But then Tink thinks of skin, ripped open, of someone else's blood on her hands, and she lets go of the chain. She'll use words instead of weapons.

'I said, *take it back*.'

'Truth hurts, doesn't it? And I should know.' Her mum hauls herself on to her elbows but she's still on the ground, looking up. 'If it's any consolation, your bastard dad broke my heart as well, hen. You think I wanted to end up like *this*? Well, you're wrong. I had dreams, you know. Nothing fancy. Just wanted a decent job, nice house, proper family. Instead I ended up with a poofter in my bed, and *you*. And now you'll end up leaving me too. And for what?' She looks at Spider now, sneering. 'For *that*? Jesus Christ. You could at least have chosen a pretty one. *That* one should have been put down at birth. And come to think of it, so should you.'

That's when Tink's hand grips the bike chain, whips it out of her pocket and quickly downwards. That's how she knows what it feels like when a bike chain makes proper contact with another human; damages them. Those are her mum's last words, because when the chain hits her face it bursts her mouth right open and she's mute now, apart from a sound that might be a cough, might be choking. There's enough blood for that now, more than Tink's ever seen. She tightens her grip, raises her arm then whips it downwards, harder this time.

But not as hard as the next time.

Somewhere between one raised arm and the next Tink hears Spider saying her name, telling her to stop. Her hands are on her but they're no longer soft, no longer tugging her closer. They're grabbing at her, hard enough to hurt.

'Stop, Tink!'

Now, she does as she's told. Even now, as she emerges from the haze of that fury, there's part of her that lights up at the sound of her name, shaped by Spider's mouth. She wishes there was a way to make time stop for good, right there.

Spider's dragging her to the other side of the room and Tink lets herself be led. For a few moments she shuts her eyes, the same way people do on roller-coasters when they see the track ahead of them plummet into nothingness. All that lies between her and the chaos she's created is the darkness behind her eyelids.

And, open.

If hell had been shackled, it now breaks loose.

Tink blinks to adjust her focus then sees her mum, stilled.

Spider yanks open Tink's fingers until she drops the bike chain. She's sobbing and shuddering, vomiting words. *Omygodwhatveyoudone?*

The answer's on the floor, bleeding.

'We need to call an ambulance, Tink!'

But Tink's shaking her head because they don't need a doctor or a policeman to confirm what's happened here. All they need is a pulse, or the lack of one.

'Is she . . .?'

'Dead? She *can't* be.' Spider lets Tink go, drops to her knees, leans over her mum. She's pressing her fingers on to her neck and wrist. Her mum's ruined mouth hangs open like a snorer on a train and her eyes stare unmoving at the spotlight on the kitchen ceiling.

Spider's got her knees in blood and one ear pressed against her mum's chest. 'She's still breathing! Call them!'

Hope. A chink of light in utter blackness.

Tink's eyes flit to the place the phone should be. It's not there.

Her mum had bought one of those fancy wireless ones so she can walk as she talks but it's not in the charger. She runs from room to room, eventually finds it under her mum's pillow. So what she'd said was true. She'd been worried, waiting for Tink to call. When she gets back to the kitchen Spider's still kneeling over her mum but she's got her hands on her chest and a look Tink's never seen before. The beauty has drained from her.

'She's gone,' says Spider. She's shaking her head, and the rest of her body is shaking too. Tink reaches for her and Spider lets herself be pulled away. Then they drop to the floor together, side by side. The two of them, staring straight ahead, their backs to Tink's mum, knees tugged to their chest, echoing the way they were sitting a few hours ago on the island, sharing beer and vodka and laughter and a love they wouldn't dare speak of out loud.

It led them there, to that first kiss.

And here, to this.

CHAPTER 50

Minutes later Jo hears tyres crunch on gravel. She turns as a silver BMW pulls into the car park of Hartfield Court and a man throws open the door. He's bald but with a dark beard, dressed in chinos and a chequered shirt, flashes of silver at his wrist. The boss. He half-runs, half-walks towards the Portakabin. The excavator driver comes out to meet him. Smoking again, looking nervous. They stand together with their backs to Jo and their eyes on that window. It's empty now, no longer frames *that* face. Was she really there?

Jo moves a little closer, straining to hear what the two men are saying, but she's still too far away and there are sirens to compete with. Police, approaching. And an ambulance. Maybe the fire crews will come as well. The holy trinity, to the rescue. The group of men are pointing at the building but keeping their distance. Filthy air rises and swirls around the wreckage of that place. It's the breath of a dragon protecting its lair: a smokescreen.

But is it thick enough to hide behind?

Jo gently pushes the fence to make a gap that's big enough to slip through, then eases her way into the site. She creeps behind the Portakabin, heading towards the back of the building. Mouth shut, eyes narrowed to keep the dust from coating them.

She holds in a cough until she's around the corner, safely out of sight from the main entrance and the car park and the Portakabin and the place the emergency services will pull up and park. She keeps walking, passes litter. Crushed Coke cans and an empty bottle of vodka. Crisp packets and the stubs of cigarettes. Paper tissues where the neds have peed. Puddles of spew. She steps around the mess and keeps going until she reaches the fire door. It's wedged open with a brick.

Jo pauses, takes in the scene.

The metal hand of the excavator hasn't yet reached this side and from where she's standing the building looks whole, solid, safe. Stable. She pulls the door, gently, and peeks inside. She's expecting gloom but it's bathed in dust-filled rays of light coming through from the other side, where the walls are partially down. But the stairs are still intact, leading upwards. She heads inside and climbs with her arm bent over her nose and mouth. The first floor looks the same as any other day and the second has some cracks and fallen chunks of plaster. But when she reaches the landing of the third floor all familiarity is gone. Instead of a window and wall at the end there's sky framed by ragged edges and holes you could stick your head through. The hallway is a broken bridge, leading nowhere. Ripped green lino hangs loose above a deep pit where once there was a floor.

Her mum's old flat is halfway along, just before the precipice. Jo edges forward, slowly, the same way she'd walk on thin ice. She steps forward with one foot and presses down hard to see if it holds. And repeat. The flat is the only one with an open door but by the time she reaches it the emergency services are pulling up outside. Sirens gulping, urgent voices being thrown across the site, one on top of the other.

A few more steps and Jo will be inside. Daylight from inside is leaking out; a pool of yellow on what's left of the corridor. She inches forward, sticks her head inside. *This is it.* She doesn't want to go in, had vowed she'd never return to the place of the murder.

'Aly?'

Nothing.

She steps into the flat, stands in the tiny hall where she used to dump her schoolbag and shoes. Here the walls and windows are whole, the sounds from out-side muffled. To her left are closed doors that lead to both bedrooms and the bathroom. Straight ahead is the sitting room and from where she's standing she can see part of the kitchen that leads off it, connected by glass double doors. The flat's smaller than she remembers but maybe that's because every inch of the sitting room walls is papered with photographs, obviously brought from the 'weird room' in Barry's flat to here when Aly moved in. So here, now, Jo's own face stares back at her from all angles. Most photos were taken when she was a teenager, snapped on Aly's fancy camera phone that everyone at school was jealous of. But a few of them are recent, show Jo on a bus, Jo standing in the doorway of the shop with a mug of tea, Jo at Jean's birthday party, sitting alone on Portobello Beach. So Aly's been watching her. Jo feels more sad than scared.

But where is she now?

'Aly?' Jo says it louder this time, knows from all the years she lived there that a voice that loud will be heard in a flat this small.

She waits, listening for a breath or a sniff or whispered shifts of position. The face she saw from outside had been looking out of the kitchen window but Jo checks the other rooms first. They're all empty. Now, she can either flee or face that fear.

The glass doors are hanging open and even before she reaches them she can see the damage on the other side. The kitchen looks as if it's been hit by a bomb. And it has, in a way. The metal scoop of the excavator has tugged at the ceiling and one of the walls. Severed cables and twisted metal hang like shit chandeliers.

The floor that used to hold their dining table is gone. All that's left is the radiator wall and a tiny island of floor in front of it, sloping steeply downwards. It's big enough for two or three people to stand on. But right now, Aly fills it.

She's hunched down, coated with filth, clinging to the radiator to stop herself sliding off that scrap of floor. Beyond it, a fall.

The floor under Jo's feet is undamaged but suddenly feels less secure, less solid. She inches forward, pushes one of the kitchen doors. It jams halfway, caught in the collapsing doorframe. She stretches one arm through the gap. 'Reach for me.'

Aly eases one hand off the radiator but grips it tighter with the other. 'I can't let go,' she says. 'Can you come and get me?'

'That floor won't hold the weight of us both.'

Aly's crying now, shoulders shaking so hard Jo worries the movement will topple the building. She's got to ger her out of there. Jo edges into the gap between the glass doors. Her mum drew her last breath close to the place where Aly is crouching. The floor that remains will still hold the blood of her. She's heard folk say buildings have memories and if that's the case it's just as well this one's being pulled down. She wishes the images from that day could be so easily dismantled, broken down to rubble that could be scooped up and slipped into bin bags and disposed of once and for all. She raises her right foot, is about to step through the gap and into the place of the murder when a hand grabs her shoulder from behind, tugs her back into the sitting room. Then comes *that* voice. 'Got you,' it says.

CHAPTER 51

Instinct kicks in. Jo whips round, shaking off the hand that grips her, primes herself for attack. Farida jumps back in the same instant, lets go, holds up both palms.

'What are you thinking, Jo? It's not safe. Why did you ask me to meet you *here*? You wanting to get us both killed?'

'I didn't *ask* you to come!'

'But you sent that text. Just after I phoned you.'

'What text? I don't even have your number in my contacts.' A realisation dawns and Jo nods in the direction of Aly. 'But *she* does. We were together on Cramond Island when you called me last night. She played your voicemail then took a photo of your number. Seems she made good use of it. She knows about . . . us. And hates you for it.'

Aly doesn't admit or deny it. She's cowering like a beaten dog, clinging to the radiator as if it's a crucifix. The distance between them is three metres, but wider than it's ever been.

'A rescue team's on its way,' says Farida. 'But we need to leave.'

'Not yet.' Jo stretches an arm between the glass doors. 'Help me reach her, will you?'

Farida shakes her head. 'It's too dangerous. We can't go any closer.'

'But we can't just leave her. *I* can't, anyway.'

'It's for your own safety. And hers. If you step in there and the floor gives way you'll both end up dead. We need to get you out, leave the rescue to the experts. I'm already breaking all the rules coming in here after you.'

'Fuck the rules.' Jo steps away from Farida and slips into the gap between the two doors. One foot in the kitchen, one in the sitting room. In front of her, Aly whimpers. Again Farida tugs at her shoulder and again Jo shakes her off. Then she leaps forward, across the gap, to the island of floor where Aly is crouched, a crying, crumpled version of who she used to be. Jo opens her arms, blankets Aly. Once upon a time she'd have given anything to be *this* close to *this* woman, every inch of them touching. Now it's like rock, paper, scissors. Aly's the rock and Jo's the paper wrapped around her. She wins. But behind them, clean and sharp and straight as a scissor blade, is Farida.

Aly's still gripping the radiator but turns her head, slowly and carefully so Jo can see the side of her face and one of her bloodshot eyes. She's still crying but now her tears run away from Jo.

Inches from the heel of Jo's trainers, the floor starts slipping away. It starts with a crack that sounds like a door banging but must be a beam or a floorboard, whatever holds this building together. She's never seen the bones of it until today. We can spend years in a place or with a person and never know what they're made of, what really lies beneath.

'Jo!' That's Farida, hunched down in the gap between the doors, one hand gripping the doorframe, the other stretched out, fingertips brushing Jo's back but not enough to get a decent grip. She's almost got her but not quite, not quite. 'Can you grab my hand?'

But Jo's already shaking her head. 'Let go,' she says, and after a moment the weight lifts from her back. Then Farida's edging away, standing up, promising to be right back, with help. But leaving. So now it's just Jo and Aly and no space between them. Jo can smell alcohol on her breath, the reek of old grapes that sour so many mouths, so many moments.

'Leave me,' says Aly, and there's part of Jo that wants to, knowing what she's done. But she's long past thinking people are good or bad, that it's a simple matter of choice.

'I'm going to get you out of here, okay?'

'I don't deserve your help. Or anybody else's. I've fucked up, Jo. *Again*. It's no wonder everybody hates me.'

'*I* don't hate you.'

'Only because you haven't read the letters.' Aly

311

shivers and the building seems to follow her lead. The floor trembles and, above their heads, plaster cracks. A lump of rubble crashes into the hole behind them. Jo snaps shut her eyes as the solid turns to dust.

'Barry made me promise *never* to tell you,' says Aly. 'And *never* to tell the police. I gave him my word but then I confessed to you anyway, over and over in those letters.'

'Confessed *what*?'

Aly doesn't hear, or ignores her. 'Somehow Barry knew I couldn't be trusted to keep quiet. So he gagged me without me knowing it, did that deal with Tony. He did it to protect me. I know that now. He was worried that if you read my letters you'd tell the police and I'd end up in jail. And if he lost me he'd lose the only family he had left.

'I did my best to get some jail time anyway, just so I could see you. But I even fucked that up. They knew who I was and kept us apart, made sure I was always sent to a different prison from you. To reduce risk, they said. But I wouldn't have harmed you. I just wanted to ask why you'd never replied to my letters. I just wanted *to talk*.'

'For Christ's sake, Aly. Just tell me what the letters say.'

Aly lets out a long, shuddering sigh. 'Remember, just after the murder, when I told you to go and find the phone, so we could call the ambulance?'

Jo nods, remembering the struggle, the spitting, the bike chain, the blood, so much blood, spilling on to the same floor where she now crouches with Aly in her arms.

'When you left the room, your mum . . . opened her eyes, saw me, tried to speak, best she could with those injuries. She told me she'd go to the police and tell them it was *me* who'd caused your dad's accident. Said I'd be jailed and you'd never forgive me.'

Jo stops, stunned. 'And was she telling the truth about that? That it *was* you, not *her*? Because that was partly the reason for the fight. I was *defending* you.'

Aly whimpers.

'I take it that's a yes? Jesus fucking Christ, Aly.'

'That's not even the worst part,' she says, and Jo can feel Aly's heart thunder under her skin, getting faster and faster. 'When your mum said that to me she was still alive. She wasn't dead, Jo. Not yet.'

Jo can hear the full stop at the end of that word and for a moment the world stops with it. Then a thousand moving parts slip slowly into place. Aly's chewing her bottom lip so hard there's blood on her teeth. When she speaks again she spits and it's red, red, red.

'I changed that.' Aly's crying now instead of speaking and Jo wishes, not for the first time, that there was a way to peek inside the head of others, to see the world as they see it. And to see the worlds they're keeping from you. 'It was me, Jo. I killed her.'

Beneath them, the building groans. And Jo's world collapses.

They'd met when Jo was just thirteen and Aly eighteen months older. Jo had been just a child, really, struggling with the loss of her dad and her mum's sad descent into alcoholism. But change had come when Aly appeared from nowhere at the bench outside these flats; handed her a can of beer. Suddenly, life had felt better. Love had come and swallowed everything else. Then it was just the two of them, and it had felt as if that was enough to keep them safe, keep them happy. Until her mum's murder three years later; Jo's guilty plea, and jail. But there was a time, between the death of her dad and the murder of her mum, that Jo had felt something like peace.

'*You* killed my mum?'

Aly bows her head.

'And you let *me* take the *blame*? You let *me* go to *prison*?'

'That's what I confessed in my letters. But I've stood by you for all these years, Jo. Surely that means something? Everyone else has left you except me. I gave up everything for you. I would have left this flat, left Edinburgh, maybe got married, maybe had kids. Would maybe have made myself *a family*. Instead, I waited for you. Surely that's love?'

Jo's not sure what love is, but it's not that. Not *this*.

'Why didn't you tell the police?'

A fat teardrop clings to the end of Aly's nose. Jo watches it, waiting for it to fall.

'I wanted to, but . . . I knew that would be the end of us. Even if I'd saved you from jail you'd have hated me for killing your mum . . . and for . . . causing your dad's accident. I knew that if I'd told the police I'd lose you for good.'

'But you lost me anyway, didn't you? And I lost *myself*. I lost *everything*.'

Somewhere downstairs there are voices, the thud of footsteps on the stairs. Then figures appear in the doorway behind them: a rescue team wearing hardhats and head torches and nervous expressions. They edge towards the kitchen; or what's left of it. Jo hears Farida's distorted voice through a radio, telling them where to go, how to locate them. *Be quick*, she says, as the floor creaks and groans under the weight of them.

Then it shudders. Everyone stops dead. Then Aly squeals and Jo closes her eyes, lets her mind skip back to the last time she was in this room. It'll be apt, some-how, if this is the place that ends her; if she's killed here, in the same place her mum was murdered.

She pictures it again: the push, the fall, soft flesh split by hard metal. Her mum's head cracked against the corner of the same radiator that she and Aly now cling to. Blood came, then death, then blame. During those fifteen years in jail, Jo had never questioned it. She'd murdered her mum and lived with the consequences.

She'd killed the one who gave her life. But now? Now it seems she *didn't*. Now it seems her mum could have been saved after all.

Beneath Jo's feet, a snap and a creak. The building heaves as if it's vomiting, determined to rid itself of those left inside, cleanse itself of impurities. The rescue team are yelling, retreating, bundling out of the room as quickly as they entered. So now it's just Aly and Jo and a truth that shreds the accepted version of what happened that day.

Her mum, dying, then dead.

Jo, convicted. But Aly, the killer.

The floor caves in. And then, together, they fall.

CHAPTER 52

In the end it's Spider who calls the police, and then they're caught between two worlds: one where Jo's an ordinary teenager, angry at her mum, and one where she's a killer.

Tink and Spider are listening to a stranger's voice, leaking from the phone. A man with a west coast accent, asking Spider if she thinks she's *in danger*. As if Tink would harm her. As if Tink would ever have harmed anyone. When Spider says no, the man on the phone asks if she's sure, and she looks at Tink for a microsecond too long before she answers. 'I'm sure,' she says, but the damage is done.

He asks if Tink is *armed* and the idea of it is so crazy that she wants to laugh. She's not who they think she is. Either that or she's not who *she* thinks she is. That's possible. Anything's possible now. They tell Spider to move outside, to wait for the police and ambulance in a *safe place*.

'Seven or eight minutes and we'll be with you.'

The man keeps talking but Tink hears none of it.

Her life is now a countdown clock. Eight minutes is four hundred and eighty seconds and that's all she's got left of this life. And still the man keeps talking, telling Spider that she's doing really well, asking her if she's at the door yet and if there are any neighbours she could go to, *in the meantime*. But the meantime is all they've got.

Tink reaches out to her and wonders if this is it: the last time they'll touch. She moves her fingers gently across Spider's knuckles, trying to commit to memory every bump and bone and wrinkle. The skin there is always dry and chafed and often bleeds in winter, but the blood there now is not her own. Tink flinches when she sees it, shifts her eyes to the doors that lead to the sitting room and the world that merrily continues beyond this flat. Her mouth is still sticky with beer and when she talks she can sense the reek of it, wafting out. She hopes Spider doesn't notice, as if a bad smell was all that would tarnish the memory of her.

'I didn't mean it,' says Tink, as if that matters now. One single act, one tiny decision, one bad move and a life is redefined. 'I was just drunk,' she says. 'Just angry.'

Spider's breathing too fast and her eyes are flitting all over the place like those pigeons who scavenge at the bins. They expect fright, attack, danger. But for now Tink's still touching her hand and Spider's still letting her. She wonders how many seconds have

passed and how many remain until she hears the sirens
that signal the end of everything. There will be police
officers and blue lights and questions and judgement
and lawyers and courts and cells but she's got no idea
how that world works in real life. She's seen it often
enough on the TV and maybe that's how it'll look but
she won't be able to switch it off when she gets bored
or tired or scared. It's inconceivable to think she could
be plucked out of her own life and dropped into
another that she does not recognise. And still that
familiar selfishness seeps out of her: worrying about
herself while her mum lies dead on the floor behind
them and Spider sits right there beside her, contemplat-
ing loss.

Tink can't tell if it's the police or the paramedics
who get there first. Their sirens are different but she's
never learned the difference between the two; never
been the reason they're screeching. A pulsing blue light
slips through the curtains.

The footsteps are heavy and purposeful. There are
voices now, just outside the front door of the flat. She
can't hear the words but she can sense the urgency in
them. Tink stays still. She wonders if she's in shock, if
her body and brain are slowly shutting down. Maybe
that wouldn't be such a bad thing.

The letter box rattles and then, they call her name.
They *know* her name.

Spider's gripping her hand but Tink's trying, now,

to edge away. The soft skin of their palms sticks together with the heat and the sweat and the blood of her mum. Then a breath of air comes between their hands and Spider tries to tighten her grip but Tink wriggles free. And that's the start of the end of it.

A policewoman is talking to them through the letter box, says her name is Effie. She's treating them like stupid children or clever dogs, coaxing them to unlock the door with a voice that's probably supposed to sound reassuring. But Tink's beyond that. There's no need for reassurance when the world's already gone to fuck.

'If you don't open up we'll have to force our way in,' says the policewoman, and then the letter box flaps shut again, a sound so ordinary and so familiar that it's impossible to believe what's coming next.

Tink looks at Spider and love fills her. We forget there's no guaranteed future, ever. There's so much Tink wants to say and wishes she'd said before but what good will it do? What they've been, what they are and what they could be – it's over.

'I'm going to let them in,' says Tink, and her eyes flit towards her mum, to the messy remains of that life. They pull themselves on to their feet, stand so close that all they can see is each other. Metres away something solid rams into the front door, hard enough that Tink can feel the vibrations of it. But it holds. In the moment of silence before the next attempt, Spider steps closer and kisses Tink gently on the lips. She doesn't kiss back.

'This isn't over,' says Spider. 'I'll wait for you. *Right here*. Always.'

Then the front door crashes open and the world floods in. Tink holds up her hands like the baddie in a film. Spider sobs. Strangers bring noise and cold air and questions.

'Joanna Forsyth Hidalgo?' She's got no idea how they know her real name. Tink nods.

And then? Cold metal on her wrists.

CHAPTER 53

It's a good day for a funeral: endless folds of clouds greying the sky and a biting wind so cold that most folk keep their hands in their pockets. The sea in Portobello is playing along as well, white horses galloping on to sand that's littered with empty shells; open caskets. Every single one a life lost. Two streets back from the water a small, scattered crowd files into the church. Collars up, heads bowed.

Jo's coat is slung over her shoulders, one arm in a sling. Somehow she'd only broken her wrist in the fall – she'd ended up three floors below her old flat, in the main entrance. Doctors said that she was very lucky to survive it; that Aly had broken her fall.

As Jo approaches the church she spots Jean with a few of the volunteers, huddling under an umbrella. Gordon's among them. He waves at her, is looking more cheerful than usual despite the occasion. He'd taken Jo aside the other day, told her she'd motivated him to stand up for himself and escape his abusive dad. He'd finally plucked up the courage to move out of the family home, age fifty-five. It's never too late to start again. And aye, the bruises on his back are now healing.

Jo keeps walking, sees Sandy Chisholm from the *Journal*, standing alone behind one of the biggest gravestones, smoking a cigarette as he talks on the phone. She's never told anyone how she found out Aly lived in her old flat at Hartfield Court, and they've agreed to pretend that frantic phone call never happened. But they both know it probably saved Farida's life.

Sandy covers the mouthpiece when she approaches, asks if she'll trust him with an exclusive about the Cramond Island Murder, as Barry's death is now known. But there's not much more to tell. Aly had been caught on camera, fleeing Cramond Island after the killing and dumping Jo's yellow leather jacket in a recycling bin. When it was retrieved it still held traces of Barry's blood and saliva. And police analysis of CCTV footage confirmed Aly had been the one to beat up Tony Burgos in that car park in Leith.

Jo's reputation – and freedom – has been saved by machines. Her heart is a harder fix, but she's working on it. She knows what can happen to those who cling to love, or wait for others to save them. Aly convinced herself she could only be happy if she and Jo were together, and set about removing all obstacles in her path: first Jo's mum, then Barry. She tried her best to finish off Tony Burgos and Christ knows what would have happened if Farida had reached Hartfield Court – and Aly – before Jo did that day. There's no doubt Aly wanted to harm Farida, maybe even get rid of her altogether. But no matter who Aly hurt, she'd never have felt any better. If Jo's learned one thing it's this: the only way to get rid of shadows is to let in some light. We are our own salvation.

As for Tony, Jo hadn't heard another word. He'd not reported her for stealing his money and there was no point in her telling the police about his dodgy deal with Barry Chisholm. She'd let the man die in peace. Unlike Barry. But soon enough the world would lose interest in his murder. Jo won't give Sandy that story but she'll buy him a cup of tea one day to say thanks for trusting her, and for helping to save Farida. Otherwise they might have been attending a very different funeral, packed with police in uniform.

But here, today, the only person dressed in black is the minister, a cheerful woman with a kind face, like a flower in bloom – bright, wide open, somehow familiar. She's standing at the front door of the church, greeting mourners with double-handed shakes. There are few, and no family. Jo keeps her hood up and her head down as she approaches. Even in God's house, she's not convinced she's welcome. She's climbing the church steps and approaching the minister when she catches the scent of freshly washed towels and realises that it could only be one person.

'How are you, sunshine?'

Jo looks up and into a face she's not seen for years. Mrs Campbell from the school office, dressed in a black gown and a white dog collar, instead of a skirt and blouse. She's holding her hand out to be shaken, and when Jo extends hers Mrs Campbell wraps it in both of hers, squeezes it. Her skin is warm and soft; a comfort. Same as before. 'It's been a while,' she says. A smile softens her lips. 'Must be . . . what . . . sixteen, seventeen years? And ten since I swapped pupils for the pulpit.'

'Suits you,' says Jo, meaning it. Mrs Campbell glows, reminds Jo of those old paintings where the saints have a halo tacked on to their head like a golden frisbee. She almost tells her but doesn't. Mrs Campbell's still holding Jo's hand even though there are people waiting behind. She's in no rush to flick her off, let her go. A novelty. Jo can sense a few folk at her back and hopes Mrs Campbell doesn't say too much, out loud. Faces from your past can be a comfort but also a threat because they know where and what and who you've come from.

'So you're the minister here?'

'Not usually. I'm retired,' she says. 'But I do the rounds in the hospital, saw Aly not long before she died and promised I'd lead her funeral service, when the time came. She adored you. I hope you know that.'

Eyes, pricking. Heart, breaking. Even if she knew how to respond to that, Jo doubts she could speak. There's an ache in her throat that no words can push past. She tightens her lips into a straight line to stop them wobbling. When she looks up, Mrs Campbell gives her hand another squeeze and looks her directly in the eye.

'There's goodness in all of us,' she says. 'Don't let anyone tell you otherwise. And don't tell yourself otherwise either, you hear me? The Lord forgives, always. But often the hardest part is learning to forgive ourselves.' Her smile is gentle, genuine. 'Come and speak to me any time, even if you're not a believer. And there's no need to see me as a minister if that makes you uncomfortable. You can call me Mrs C, if you like. I'm the same person I was back then, before you lost your mum and dad. Before any of this. And you know what? You are too. Learn from your past but leave it behind. Move on.'

A gentle smile, and Jo returns it. There's warmth in her chest. Hope; there after all.

Inside, most rows are empty but Mrs Campbell gives Aly a good send-off. Jo sits at the back and leaves early, walks into a morning that's cold and damp and perfect exactly as it is.

She walks to the graveyard, thinking of the first time she came here with Aly all those years ago. They'd never imagined the note and flowers on her dad's grave had been left by her mum until they'd seen her there so unexpectedly on the day of the murder. She'd been taking the bus to the same place as them, secretly grieving that loss. Jo can see now that her mum had been angry because the flowers in her hand had exposed the truth of it. She was sad too, suffering too. But her mum had buried that pain for so long it had mutated into an anger that neither of them fully understood. As a teenager Jo saw the claws but not the hurt that lay behind them. She'd rejected her mum because it was easier than looking for ways to connect with a woman who felt like a stranger. And as it turned out they'd had something in common after all: a man to miss.

She wonders often how different all of their lives could have been if only she'd left Aly on the pavement and taken the bus home with her mum that day. Maybe they could have had a conversation instead of that conflict.

But when Aly had told her to run, she'd run.

Arthur steps out of his little shed as she approaches, raises a smile and a mug that steams in the morning air. His skin's crushed as crepe paper, his grey hair almost gone. He calls to her. 'Bit unsettled today.' He points up at the sky, shaking his head like it's a mischievous child. 'But the weatherman says it'll brighten up.'

She gives him a thumbs-up but keeps on walking, leaning into the bitter wind.

The gravel crunches under her feet. Thirty-three

steps and she reaches the gravestone she's looking for. *That* name and *that* date. She kneels down, runs a finger over the letters and numbers that had both made her and been her undoing. Her mum gave her life, and her murder turned Jo's whole world on its head. She was orphaned, imprisoned, unforgiven.

And unforgivable, until now.

Maybe people come to graveyards not to say goodbye to the dead but to bring them a little closer. Jo crouches down, reaches out, presses her hands on to her mum's gravestone for the very first time. It should be cold, should be hard. But here, now, nature has taken charge.

Moss makes soft the stone.

CHAPTER 54

Jo looks up in the same moment as Arthur whistles to her. His cheerfulness is out of place here and that's what she likes about him. He lives simply, reacts how he wants to react, doesn't follow the invisible rules humans create to make life more difficult. We try to control life and instead we complicate it. Arthur's standing outside his little cabin, punctuating his words with gentle laughter as he points in Jo's direction, one hand held out to guide the visitor towards the correct grave. Farida towers over him and when she walks her boots fall heavily on the soft ground. Jo stands but stays where she is, keeps her mother's grave between them.

'So you came?'

'Only took me fifteen years.'

'Better than never,' says Farida. 'And your dad?'

'His grave's in the corner.' She glances towards the oak tree that's even taller than before, and always renewing itself. 'Close enough.'

Farida sniffs then steps forward. 'And what about us?'

'We're as close as we'll ever be.'

'Perhaps.' Farida glances over her shoulder, towards Arthur and the car park and the city that lies beyond them. A force of habit, maybe, making sure they're not being watched. But Jo can see clearly now: that's how it would always be. When she brings her eyes back to Jo her face has softened, a little. 'Thing is, I care,' says Farida.

'About?'

'You. A lot of things. More than you imagine.'

'I sense a *but*.'

'Maybe the doubt is yours.'

'Aye,' says Jo. 'But there's more than enough for both of us.'

Some things don't change, despite the law: heads rule hearts, shame steals the simple joy of a touch that matters. Sometimes, for some people, solid reputations hold more weight than heartstrings, gently tugged. But that's the magic of things like love, and desire. They're invisible but somehow you believe in them anyway.

And, sometimes, you let yourself be led.

'Give me a minute and I'll walk you to your car.' That's Jo. Farida steps back, turns away as Jo kneels down in front of her mum's grave again, glad she came but knowing she won't come back. When she stands, the grass stays where it is: flattened, bent over, pressing into the earth. Her presence, noted. And, in a place like this, that's enough.

She and Farida walk side by side but wordless. Jo's

grateful for the crunch of gravel, the whistle of Arthur, the birdsong that drifts down from the trees. Somewhere in the car park a tin can clatters and Jo thinks of her and Aly, downing beers up the park and tossing the empties over their shoulder. Tink and Spider, hiding behind nicknames and drinking to feel *happy, faster*. But it didn't work then, and it still doesn't.

Farida's is the only vehicle there, the threat Aly wrote on its door now scrubbed clean. They stop there, both of them standing on the driver's side. The sun-blackened windows hold their reflection. Jo catches a glimpse of herself and, for the first time in years, doesn't look away.

Farida pulls out the keys to her pickup. 'Can I run you home?'

'I'll make my own way.'

'Sure?' The faintest ripple passes over Farida's face. Once you get to know her you realise she's made of still water, not stone.

Jo nods, steps closer. Farida lets her.

Then there are closed eyes and a kiss that spells *The End*. Jo lets go first; smiles then walks away. When she reaches the main road the traffic lights are red. She looks both ways then keeps on going. She doesn't look back; doesn't need to. Up ahead, the road is clear.

Acknowledgements

I started this book in December 2023, just before embarking on a three-week renovation job at our Barcelona flat which turned out to be a fairly disastrous three-month project instead. As a result I wrote most of the first draft while living full-time in our beloved pop-top campervan. So my first thanks goes to our old van, Katie, for being our refuge. And of course, massive love and *muchas gracias* to Mari, who was literally locked inside a small metal box with me for months while I battered out the first draft with my trademark noisy typing.

Draft one was done by the summer of 2024 but thankfully the only person who'll ever read that version is Claire Christie, my wee-est big sister and ever-faithful first reader. Claire was the first of several brilliant women who've helped me transform this story.

A deafening drum roll and wild applause, please, for my infatigable agent, Caroline Hardman, my super-sharp (and yet very sweet) editor at Mountain Leopard Press, Jenni Edgecombe, and the world's most brilliant copy-editor, Linda McQueen. Thanks also to all those behind the scenes at my publisher – the cover designers, marketing team, proofreaders and everyone else who was involved.

Next thank-you goes to the readers and bloggers and bookshops who've rallied behind me ever since my debut was published in 2020. Release the fireworks! Thank you for buying, borrowing, reading, lending, and selling. Thanks for recommending my books to your pals and followers and customers. Thanks for taking the time to pre-order and write reviews. Everything you do makes a real difference to me and other writers.

Huge shout-out to my dear friend Liv Matthews for supporting me in so many different ways. My writing life wouldn't be the same without you. And yes, my prison officer Tony Burgos has just read Liv's latest novel, *To Love a Liar*. He agrees it's awesome.

Talking of prisons – a big thank-you to fellow writer Claire Wilson for sharing your knowledge of life on the inside. Any mistakes are mine. I deliberately avoid naming a specific prison in the novel but to remove any doubt: the now-closed Cornton Vale Prison in Scotland housed both youth and adult female offenders. Youth prisoners would be moved to an adult block when they turned twenty-one. And yes, it's feasible that prison officers like Tony could have moved between the youth and adult sections.

So many writers have helped me bring this all together. Thank you, authors! Impossible to mention everyone but a special mention goes to Frances Quinn, Trevor Wood and Lou Hare for reading the book at record speed and sharing your thoughts.

If you're wondering why I set this book in a charity shop, it's because I worked in Barnardo's in Aberdeen for two years. Absolutely loved that job, mainly thanks to my boss, Diane Tunks, who made sure we laughed every single day. She doesn't chain-smoke or wear a bum bag or remotely look like Jean, but she's got that same good heart.

Thanks also to all my friends who've patiently listened and encouraged me whenever I was having a wobble during the writing of this book.

I mostly edited the book at MOB co-working office in Barcelona. Huge thanks to all my buddies there for many moments of light relief over coffee or beer or Honest Greens. Another huge *gracias* to Antonio Jorge and all the crew at Espacio Interior for all the insights and *abrazos*. To Las Hachas – *os quiero, chicas. Seguimos afilando!* To Marion Todd and the Caledonia Crime Collective, thanks for always being there for a WhatsApp whinge. Ta to the Cumnock lassies (and Rowan) for keeping me right. And Sophie, I owe you a barrel of vermouth.

ACKNOWLEDGEMENTS

Last but not least, three cheers for my family! To my beloved parents and siblings, and my awesome nieces and nephews: you all rock.

I do like an encore so I'll bring Mari back on to the stage to say: you are the only thing in any room you're ever in. Equipo Alba forever.

About the Author

Emma Christie is the author of four psychological thrillers set in Portobello, Edinburgh's thriving seaside neighbourhood.

Her debut novel, *The Silent Daughter*, was short-listed for Bloody Scotland's McIlvanney Prize and for the Scottish Crime Debut of the Year 2021. Her second novel, *Find Her First*, published in 2022, and in 2024 her third novel, *In Her Shadow*, was chosen as a *Times* 'Thriller of the Month'. *Watch Your Back* is her fourth novel and, no, she can't quite believe it either.

Emma lives in Barcelona with the love of her life, Mari. At weekends they can often be found exploring the mountains and coastline of Catalonia in their campervan, Poncho.

Find her online at www.emmachristiewriter.com or across social media @theemmachristie.

DISCOVER EMMA CHRISTIE

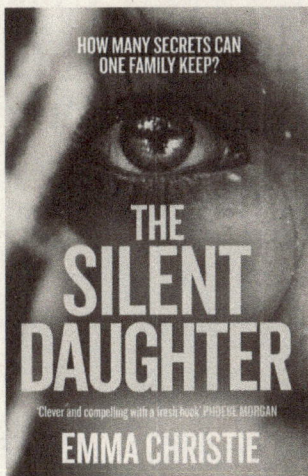

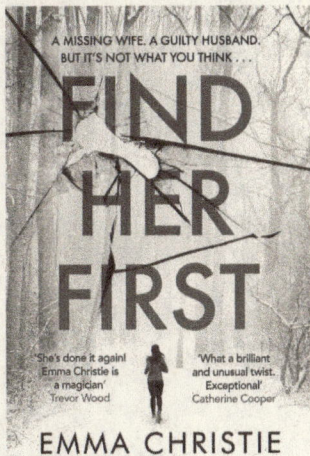

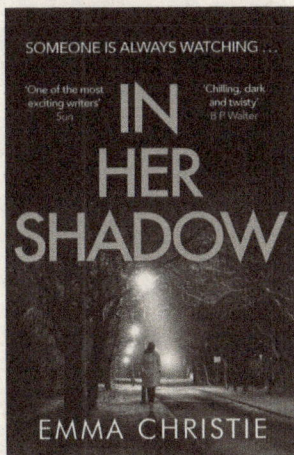

AVAILABLE NOW

RAISING READERS
Books Build Bright Futures

Dear Reader,

We'd love your attention for one more page to tell you about the crisis in children's reading, and what we can all do.

Studies have shown that reading for fun is the **single biggest predictor of a child's future life chances** – more than family circumstance, parents' educational background or income. It improves academic results, mental health, wealth, communication skills, ambition and happiness.[1]

The number of children reading for fun is in rapid decline. Young people have a lot of competition for their time. In 2024, 1 in 10 children and young people in the UK aged 5 to 18 did not own a single book at home.[2]

Hachette works extensively with schools, libraries and literacy charities, but here are some ways we can all raise more readers:

- Reading to children for just 10 minutes a day makes a difference
- Don't give up if children aren't regular readers – there will be books for them!
- Visit bookshops and libraries to get recommendations
- Encourage them to listen to audiobooks
- Support school libraries
- Give books as gifts

There's a lot more information about how to encourage children to read on our website: **www.RaisingReaders.co.uk**

Thank you for reading.

hachette
UK

1 OECD, '21st-Century Readers: Developing Literacy Skills in a Digital World', 2021, https://www.oecd.org/en/publications/21st-century-readers_a83d84cb-en.html
2 National Literacy Trust, 'Book Ownership in 2024', November 2024, https://literacytrust.org.uk/research-services/research-reports/book-ownership-in-2024